# Accla___
# Heidi Mc___

"Heidi McLaughlin has done it again! Sexy, sweet, and full of heart, *Third Base* is a winner!" —Melissa Brown, author of *Wife Number Seven*

"If you're looking for a book with a baseball-playing bad boy with a reputation for living outside the box, and a love story to melt even the coldest of hearts, *Third Base* is going to be your ticket."

—Ashley Suzanne, author of the Destined series

"*Third Base* hits the reading sweet spot. A must-read for any baseball and romance fans." —Carey Heywood, author of *Him*

"*Third Base* is sexy, witty, and pulls you in from the first page. You'll get lost in Ethan and Daisy, and never want their story to end."

—S. Moose, author of *Offbeat*

"Heidi McLaughlin never disappoints."

—Nicole Jacquelyn, author of *Unbreak My Heart*, on *Blow*

"McLaughlin will have you frantically turning pages."

—Jay Crownover, *New York Times* bestselling author, on *Save Me*

"When it comes to crafting a story that leaves you breathless, no one does it better than Heidi McLaughlin."

—Rachel Harris, *New York Times* bestselling author, on *Save Me*

"Heidi McLaughlin has once again delivered a heart stopping masterpiece."

—K. L. Grayson, bestselling author, on *Save Me*

**Also by Heidi McLaughlin**

*Third Base*

# HOME RUN

## HEIDI McLAUGHLIN

FOREVER

NEW YORK    BOSTON

Copyright © 2017 by Heidi McLaughlin
Excerpt from *Grand Slam* Copyright © 2017 by Heidi McLaughlin

Cover illustration by Claudio Marinesco. Cover design by Elizabeth Turner. Cover copyright © 2017 by Hachette Book Group, Inc.

Forever
Hachette Book Group
1290 Avenue of the Americas
New York, NY 10104
forever-romance.com
twitter.com/foreverromance

Originally published in ebook by Forever in January 2017.

First Trade Edition: June 2017

Forever is an imprint of Grand Central Publishing.
The Forever name and logo are trademarks of Hachette Book Group, Inc.

The publisher is not responsible for websites (or their content) that are not owned by the publisher.

The Hachette Speakers Bureau provides a wide range of authors for speaking events. To find out more, go to www.hachettespeakersbureau.com or call (866) 376-6591.

Library of Congress Cataloging-in-Publication Data

Names: McLaughlin, Heidi (Romance fiction writer), author.
Title: Home run / Heidi McLaughlin.
Description: First Trade Edition. | New York ; Boston : Forever, 2017. | Series:
   The boys of summer ; 2
Identifiers: LCCN 2017002977| ISBN 9781455598274 (paperback) | ISBN  9781455598281
   (ebook) | ISBN 9781478915966 (audio download)
Subjects: LCSH: Man-woman relationships—Fiction. | Baseball players—Fiction. |
   BISAC: FICTION / Romance / Contemporary. | FICTION / Contemporary Women. |
   GSAFD: Love stories.
Classification: LCC PS3613.C57535 H66 2017 | DDC 813/.6—dc23 LC record
available at https://lccn.loc.gov/2017002977

ISBN: 978-1-4555-9827-4 (trade pbk.), 978-1-4555-9828-1 (ebook)

Printed in the United States of America

LSC-C

10   9   8   7   6   5   4   3   2   1

*To Gumpa,*
*I look forward to catching a game with you!*

# HOME RUN

# BOSTON RENEGADES

It's time!

Spring training is upon us, fine folks in New England. While our Renegades head to Fort Myers and the faithful allegiance of fans follows, there are a few of us who will remain here in Boston. However, game stats and spring training updates will happen as usual.

It'll be interesting to see what manager Cal Diamond does this year with both Steve Bainbridge and Cooper Bailey on the roster. You can't go wrong with starting either of them, as both of their numbers last season were solid. Diamond has a tough decision ahead of him, that's for sure, and so does general manager Stone, considering he's fielding requests for a player trade that includes Bailey.

Expected to move into the starting catcher position is Jose Gonzalez, unless the off-season acquisition of Michael Cashman proves to be a better choice.

Be sure to watch for designated hitter Branch Singleton during spring training. The scuttlebutt around the clubhouse is that he's been working out there daily, and the coaching staff is expecting his batting average to soar this season.

If you're in Fort Myers and want to contribute to the BoRe Blog, please email us!

## GOSSIP WIRE

Travis Kidd is still up to his old antics, and nothing seems to stop him. He was recently spotted at BU hitting up a sorority. Rumor has it, he was caught streaking by the Pub Safe patrol, but being a fan of his, they let him go.

The BoRe Blogger

# ONE

## Cooper

Over the years I've had many dreams. I'm not talking about the ones you experience when you're sleeping, but the kind of dreams that can become reality. When I was young, my mother passed away, leaving my father alone to raise me. This wasn't necessarily a bad thing, except I probably didn't experience everything I could have. To cope with the loss of my mother, my dad and I turned to baseball. We'd play catch in the yard every night before sitting down to dinner, which usually consisted of sandwiches or cereal.

Hours of tossing the ball around the backyard turned into fielding grounders, catching pop flies, and spending time in the batting cages. What started as a way for us to cope with our depression turned into something I really enjoyed doing, and when the scouts started paying attention, I began dreaming of the big leagues, the pomp and circumstance of playing in the majors. I dreamed of winning a national championship at a prized SEC school and running out of the dugout as my name was announced during the All-Star Game. When the Boston Renegades drafted me, my dreams started to become reality; the only thing standing in my way is Steve Bainbridge. The veteran center fielder was hinting at retirement last year, leaving the door open for me, which is part of the reason the Renegades went after me in the draft. At the end of last season, Bainbridge changed his mind, putting my spot on the team in limbo. Still, the organization called me up, and here I am, about to make my major league debut.

Now as I step out onto the wet field, my cleats sink into the dewy grass. I'm not supposed to be out here today, but I couldn't resist the temptation. I'm so close, yet so far away, from starting my major league career.

Spring training is a rite of passage for any baseball player, but for a rookie like me, this is *everything*. When I arrived in Fort Myers, the itch to get out onto the field was something I had never experienced before.

I tilt my head back and let the early morning Florida sun warm my skin. In the distance, the sound of lawn mowers coming to life, the swooshing sound of the nets being raised behind home plate, and the smell of glove oil all surround me. There are a few things missing that would make this better, such as the smell of hot dogs and popcorn and the sounds of the fans gathering in their seats.

"Rookie, look at you being the first one out here." Travis Kidd, our left fielder and someone I will have to work closely with, calls out to me as he steps onto the warning track. As the center fielder, I'm tasked not only with backing up numerous positions, but I must also have the ability to run fast and judge the depth of a ball. My high school coach once said that you could tell where a ball was going by the sound it made when it left the bat. He was probably right, and I'd love to do that now, except we use wooden bats and not aluminum. Switching from aluminum to wood took some getting used to. I had a faster swing in college and could smack the shit out of the ball. Now, the ball and bat have to hit just right, and you have to really put some power behind your swing in order to get the same effect.

"He's eager," Bryce Mackenzie says. Mackenzie is in charge of second base, another position that I'll have to work closely with.

Next to walk out of the dugout is Steve Bainbridge, who doesn't even try to make eye contact with me as he steps onto the warning track. Being a fan of baseball makes me a fan of his, but right now he has the job that I want, and I'm here to take it from him.

Last year when I was called up, we had a team-wide meeting. Everyone was very nice, genuine in welcoming me to the club. Well, everyone except for Steve Bainbridge. I get it. I do. In his eyes, I'm the enemy. I'm here to take his starting position and make him a "has-been." Some call me unlucky because he's a fan favorite, but I call it the luck of the draft. The general manager, Ryan Stone, chose me. He wanted me here to make a difference, to help lead the Renegades to the pennant.

Other team members start to filter out of the dugout. It's six a.m. and time for us to start conditioning. I imagine our conditioning will be similar to that in the minors since they try to follow the same regimen.

"Morning," Scotty Johnson, the Renegades trainer, says as he stands in front looking at each and every one of us with an evil glint. I've seen an expression like that before, on my college coach, and know it means there will be hell to pay today. The holiday beer guts are about to be a thing of the past. "I don't know about you, but I feel like running today."

No one says anything, because we know what's coming.

"All right, here is what we're going to start off with. Two laps around the field and into one hundred Superman planks followed by two more laps. When you're done with that, you're going to give me five-minute wall squats with a medicine ball between your knees and then one hundred burpees. This is on repeat until I say stop. Last year, you looked like shit. You were out of shape, and most of you couldn't outrun a throw to first. This year, I'm going to make damn sure you'll be able to." He blows his whistle, and we're off.

I'm confident that I'm one of the fastest players on the team, but I have to pace myself. The last thing I want to do is become gassed or piss anyone off. Branch Singleton is by far the quickest, and right now he's all the way at the back of the pack. Everyone is paired off, except for me. I get it. I'm the outsider. Even Michael Cashman, who was acquired in the off-season, is running with another teammate.

"They're a tough group, but keep your head up." I take a sideways glance to see who's running next to me. Ethan Davenport, the third baseman.

"You would know, right?"

"Yep. Rookie year is tough, even tougher for you because of their loyalty to Bainbridge."

"Yeah, I'm sensing that. I guess I thought they'd see it wasn't my choice?"

Ethan shakes his head and keeps stride with me. We're both huffing and puffing by the time we finish our second lap.

"Everyone has a choice," he says. I half expect him to leave me so he can go work out with his friends, but he doesn't. He takes a spot on the grass next to me and starts his planks. "The thing is, Bainbridge is still hanging on. He's going through some shit at home, and this is the place where he can escape."

His marriage problems have been widely reported. My agent says I can use that to get into Bainbridge's head and get him to mess up. Each screwup is an opportunity for me to take the starting spot. While the viewers and fans think baseball is about family, it's not always that way. The more television time you have, the more sponsors you end up with. Sponsors are the way to supplement your income and prepare yourself for early retirement if you're unlucky enough to have a career-ending injury.

Except that isn't how I function. I want to play baseball and I want to play for the Renegades, but if they don't need me, I'll have no choice but to ask for a trade. The game has always been my priority.

"Have you moved to Boston yet?"

I grunt through my planks, finishing before Ethan does. I decide to wait for him so we can run together again.

"I haven't yet. I started looking, but nothing has caught my eye. I'm not sure where I should look, either."

"I went through the same thing when I first came to Boston. I rented for a bit before buying a condo. When we get back, you can stop by and check it out if you want. My wife won't care if you crash for a few days."

"Wife?" Ethan and I aren't far apart in age, and I can guarantee you that a wife or girlfriend isn't in my near future.

Ethan smiles. "Yeah, we got married after last season. She's cool. You'll like her."

I shrug and continue my run. We catch up with a few of the other guys: Preston Meyers, who plays right field, and Kayden Cross, who covers first. Ethan keeps me in the conversation, and before I know it, I'm laughing right along with them. Minus the workout, I have to say today is shaping up.

———◆———

"Here are your playbooks," Cal Diamond says as he hands them out. There was some scuttlebutt last season that he was ill, but he looks healthy to me. I'm looking forward to playing for him.

"Also, we have some public relations matters that we need to take care of. The Major Leagues are pushing an initiative to give back to the communities, and Stone wants to start in Fort Myers."

There's a collective groan throughout the room. I've been doing this for a while, so I'm okay with whatever we have to do. In the minors, we set aside a few minutes here and there to sign autographs before and after the game. Some of the kids there can't afford the big-league prices so we try to make it special for them.

"Later this week, we'll be giving a tour to some kids at the zoo. I know most of you haven't been to the zoo here, so the best thing to do is to let the kids guide you. There will be ample time for autographs and pictures. It's just one of those things you have to deal with. You'll have lunch with the kids and end the day with a photo op with the staff. The zoo is closed to the public when we go, so you won't need to worry about people tagging along that shouldn't be there.

"Another event you'll be doing is senior prom."

This time, the groans are louder. Diamond smiles and shakes his head.

"Wrong kind of prom. This senior prom will be held at the community center, and it's for the residents of the retirement home. Now just because they're of age doesn't mean there will be drinking. I don't care what they try to slip you. You're expected to dance, talk baseball, and entertain. I've been to a few; they're fun. You just need to remember that the people attending probably haven't done this type of thing in a long time.

"And don't forget about the charity golf tournament. You're all expected to be there."

Diamond continues to go on about the expectations while in Fort Myers, how he has an open door policy, and he reminds us that we take the field in two weeks. It's crazy to think, but all-day conditioning and practicing will get us ready for preseason play. Everything else we'll fix along the way.

"Before you leave tonight, don't forget to pick up your uniforms. This year, we'll be wearing three different hats instead of the normal two. And don't forget your autograph sessions. Your schedule is in your binder."

I flip through the binder as everyone gets up to leave. I look around and find the other rookies doing the same thing. We're in this boat together, even if we're miles apart on the playing field.

"Hey, rookie?" I look up at the sound of Davenport's voice. "We're heading to dinner. Do you want to come?"

The truth is, no, I don't. I'd rather go back to the apartment and learn the plays, but to tell him no would be foolish.

"Yeah, of course," I say, scrambling to gather my things.

# TWO

## Ainsley

"Do you miss this?"

Glancing over at Bruce and seeing a smile that likely matches mine answers his question. It's only a matter of seconds before I turn my gaze back to the fifteen-foot cow who is pacing her sawdust-laden stall, waiting for her first calf to be born. I have been anticipating this moment since I first thought Jambo was pregnant. Later, an ultrasound confirmed what I and my co-workers thought: We were going to have a calf among our giraffe population. That was almost thirteen months ago, and so much as has changed for me since.

"I do. I miss being with them so much. The giraffes have always been my favorite. Even in college, I found myself focusing on them, their habitat, and their interaction with humans." About the time Jambo's pregnancy was announced, I had to step down from my job as a zookeeper due to the long hours and always being on call. It wasn't an easy decision, but my mother is fighting cancer, and it's more important that I'm there for her. Still, it's times like this when I truly miss my job, even though I still hold a position in the front office of the zoo. Being hands-on with the animals, particularly the giraffes, is my passion.

"Thank you for calling me, Bruce," I say, focusing my attention on Jambo. I knew she was due to give birth, and when Bruce called to tell me that she had started pacing, I raced down here, not caring that it was two in the morning and thankful that my mother's part-time in-home nurse agreed to come when I needed her. I didn't want to miss this experience.

"You deserve to be here, Ainsley. Jambo is your baby."

He's right, she is. She was over a year old when she came to live at the zoo, and it took us a while to bond, but once we did, I could call for her from across the yard and she'd trot over to me. This proves especially fruitful when I occasionally volunteer to lead the feeding sessions. Even though I can enter their sanctuary at any time, sometimes it's better for me to try to distance myself, yet I can't always stay away.

"There's enough padding, right?"

"Of course. I set the large mat down last week and put down about eight inches of sawdust myself three days ago, with a fresh layer this morning. The calf will be fine, Ainsley. Don't worry."

"I know. I can't help it, though. Jambo is a first-time mom, and I want everything to be perfect for her."

Bruce doesn't say anything. He doesn't have to. He knows what I'm thinking. We've all been so worried that something would go wrong after a calf at another zoo was delivered stillborn a few months ago. Since then, that giraffe has had trouble integrating back into the yard with the others. Even animals suffer from depression, and it can be hard to treat them properly.

"Bruce, look." I point toward Jambo as hooves start to appear. Bruce mutters the time, and I know he's writing it on his clipboard because that is what I'd be doing if this were still my job. Tears well in my eyes as I watch an animal I love dearly bring her first child into this world.

Watching her give birth is in complete contrast to how I spent my day, sitting beside my mom while she received her chemo with her eyes closed and her hand pressed tightly into mine. I spent most of my day re-reading the same pages of the magazine I brought because it was the only thing that could keep my attention long enough.

My mother is dying, while Jambo is giving birth. It seems like an odd form of irony when I think about it. Shortly after the news broke about Jambo's pregnancy, my mom was diagnosed with stage-four gastric cancer. I have yet to come to terms with her prognosis: I'm still waiting for a drug to miraculously become available that wipes out every nasty cancer cell ever discovered, but I know deep in my heart that it won't happen.

The chaplain always seems to come around when my mother is receiving her treatments. At first, it didn't bother me, but now it does. He says to pray, and I question: for what? Do I pray that this is all a dream and that, when I wake up, everything is back to normal?

Or do I forgo praying and instead pinch myself to wake up from this nightmare? Neither option right now seems to be the correct answer.

My mother, she's all I have. My father bailed before I was born, and she raised me by herself. My grandparents are around, but they can't help. They try, but they're old and frail, and watching their only daughter die isn't something they're taking very well.

So I'm there for her with no questions asked. It's where I want to be. It's where I need to be. She didn't have to keep me, but she did. So I'm there with a smile on my face, tending to her while her body is pumped full of drugs that are going to make her puke her guts out later, make her hair fall out and cause her to cry each time she looks in the mirror, and make her weak, even though she's the strongest woman I know, because she was *always* there for me.

In the past year, so much has changed. My mom has gone from a healthy, active woman to a frail, sickly shell of who she used to be. Retirement was supposed to be her time to shine. Her plans were to travel, play golf, and enjoy life, all while trying to find me a rich doctor to marry. She can pretty much guarantee I won't be marrying a doctor, not unless he's the one who finds the cure to keep her in my life another forty years or more.

Not a week after she retired, she called me complaining of a stomachache. I brushed it off. I mean, how many have I had one that went away hours later? A month after that phone call, she showed up at my apartment with the news. I was so excited to tell her about Jambo, but I could see by the look in her eyes that she had something important to tell me. I cried in her arms; *she* was consoling *me*, promising me that everything was going to be okay.

It's not.

Her last scan showed that the cancer is growing. The last round of chemo didn't work so they're trying a new kind. Who knew there were different kinds? It's like a vending machine full of drugs, and your selection is B-15. Only to find out you chose wrong.

The staff and I are on a first-name basis. I tried to keep a wall up, not wanting to get to know any of them, but after you spend days, even weeks in there, you can't help but ask personal questions and answer theirs in return. My favorite nurse is Lois. She's very caring when it comes to my mother, making sure that she's always comfortable. When I'm running late, Lois steps in and reads to my mom for me. With our many hospital stays and chemo visits, we've sailed through an array of romance novels, and while my mother loves the stories, some of them make me blush.

"Ainsley, are you watching?"

"I'm sorry, what?" I shake my head, clearing myself from my day-dream. Only it's not a dream, but the stark reality in which I live at the moment. My eyes focus back on Jambo as the face of her calf appears. More tears of happiness emerge, and I can't help but start to clap for her. The calf moves slowly out of its mother until the six-foot baby is on the ground with the padding cushioning its fall.

"Oh my," I say, covering my mouth. "We have a baby, Bruce." You would think that I had given birth myself with how emotional I am at the moment.

"That we do. From start to finish, Jambo did this in under an hour. Not bad for a first-time mom." Everyone around us is cheering.

"Now we wait and see if she nurses or if we have to guide them to each other." My hands clasp together with my thumbs resting against my lips. I study Jambo as she looks at her calf warily.

He or she is covered in sawdust, and the sight is comical and ador-able. Jambo takes tentative steps as she nears her calf. She nudges her baby a few times and then starts cleaning.

"She's a natural," I say. "And the calf is beautiful."

"She is," Bruce says, standing next to me. "I'll be right back. I want to check the temperature in the room."

My mother is always cold. It's a side effect from the chemo. We live in Florida and are likely the only people who don't use our air condi-tioner. In the hospital, they provide warming blankets, and I looked into having one of the machines in our house. The dryer doesn't warm them enough, and I'm afraid an electric blanket will burn her if she keeps it on too long. It's a no-win battle sometimes. Our condo is sti-fling, and sleep often evades me, especially when it's hot.

On good days, my mom will get dressed, put on makeup, and go to lunch with friends, but those days are few and far between lately. I feel like her lack of motivation is being caused by some form of depression, and I've asked her to see a doctor, but she refuses. She's stubborn and determined not to be a burden. I can't get it through to her that she's not a burden and I only want what's best for her.

I gasp again when the calf stands, and Bruce hollers "woohoo" from around the corner. Over the next few days, this calf is going to be mischievous and will test Jambo as a mother. I already know that I'll try to be down here as much as possible, even if it means giving up my lunch hour to spend time with mama and her baby.

"Yes, move toward your baby, Jambo," I say, trying to encourage her to let the calf nurse. "Oh, Bruce, look." I point as the baby latches on, much to the delight of all our staff. There's a collective sigh among us, knowing that the first steps of motherhood have been taken by Jambo and were done so easily.

I choose to sit on the floor and rest my head against the wall, not ready to leave. Right now, I don't care if I'm lacking sleep or my alarm will sound in a few hours. Everything I witnessed in the past couple of hours is giving me enough adrenaline to conquer whatever tasks lie ahead. Including the fact that, once the sun rises, the Boston Renegades will be here for media day, along with a hundred or so underprivileged third-graders from various schools in the area.

That alone should scare me into leaving, but it doesn't. Sitting here, watching Jambo nurse her calf, is the most calm and peaceful I have felt in a long time, and right now I could use a heavy dose of this type of happy to get through everything I'm facing with my mother.

# THREE

## Cooper

I dive into the swimming pool and stay under as long as I can before I begin to stroke. Swimming is my way of loosening up my sore muscles and keeping them from getting strained. I can't afford to get injured during spring training or not to be in the best shape of my career. Everyone is watching me. They're waiting for me to come out and hit the shit out of the ball, or to fuck up. The critics out there are wagering on whether I can make it in the majors or not. They say Stone kept me in the minors for a reason, and now I have to prove them wrong. Their opinions shouldn't matter, but they do.

With each lap I complete, my mind becomes clearer. My body cuts through the lukewarm water, creating a path so I can glide easily into my next stroke. This is the only time I have to myself before I'm "on." Before I'm officially Cooper Bailey, Boston Renegade. I know it's going to be different, with a lot more expectations, and for that I'm ready. I'm ready for what today is going to bring, with a whirlwind of activities, and I want to be my best. I want to stand out among my peers.

After the first day of conditioning I thought the guys like Davenport, Meyers, and Cross wouldn't talk to me again; however, they have and we continue to go through our workouts together. They're making me feel welcomed, and I've even been razzed by Kidd with some off-the-cuff one-liners that had me bent over gasping for air because I was laughing so hard. But there are still some guys in the clubhouse who give me sideways glances. I get it. I just hope they know I have no control over who gets the starting spot—that is all determined by the performances of Bainbridge and myself, and in the hands of Cal Diamond.

I know in a semi-perfect world, Bainbridge and I would split the spot, but that doesn't work for me. There are goals I want to achieve, accolades that I want to receive, and you can't earn those if you're sitting the bench for half the season. Part-time players don't earn batting titles or the Gold Glove. And if I'm sitting the bench, I can kiss my Rookie of the Year nomination goodbye. I'm sure Bainbridge feels like he's in a similar boat, perform or get benched. The difference is he's been there before. He's received the awards. It's time to let the young ones take over.

I finish my laps and head back to the apartment. I'm sharing it with a couple of the other rookies, both of whom are just out of college. Technically this is my second year, but it's my first in the majors. The guys I'm living with are straight out of college trying to make the forty-man roster. Last year I wasn't even invited to spring training due to a late-season muscle tear that left me sidelined. My arm is good to go now. I've been working my tail off to make sure something like that doesn't happen again.

As I climb the steps back to my place, I pause and look around the courtyard. This place is nice, nothing fancy, and it's cheap. It's what we can afford. We all get signing bonuses; mine was received last year, but that doesn't mean we're rolling in the cash like the other guys, so we live on the inexpensive side. There used to be a time when the organization paid for the players' housing and transportation. Athletes didn't have to worry, unlike now. If it weren't for me, the other two living with me would be catching the city bus or asking one of the other guys to pick them up. Luckily, I drove my car down here, but I won't be it driving back. Once spring training ends here, we have a few games up north to play and we'll be flying directly there.

After I get ready, the guys, Brock Wilder and Frankie Guerra, all pile into my car and we head to our training facility. There's a coach bus waiting for us when we arrive. The other Renegades are all dressed similarly with khaki shorts, our red polo shirts, and ball caps. We don't look much like baseball players, more like golfers.

I take a seat next to the window and pretend I'm interested in something in the parking lot. From my experience on team buses when I was a freshman in college, it's best not to make eye contact with anyone. The last thing I want to see on anyone's face is a look of disgust when I'm still trying to find my footing.

The seat next to me is taken, and a quick glance sends me into a partial panic attack. I shouldn't be scared or even nervous to sit next to Steve Bainbridge, but I am. When it comes down to my love for the game, he is one of the best. I've modeled some of my skills after him, and here I am gunning for his job.

"I thought I'd introduce myself," he says, extending his hand to shake mine. His grip is firm, strong, really, and meant to send me a message. Message received, but not processed. What's that saying—keep your friends close, but your enemies closer? I'll be his best damn friend if that's what I have to do. I'm not afraid of being underhanded in order to get what I want.

"It's nice to meet you," I say to him with pure honesty. Two years ago, I'd have been lining up for his autograph. By the end of spring training, he'll be asking for mine.

If I was expecting a conversation on the way to the zoo, I'm sorely mistaken. Bainbridge stands with a huff and moves to the back of the bus; his seat is filled immediately by Travis Kidd.

"His bark is worse than his bite."

"Okay?"

I shake my head and focus on the scenery outside. Everything here is green and lush, unlike Boston. In New England it's cold, dreary, gray, and gross. I long for the dry heat of Arizona, where I can play ball every day of the year unless it's raining.

"It means he's really a nice guy once you get to know him."

"I'm sure he is."

Kidd doesn't say anything after that, riding next to me in silence. From what I've heard, and believe me, rumors travel fast in the club-house, Kidd is a major partier in the off-season, and doesn't hold back much during the season, either. My dad has read articles about him, cautioning me from that type of behavior. He's reminded me that my image is everything, and once the public sees you doing something stupid, it's hard to come back from that. Keep my nose clean, that's what I'm supposed to do.

"Hey, rook, tonight a bunch of us are hitting the bar. We have late practice tomorrow. You should come." I'm surprised by the invite from Kidd, but pleasantly happy as well.

I shake my head slightly. "I don't do bars during the season."

He laughs and slaps his hand down on his leg. "There will be lots of women."

"I don't do women, either." The second the words are out of my mouth I regret them. His face pales before he starts to nod.

"I get it—"

"No, it's not like that," I say, interrupting him. "What I mean is, I don't date or anything like that. I'm focused on my career right now. Shit's hard enough, and I'm trying to make the roster. I need to keep my priorities straight."

"I was that way, too, my rookie year, until about midway through the year and we were in a slump so I had to drown out my sorrows. Once those floodgates open, man, you can't stop them."

"Let's hope we don't hit any slumps." My goal, like everyone else's on this bus, is to win. Put up high scores, outpitch the other team, run the bases harder, and challenge the opposing players to get us out. Make them work for their victory and hand them nothing.

Last year the Renegades didn't even make the wild card race and they were projected to. The season was a letdown, and I half expected to be called up much earlier. Sports analysts have said the Renegades tanked last year because Cal Diamond was supposedly sick and not truly focused on the game. Others say we're too young and need some veterans. If the latter is true, it explains why guys like Bainbridge are still around, but doesn't give much explanation as to why I'm here. They could've easily traded me and secured future draft picks if they're looking to keep veterans.

The guys start hooting and hollering when we pull into the zoo's parking lot. Yellow school buses and lines of kids surround us. Kids aren't my favorite things in the world, but I can smile, sign autographs, and act like I'm having a good time to do my part and make the organization look good.

As we file off, the kids start pointing. A few scream when Singleton, Davenport, and Bainbridge step off the bus. Steve walks right up to them and starts shaking their hands. It takes me a minute to realize what he's doing. *This* is why he's a fan favorite. *This* is what I need to emulate in order to be successful on both sides of the fence.

I start shaking hands. Most of the kids don't know who I am, and I'm okay with that. I answer their quick questions and even ask a few back, letting them know that I'm as interested in them and that I care.

We're ushered inside the zoo and met by staff. My eyes immediately fall on the woman who seems to be in charge. She is standing in front of a group of people all dressed in different shades of khaki green. I have never seen someone so poised and self-assured; it's mesmerizing how she commands the attention of everyone around her. Her smile lights up an already bright day, and I find myself stepping closer so I can get a better look at her.

"Good morning. My name is Ainsley Burke and I want to thank you all for coming out today. The third graders that you met on your way in are from underprivileged schools, and coming to the zoo is something they usually only have the chance to experience during field trips. At noon, we'll meet at the cafeteria, where we'll have lunch before finishing the second half of the tour. There are about one hundred kids here today, and you'll be in groups of five. That puts two players with each group. You can switch groups at any time, or wait until after lunch."

Her name is Ainsley. I say it over and over again in my head as I stand here staring at her. She smiles at me, but her eyes move away quickly as she watches my teammates filter to their locations to meet the children. The activity around me is a vision of blurry bodies while she stays crystal clear. The only thing missing is the epically cheesy music that either signifies a connection or our untimely doom.

"Bailey!"

I snap out of the trance I'm in to look for the source of my name being called. Davenport is waving his hand in the air, beckoning me over. With another glance at Ainsley, I step toward him, but not before looking back at her. That's when I see it. She's watching me, and when our eyes meet, she blushes and runs her hand over her copper blond ponytail. Is it an automatic response that her head tilts down as she tries to hide the grin on her face?

"Dude!" Davenport says when I reach him.

"What?" I ask, feigning indifference, but on the inside I'm busting with excitement. What I'm feeling isn't foreign. I've liked women before, even dated a few in college, but never did I have the physical urge to stare at someone, to memorize them before they faded away. Something must be wrong with me.

"You were eye-fucking her like there's no tomorrow."

My brows furrow at his comment, and he looks at me oddly.

"Are you a bat boy?" he asks, whispering in my ear.

"What?" I choke out. "You know I play center field."

He shakes his head. "You know," Davenport says, waggling his eyebrows and pointing down to his crotch. Did he really ask if I was a bat boy?

I shake my head. "No, man, that ship sailed back in high school."

Davenport wipes his forehead and lets out an exaggerated "phew" before glancing over in the direction where Ms. Ainsley Burke is standing. She's talking to some other woman, a teacher maybe, and when she looks in my direction, she smiles.

"Well, I think she wants your juice packer." A hand is slammed down on my shoulder as Kidd steps next to me. Davenport starts laughing while I try to contain myself.

"What did you say?"

Kidd shrugs and continues to look at Ainsley. "You know, your cooch lover. She wants to ride the jerk boner. Just don't do her in the cheap seats," he says, patting me on the shoulder before whistling at someone to get their attention.

"What the hell did he just say?"

Ethan shakes his head. "The one thing you need to learn about Travis is that he has this whole array of slang words for everything sexual. Cheap seats means having sex on the floor."

"Ah," I say, pretending to understand. "And bat boy?"

"Virgin, man. And if you are, don't you dare let Kidd find out. You'll never live it down, and you'll become his new favorite hobby."

Before I can respond, the kids start filing in. I'm sure they were told not to run, but you can see them speed-walking to get to their player. Davenport and I are with three girls and two boys who all seem very excited to be here. I was excited, until we had to leave and I could no longer openly gawk at Ainsley.

# FOUR

## Ainsley

The sound of loud cheering has me peering out my window. The charter bus carrying the Boston Renegades has pulled to a stop and the players are stepping off, much to the delight of the children waiting to meet them. Looking back into the mirror, my eyes roam over my ragged look, and I try to bring some life to my cheeks by pinching them. With my reddish blond hair in a ponytail and a very light dusting of makeup, this is as good as it's going to get for me today.

And today, of all days, is media day with the Renegades. I knew this at two in the morning when I raced back to work to watch a miracle unfold. I couldn't leave, though, not once I caught sight of the calf. Even though I enjoy my job now as the zoo's event and staff coordinator, I miss working with the giraffes every day, and watching the birth of our newest member really hit home. However, I have no doubt in my mind that this event today will be just as joyous. I can only imagine how fun it's going to be, watching the children's faces when they meet their favorite athlete. Probably much like mine when Jambo gave birth in the early hours of the morning.

When I contacted the Renegades' general manager, Ryan Stone, with my idea, I thought he would hang up on me. Instead, he loved it and promised that the team would be at the zoo. He went on to say that it's important for the team to give back to not only the community at home, but also the community they call home for their preseason. I couldn't agree more.

Peeking out my window again, I watch the players move down the line, stopping and shaking hands with each and every kid, likely making this a dream come true for some of them.

I grab my radio, exit my office, and step out into the blazing sun. It's unseasonably warm for March, making me hope this isn't a sign of things to come. I'd rather not experience a scorching summer this year.

"This was a great idea, Ainsley," Bruce says through a yawn.

"You should've gone home. I could've found someone to fill in for you."

"Nah," he says, shaking his head. "I want to be there when they see the calf through the window."

*Me too.*

"It's good that they agreed to this. I know it was a risk asking, but the Renegades are so popular I thought everyone involved could benefit from this event."

"Did you think they would tell you no?"

I shrug, not really knowing the ins and outs of what professional teams or athletes normally do. Sure, I read things on the web about money being donated or an athlete paying special attention to a child who is battling an illness, but to take a day off from training to spend it at the zoo is probably, at least in my opinion, unheard of. In what research I could do, I didn't find any reports or documentation that this sort of event had been done before. Golf games, bowling, and the like are done all the time, and I honestly didn't think my idea stood a chance. Thankfully, the Renegades had no qualms about proving me wrong.

"Most of the players come from nothing, so they're making sure the communities who support them are taken care of. They want to make sure that kids have the same opportunities to succeed," Bruce says, opening my eyes to a different side of athletes.

"That makes sense," I say as I stand next to him, watching the players interact with the kids. Autographs are signed, and teachers are taking pictures, and even a few of the players are snapping their own shots. It's nice that they're not on a time limit, but I'm antsy and want to get this event started. The nerves are starting to set in, and I want to make sure everything is perfect.

A few of the players make their way into the zoo, shaking hands with the staff as they pass by. I hear my name in the distance and turn to find an older gentleman walking toward me.

"Are you Ainsley Burke?"

"I am. Are you Cal Diamond? Mr. Stone said you'd be my point of contact today," I reply as we shake hands.

"Thank you for having us."

"It's my pleasure." We step off to the side and go over the plan of action for the day; he reiterates what I agreed to with Stone.

"I want to make sure the focus is on the children and not the end result with the media," I tell Cal, who nods in agreement.

"Of course, that is why we're here. Honestly, the guys could care less about the media today. They're excited to be here and away from training."

"That's good to hear. We're excited to be hosting them and especially for the children. They seemed very excited out in the parking lot."

We exchange cell phone numbers, in case either of us needs to get in touch with the other, and I remind him that I always have my radio with me, and any one of the staff members can get in touch with me if I'm needed.

Today is going to be different from any other day. For one, the zoo is closed to the public. Two, everything is free, including one souvenir of each child's choice. Three, we're going to make sure the animals are outside for the children's arrival so they can have optimum viewing pleasure. Hearing their laughter, seeing their faces light up when an animal, particular a giraffe, comes near, is worth the extra work we're putting in today.

I stand at the entrance of the zoo, looking over the courtyard where everyone is gathering. The players are mingling with a few of the staff, taking pictures and chatting about who knows what. A sense of pride washes over me as I see so many happy faces. It's important to me that today goes off without any issues and that it's a success. I radio the different exhibits to make sure they're ready, and all are eager to let the kids in.

The Boston Renegades will be the kids' tour guides. The best way to handle this was to leave the responsibility up to the teachers about who their students went with. It's honestly something I wouldn't have been able to do, considering I don't know any of the players. Well, except for one.

There was one that caught my eye when I was perusing the roster that was sent over by the organization. It was the way he looked at the camera for his photo, not cocky but self-assured. I found myself looking him up online, trying to figure out what my attraction was, and found very little. If he has a girlfriend, there's no mention of her. If he's been in trouble with the law, it's not been stated. He seems to be a squeaky clean rookie, who was, by all accounts, a superstar in the minor leagues.

And while my interest is piqued, I remind myself that I don't date athletes. I tried that once, and the failure was so epic that it's something I'll never forget.

"Bailey!"

His name is yelled, and it makes it easy to follow him. Our eyes meet, and even though I pretend I'm looking elsewhere now, he somehow knows I'm still staring at him. And if he didn't, then he does now, because my cheeks are on fire and the only thing I can do to quell my embarrassment is run my hand over my ponytail in hopes that my arm is shielding me from him, but that doesn't work because I smile automatically at the thought that he is watching me.

As much as I want to turn away, I don't. I take in the way he interacts with his teammates, the laughing and carrying on, and wonder what it's like to be so free. I haven't laughed in months, not since my mother first got sick, and the most joy I have felt in a long time happened this morning.

I give the signal, and the gates open. The kids move in an orderly fashion, but even I can see they're trying to get to their assigned player. Their chatter is refreshing as they tell their friends how excited they are, and the teachers seem relieved that they're getting a break, more or less.

"Excuse me?"

I feel a small tug on arm and look to find a little girl smiling back at me.

"Hi, what can do for you?" I ask, bending down so I'm at her eye level.

"Do you know if Jambo had her baby yet?"

I can't help but smile and nod my head enthusiastically. "She did, earlier this morning. And Zookeeper Bruce is so excited to for you all to see, but remember, don't tap or bang on the glass because you'll scare Jambo and the baby."

"I won't," she says, running off to meet with her group.

When I stand back up, the groups gather and are ready to start their day. With one quick look around at all the smiles, I remind myself that I did this. I brought these groups together.

"Remember to use your maps today, and don't forget to refill your water bottles along the pathway. Be mindful of the critters that you'll meet during your journey, and pay special attention to any of the staff you see standing around; they might have someone special with them. And please make sure to visit the giraffes. Not only will you be able to feed them, but you'll see Jambo's new baby," I proudly tell them. The last part is met with a loud cheer, and not only from the children. "The gates are officially open. Have fun!"

The groups start to move away slowly, and I once again find myself watching for one in particular. When he looks over his shoulder, I pretend I'm paying attention to everyone and not just him, but I think he sees right through me. From afar, I can gawk, maybe even fantasize when I'm feeling up to it, but the reality is that nothing will ever come of this. He's not my type. And he already has two strikes against him—forgive the pun, but it's true. He's a baseball player, and they're nothing but trouble.

# FIVE

## Cooper

I am likely going to hell when I die. I don't know how long it's been since Davenport and I took our small group away from the entrance, the place where I fell under the spell of Ainsley Burke, but every few minutes I'm looking over my shoulder to see if she's checking up on us.

And the reason I'm going to hell is because I'm secretly hoping one of our students hurts themselves and I have to rush them to the office for first aid. These thoughts make me a shitty human being.

Or our small group could easily become a band of misfits and troublemakers, giving her an excuse to come check on us and to make sure we don't need anything. Forget the fact that my group is pretty awesome and the kids seem to be excited, so it's not like we're drawing attention to ourselves. At this rate, I'll be lucky to see her at all.

"Stop looking for her," Davenport says.

I shake my head, scoffing at him. "I'm checking out the surroundings. I've never been here before. What if there's a flying monkey or something waiting to attack?"

The kids laugh, and one little girl steps a bit closer to me and smiles. Her toothless grin and big brown eyes remind me of why I'm here, to make sure these kids have a good time. I shouldn't be worrying about whether Ms. Burke is going to come check on us or even seek me out. If she's someone I want to know, I'm going to have to be the one to make the move.

I fall in step behind the little girl as we move to the next exhibit. Walking at the zoo is a massive workout for these kids and their little legs. The terrain is such that you're always climbing or descending a hill, giving your legs ample exercise. Renegades management is smart, having us do this. Today may be our day off from conditioning, but we're still getting some cardio training in.

When we reach the monkeys, Davenport yells about something overhead, and I go scrambling. The kids laugh, making fun of me as I take cover under a tree. I laugh, letting them know that I'm only joking and chase after a few of them as I act like one of those beasts from *The Wizard of Oz*.

By the time lunch rolls around, I'm exhausted, as most of the guys are. We're dragging our tails into the cafeteria to sit on hard plastic chairs and eat fried foods. The teacher for our group comes around, asking if any of the kids would like to switch players. The boys raise their hands, and I don't blame them. There are better, more seasoned players than Ethan and me, but the girls stay. My little friend from earlier hasn't left my side, and has kept pace with me since she smiled at me.

She taps me on the arm and points. I follow her direction to find Ainsley talking to one of the teachers. She makes quick eye contact and smiles before continuing her conversation.

"That's great, you have one of our charges being a lookout for you."

I throw one of my fries at Ethan, only to hear the words "food fight" being muttered by a few of the boys at our table.

"No food fight," I tell them, trying to calm them down. "Davenport wanted some of my fries is all."

The young boys look at me like I'm crazy. I am. The last thing I want to do is start a food fight on a field trip. Somehow I don't think our GM would be appreciative of my actions.

"My dad says you'll never start over Bainbridge," the lad next to me says as he stuffs his mouth. I glance down at him and realize I could take him if push came to shove.

"Who does your dad play for?"

The boy pauses mid-food shove and shakes his head. "He doesn't play baseball. He works in an office."

"I see. And you believe him?"

He shrugs. "Sure, why not?"

"I don't know, that's why I'm asking. What do you think? Have you seen me play before?"

He shakes his head.

"Has your father?"

He shakes his head again.

"So you and your father haven't seen me play, but both feel like I'm not good enough to start over Bainbridge?"

Davenport kicks me under the table, and I glare at him. I'm not pissed at the kid, but at the father for saying crap like this. How does the father know I can't start over Bainbridge if he's never seen me play? Clearly, if you're looking at my stats from last year, I'm far better on paper than Bainbridge.

"Don't forget you're allowed to make up your own mind. Maybe you can come to a spring training game and watch. Then you can form your own opinion."

"Yeah, maybe. I'll ask, but my parents usually say no."

It dawns on me that a lot of these kids aren't from middle-class families. Most receive state aid and supplemental income.

"Tell you what, if you want to come to a game, you give me a call, and Steve and I will set some tickets aside for you."

His face lights up like a kid on Christmas morning, and he wraps his arms around my midsection, pinning my arms to my side.

"Thanks. I'll tell him."

I hand the boy a card with my agent's number on it. "Just call this number if you want to go. He'll be expecting your call."

As soon as lunch is over, we're back to walking. The last half of the zoo seems to go a bit faster than the first, and the kids are all dragging behind by the time we reach the entrance again. They're going to sleep the whole way back to their school, that's for sure.

My new friend, also known as my lookout, gives me a hug and thanks me for being her walking partner. As she heads toward her teacher, I realize I should've thanked her for being my eyes today. We could've been partners in crime if we'd had more time together.

When the kids line up with each of their schools, it's time for a photo op. The media is escorted into the zoo, and the cameras start going off. The sound is annoying, but one I'll have to get used to. We assemble around the kids and take an array of photos with each class. Afterward, the staff gets their chance.

"You should stand by her, put your arm on her shoulder," Davenport whispers into my ear as he motions toward Ainsley. I like his idea and maneuver my way toward her. She sees me, and from where I'm standing, I think she smiles. There's a soft glow to her skin, and I find myself wanting to reach out and touch her cheek. It's dimpled and leaves me wondering how I can make her smile just so I can see it. Her nose is small, yet it's perfect for her face. I like that she's not covered in eye makeup, and I can see the fine lines that come with laughing too much. Standing this close to her, my heart starts beating faster, and my palms are sweating—of course it's eighty degrees out—but it's the thickness of my tongue that has me speechless and swallowing hard when she runs her hand over her reddish blond ponytail, moving her hair to the side as if she's giving me a clearer view of her. She hasn't stopped smiling since I've been standing here, and while she could be getting ready for the photo, part of me is also hoping it's because I'm next to her, and that's what I'm going with because it makes me feel good about myself.

At the last moment, I set my hand on her shoulder and squeeze, keeping my eyes forward even though I just want to stare at her. The media coordinator tells the photographers that their time is up. A few of them grumble and continue to shoot while most of us stand here, smiling, but the veterans all turn their backs.

I don't move, and neither does my hand, until she turns to face me.

"I'm Cooper Bailey," I tell her, even though I'm not sure she wants to know.

She steps back and offers me her hand, and once I take it, I can't let go. This is very unlike me. I've never chased a woman before so I feel a bit unsure, but the feel of her hand in mine makes me feel like I'm soaring through the air. The exhilaration I feel from holding her hand is downright crazy.

"Do you want to let go of my hand?"

"No, not really," I tell her honestly. I loosen my grip, giving her the opportunity to slip away if she wants.

She doesn't want. "My name is Ainsley." Her voice is sweet and soft, sending a chill down my spine. Behind me, I can hear the guys snickering, so I let go of her hand and adjust my ball cap.

"They're probably waiting for you."

I look over my shoulder to see Travis Kidd acting like a woman. The jackass is blowing kisses and posing like a supermodel. I shake my head, wondering how immature he really is.

"They can wait," I say without looking at her. When I turn back, she's still staring at me, and I like it. I like the way her eyes connect with mine. It's as if she's trying to figure me out.

"Can I call you sometime?"

Ainsley looks down at the ground and crosses her arms over her chest. "Listen, I'm sure you're a nice guy and all, but I don't date baseball players. You guys all come in here, acting sweet and caring about the kids, but will be gone in two months. We're forgotten all about until next season."

From her spiel, I can tell someone has hurt her in the past, but I'm not willing to give up. There's no way I can now.

"Whoa, why the one-eighty?"

"Excuse me?"

"I mean, a second ago I sort of thought … never mind." I shake my head and start to walk away, only to turn back. "I don't know about the other guys. I only know me, and I'm not like that. I'd like to prove myself. Just one date to show you that I'm genuine?"

She shakes her head no again, but there's a glint in her eye that tells me she's thinking about it. "I'm sorry, I can't." Ainsley is walking away before I can even think to form a rebuttal. Kidd is there to pick up the pieces and remind me that I just had my first strikeout of my Major League career. Wonderful.

I drag my sorry ass out toward the waiting bus with my head hanging in shame. I thought for sure I'd at least get her number and be able to convince her that I'm not an epic douche like some of the other guys.

Just as my foot touches the bottom step, my name is called from behind. In a heart-stopping moment, I think it's Ainsley, only to find another female worker running toward me. I step away and wait for her to get to me.

"Here," she says, slapping a piece of paper into my hand. When I look at what's written on it, I'm surprised to see Ainsley's name and what I'm assuming is her number. "She'll kill me if she knew I did this, but it's her cell. Sweep her off her feet. She deserves it." The woman winks before running back toward the zoo.

"Well, you lucky dog," Michael Cashman says as he slaps me on my shoulder.

I look at the piece of paper then back at the zoo entrance and smile. Now the challenge is to get her to return a text message or go on a date.

# SIX

## Ainsley

I'm great at pretending. It's what I do best, even when my actions break my own heart. Okay, the heartbreaking is a little overdramatic, but it feels the same. From the first time I saw Cooper Bailey staring at me this morning, right up until he asked for my number, I felt good about myself. Someone was actually interested in me. It's a satisfying feeling when you catch the eye of a good-looking man, but that's all it can be.

When he came over and stood by me to seal our first and only meeting with a photo, I thought I was having an out-of-body experience. My entire being gravitated toward him while my brain reminded me to be pleasant. That it's my job to be nice. But my version of nice went way too far when I smiled at him, not once, hell, not even twice, but every time I've seen him today. I couldn't help it. I don't know if it was the way he entered the zoo, with an air of confidence, or the way he looked at me like he's known me forever. Things became bad when I saw his five o'clock shadow and turned even worse when he went to adjust his hat and inadvertently flexed his arm.

Cooper Bailey, or any other athlete, is off limits. They're trouble and not just with a capital T. It's the whole damn word that needs to be capitalized. It's been my rule for as long as I can remember, and living in Fort Myers makes my point even more valid because most of the baseball players march around town like they're God's gift to women. Some of us fall for them, but there are the few of us who are immune to their charms.

A few of us call them the spring flings. They're here to entertain us, make our streets look damn fine with all the man candy, and bring in the revenue we need to kick off our summer. Many of my friends belong in this category. I, however, am not one of them.

Then they leave. And in their wake, they leave broken hearts, pissed-off husbands, and a few unlucky, or maybe lucky, depending on how you look at it, pregnancies. I've been here long enough to know that you don't mess with the baseball players. It's safer for all those around you.

So when my body becomes a traitor and my heart is beating five times faster than normal, I expect my brain to be the voice of logic, and it was, for the most part. It was easy to say no to Cooper when he asked if he could call me sometime, because I don't want the heartbreak come April when he leaves. I'm too old for a relationship that is only going to last a few months, or even a few dates. I want to settle down. I want that house with that stupid picket fence and a mailbox out front, with flowers growing along the walkway and the sense of love inside my home. You can't get that when you date an athlete. I should know.

As I hear the chartered bus pull away, I sigh in relief, knowing that I've done the right thing. Would it be fun to date a man like Cooper Bailey? Probably. I'm sure he could show me a good time, but having a predetermined expiration date is like having a neon sign over your head that reads "loser."

Of course when I sit down, the Boston Renegades baseball roster, complete with the photos and bios that I needed for media day, is sitting right on top for my viewing pleasure. None other than Cooper's profile is highlighted, by my stupid yellow marker. His résumé is impressive, but that doesn't negate the fact that he's an athlete, and that is a road I will not travel down.

My co-worker and overall best friend, Stella, slams the office door, getting my attention. Stella is by all accounts a spitfire, live-on-the-edge type of girl with her long blond hair and green eyes. She's been untamable since I met her back in middle school.

"What has your panties all twisted around?" I ask.

Stella stands in front of me with her hands on her hips, rosy red cheeks and a scowl that would make anyone cower, except for me. I've been on the receiving end of a Stella tirade before; they're not fun, but I've learned to work through them.

"He's cute."

"You'll have to be a little more specific, Stella. We had forty men, not including coaches, here." As slyly as I can, I slide a piece of paper over Cooper's face. The last thing I want is for her to see me looking at his picture or notice that I've spent time focusing on him specifically.

"You're right, but not all of them are good-looking. I mean a few of them . . ." She shakes her head as if she's laughing at her own inside joke. "Anyway, I gave him your number. You can thank me later." Her words are to the point and without pause as she digs into my candy dish to take a handful of Starbursts.

My mouth opens and closes, only to open again. When I try to speak, nothing but a squeak comes out. With my nails biting into my palms, I prepare to ask the question I already know the answer to and so does my heart.

"You gave who my number?"

"The cute one." She thumbs over her shoulder, pointing toward the window. Five minutes ago, she would've been pointing toward a slew of buses, but they're gone now, and the parking lot is empty except for the employees' cars.

"Well, that narrows it down. I'll be sure to ask the caller if he's cute if and when he decides to call me. Do you mind giving me a name so I know who I should be expecting?"

"*The* one. I don't know his name. Let me see the roster."

"I don't have one," I lie, strategically placing my arm over the hidden roster.

"I smell a pile of stinky shit. Give it to me, Ainsley," she says with a bite of authority and her hands on her hips.

"We work in a zoo. We often smell odors we wish we didn't." I'm being childish in the worst way, but I can't help it. I don't want Cooper Bailey or any of the other Renegades calling me, except I do and I shouldn't feel this way.

Stella leans over my desk, and my fingers press down on the stack of papers. Yet my eye contact with her never wavers. If I don't look down, she'll never know what I'm hiding. Everything moves in slow motion. The closer she inches, the more my heart races. I don't understand what the big deal is. If I wanted him or any of the others to have my number, I would've given it to him. She didn't have to do it on my behalf.

Her fingers come in contact with my upper arm, tickling me until I have no choice but to use my hands to defend myself. She grabs the papers and doesn't even have to sift through them, since the paper on top gave way in her bid to humiliate me.

"This one," she says, pointing to Cooper's picture. "I don't know why you're playing coy. I saw you talk to him, and you've highlighted his picture. I don't see any of the others with yellow lines boxing them in. Shit, the only things missing are little hearts and stars."

I want to add that I looked at him—stared at, really—thought about him and imagined what it'd be like to have his arms hold me, but I refrain. I don't need to give her any more ammunition.

I snag the roster back and toss it into my drawer, slamming it closed. The logical thing would be to throw it away, but I'm not logical right now. I'm determined. "You know I don't date athletes."

"Ainsley, that was *years* ago."

"It doesn't matter when it happened, it happened. I was in love, he was the quarterback, and we were engaged. Athletes are all the same."

"Not all guys cheat."

I laugh, because she knows that's not true. "It's a moot point, Stella. I'm not interested. Besides, I have too much on my plate right now with my mom being sick." I stand and push my chair in, grabbing my purse so I can leave. "I never thought growing up without a dad would be a big deal, but it is. Taking care of mom by myself is tiresome. It'd be nice to have a little help every now and again."

"I help as much as I can," she reminds me.

"I know, and I appreciate it, but it's not the same. I know my mom is lonely. She wants me to get married and give her a grandchild, but it's not going to happen. The doctors aren't very optimistic about her prognosis."

"Maybe Cooper is willing?" Stella states as she shuts off my light and closes the door behind us. We walk out of the office, saying good-bye to the other staff members before heading toward the parking lot.

"No man is willing to knock someone up to appease a dying woman's wish."

"In vitro?"

Shaking my head, I fish my keys out of my purse. "No, she'll just have to hang on until I meet the man of my dreams."

# SEVEN

## Cooper

"Keep your front leg planted and use your hip more, Bailey. You're not a power hitter." The Renegades' batting coach, Mickey King, demonstrates the movement that he wants to see from me. I should be pissed about the criticism, but I'm not. I'd rather rack up the RBIs or get on base and let the others bring me home. My base running speed is one of the fastest on the team, and I have the ability to steal any base. So what if I'm not hitting a ball out of the park every game?

Digging into the dirt, my leg twists twice before I settle into my stance. I've been practicing for the past twenty minutes, hitting meatballs all over the park. King doesn't like my stance and says that I'll have a hard time with the left-handed pitchers when I face them and I need to adjust. I didn't have a problem in the minors. A decent number of the pitchers we faced were Major Leaguers rehabbing until they got called back up.

The pitch comes, and I keep my front leg planted and twist my hip as King instructed. The ball sails, caught easily by one of the outfielders waiting their turn.

"You're stiff. Loosen up." King rubs my shoulders quickly, patting and stepping away. He's wearing catcher's gear so he can watch me from behind and is probably praying he doesn't take one to the junk while he's squatting.

My right cleat digs in, followed by my left. I swing the bat a few times, trying to loosen up and prepare for the next pitch. It's delivered. I swing, and the beautiful sound of the ball hitting the sweet spot of my wooden bat fills my ears. The ball travels along the left field line, staying fair but far enough out of reach that, if this were live, the ball would be hard to get to. I'd be on second by now with a stand-up double.

Behind me, King hoots and hollers, telling me that this is what he wants to see every time I'm in the batter's box. I step again and take the pitch with a similar result. This continues for another twenty minutes until he tells me to head to the trainer and get some ice for my shoulders.

Bainbridge is in the dugout, waiting his turn, along with a few of the other guys. I nod to most of them, but things between Bainbridge and me are going to go from bad to worse in less than a week, and there isn't shit I can do about it. Right now, I'm performing better in the outfield, running the bases faster and more aggressively, and my batting is only going to improve now that I know what King wants. It would make sense for me to start over Bainbridge.

We don't exchange glances after I stow my gear and head to the training room. Words are mumbled as I pass by, but I pay them no mind. The guys on the team are loyal to Bainbridge, and that's the way it should be. They're lucky no one is vying for their spot or they'd be freaking the hell out like he is.

In the training room, Davenport and Hawk Sinclair, one of our starting pitchers, are taking an ice bath, while a few of the other guys and staff filter around the room. The trainer tells me to have a seat on the table, and he'll be with me in a minute. Slipping off my jersey, I sit there wondering if I should strike up a conversation with the guys.

For the most part, Davenport has been a good buddy to me, Kidd too. But I still feel like the odd man out, especially considering Bainbridge.

"Yo, Bailey, how's that hot piece of ass from the zoo?" Sinclair asks, causing Davenport to look over at me. They're both waiting for an answer, one that I don't have for them.

"Uh, not sure." I run my hand over the back of my neck and shake my head. Water splashes, and a very naked Davenport steps out of the tub, wrapping himself in a barely big enough towel.

"You got the chick's digits. Have you used them?"

Shaking my head. "Nah, man. Not yet."

"Why the fuck not, Bailey?" Sinclair asks, standing in the tub so the room can see all his glory. He doesn't care that his dick is hanging out for everyone to see, and the fact is that he's standing there with his hands on his hips, mimicking the way Kidd was acting at the zoo. It's hard to take a man like Hawk Sinclair seriously when he's like this. Hell, it's hard to take any of them seriously most of the time.

"Dunno, she didn't exactly give it to me."

"Who the fuck cares? Call her," he bellows. "She was fucking hot. You could be tapping that ass before we have to get down to business."

"Our first game is in a week," I remind him, but he blows me off.

"Preseason doesn't count for shit."

That's where he's wrong. I only have this window to really prove myself. If my performance is mediocre, that won't bode well for me when we get back to Boston. If I do well, I make it harder for Diamond to put together his starting lineup.

"Shut the fuck up, Hawk. Every day we're out here is important. You're just burnt out because you've been here longer than the rest of us," Davenport says, pulling up the stool next to me.

"I don't have time for a relationship," I mumble as Sinclair leaves the training room. That is my go-to excuse. It always has been. Despite the fact that I asked for Ainsley's number, I can't say if I would've used it or not.

"I thought the same thing, but, man, once I met Daisy, I chased her ass big time. Some of it backfired, but in the end, it worked out for the best," Davenport answers the statement I threw at Sinclair's back.

"Maybe there's something wrong with her."

"Doubt it. You know she's compassionate, or she wouldn't work at a place like that. Plus, did you see her with the kids?"

"Does your wife know you're pregnant?" I ask Davenport, whose face turns bright red.

"What the fuck are you talking about? Just because a man is in touch with his feminine side doesn't make him a pussy."

I stifle a laugh, which only seems to piss him off even more. I couldn't help it, the way he was going on about compassion and shit like that. If I didn't know any better, I'd think he'd wanted to ask Ainsley out on a date himself, but I've heard him talking to his wife. I can't imagine ever talking to someone the way he does, but I think it'd be nice. He's not mushy with her on the phone, but sweet and caring. I know he misses her, especially since they haven't been married that long and now he's away from her until April, unless she comes to visit. "I'm just giving you shit."

Davenport throws something white at me, smacking me in the face. I can only pray that it's a towel and not someone's dirty jockstrap. I bat it away but don't look at what it was. Some things are better left unknown.

"Seriously, though, call her. If there's one thing I learned from dating Daisy, it's don't wait."

"She wasn't interested."

Davenport stands, cinching his towel at his waist. "You asked for her number at her place of employment. I probably would've said no, too. You have her number, call her. The worst thing that is going to happen is she says no again. You don't have anything to lose. Or you're looking to get laid, go to the bar, tell them who you are, and you're guaranteed to find a cleat-chaser." He pats me on the shoulder and walks off toward the clubhouse. He's right. I have nothing to lose by calling her, except my dignity if she tells me no again.

After practice, instead of going into my apartment, I stay out in my car for some privacy. I'm worked up, my heart is pounding, and I'm afraid I'm going to make a fool of myself. If so, at least it's done over the phone and not face-to-face.

What I didn't tell the guys is that I have her number memorized. I studied it until I could recite the digits written on the piece of paper. I even tucked the piece of paper into my wallet and made sure her name and number were stored in my contacts. All for a woman who told me no from the get-go. If that's not desperation, I don't know what is.

My thumb hovers over her name, *Ainsley Burke*. She's the first Ainsley I know. It's unique and stands out, fitting for her. Shutting off my car so it doesn't overheat and with the windows rolled down, I finally press the phone icon that will connect me to her, hopefully.

Three rings and the line opens. Her voice, the same one that I remember so clearly in my head, says hello, and I sit here like a fucking moron.

"Hello?" she says again, clearly irritated.

"Uh...hi, hello."

"Who is this?"

"It's ... uh." I swallow hard and chastise myself for being an idiot. *Just talk to her.* I clear my throat and man up. "Sorry, it's Cooper Bailey. Your co-worker gave me your number, which I know you didn't want me to have, but—"

"But she meddles in my life and business, and you've decided to call after two days."

"Yeah, something like that."

"The answer is still no."

And just like that, our conversation is over. She's already turned me down, and I didn't even ask her anything. I can play it off like a hurt puppy or I can be coy. I glance at myself in my rearview mirror and shake my head. I've never been afraid of a woman until now, but that shouldn't stop me from pursuing her.

"That's good. I wasn't calling to ask you out."

"You weren't?"

"No. I was calling to thank you for organizing the event the other day. You see, this is my first time in Fort Myers, and you and your staff really showed me some southern hospitality. After my day there, I'm excited to start playing so I can get a feel for the hometown crowd."

"And this is why you called?"

"Of course."

"Hmm," she says, pausing. "Well, I guess I owe you an apology. I'm sorry for jumping to conclusions and assuming you were calling to ask me out. It's just..."

"No, I get it. I was sort of an ass the other day and shouldn't have put you on the spot."

She laughs lightly, sending a jolt through my system. Man, what I wouldn't do to hear a full-on laugh from her because of something

I've said, and now that I have her on the phone in a somewhat jovial mood, the last thing I want to do is hang up. "Listen, I'm really in the mood for some Italian, like the-best-food-you've-ever-had-in-your-life-never-eating-carbs-again-Italian. Do you know a place like that near the ballpark?"

"Well, that depends. Are you looking for casual or fancy, and do you want American Italian or legit Italian?"

Well, that question quickly backfired. I was hoping she'd tell me that she'd show me where to go, but no, she has more questions. The only thing I can do is play along, because the longer I keep her on the phone, the longer I have a chance to get to know her.

"Probably casual and American. I left my tuxedo back in Boston." I laugh, hoping that she gets my sense of humor. When she does, I fist-pump and give myself one point for hearing a happy sound out of her.

"Right, so you want LaMotta's. They have the best pizza, and the meatballs are giant."

"You like big balls?" I realize the horror of my words the second they're out of my mouth. "I'm sorry, that's not what I meant. I spend my days around ball players, and we're not exactly polishing china during the day."

"It's fine, but yes, I do enjoy a good meatball, and LaMotta's is the best."

"LaMotta's, got it."

"What else have you done since you arrived?"

Bingo, now we're talking. I fill Ainsley in on my lackluster life, mostly due to training and not knowing anyone here. I'm hoping she takes pity on me, and if it's not tonight, then maybe tomorrow when I call her back asking for directions to her favorite restaurant. As long as

I'm talking to her, it's a step in the right direction. She may have told me no tonight, but that could change in the next few days or weeks.

"Hey, Cooper?"

"Yes, Ainsley." I know the way I answer her can probably be construed as seductive, but hearing her say my name does things to me that shouldn't be happening in the parking lot of my apartment complex.

"I need to go. It's getting late, and I have an early morning meeting."

My heart drops, but she's right. My alarm clock will be going off sooner rather than later. "Thanks for all the info on the area."

"Yeah. If you check out LaMotta's, let me know."

"Will do. Good night, Ainsley."

I hang up after she says goodbye, and fist-pump again in excitement. She left it open for me to call her again, and I plan to do just that. I'm up for the challenge of getting this woman to go out with me, even if it's just one date.

# EIGHT

## Ainsley

"TGIF," Stella sings as she comes through the door. In her hand are a box of donuts and a bag of muffins, her usual "care package" for the staff on Fridays. I pay her no mind, still pissed at her for giving Cooper Bailey my number.

Well, I'm mad that she gave it to him because I've been up late for the past three nights, missed two of my favorite television shows, and am afraid we've run out of things to talk about on the phone. I have found that I rather enjoy talking to him, but dating or even dinner is out of the question.

Stella waves the open box of donuts under my face. I pretend to be busy and shake my head. She sits in the chair across from my desk with a huff.

"What's wrong? You're usually good for at least one Boston creme."

The irony isn't lost on me that Boston creme is my favorite donut and the one guy who is interested in me plays for Boston.

"I haven't been getting much sleep."

She shuts the lid and leans forward, sorrow written all over her face. I don't have the heart to tell her that it's not because of my mom, at least not this week, but because I keep getting these phone calls that last for hours.

"What do the doctors say?"

"About Mom?" I question, causing her look at me suspiciously. "They changed her chemo because the last round didn't work. We won't know much more until they do another CAT scan."

"Is she in pain?"

"No." My answer is very nonchalant, and I avoid making eye contact with her because I know she'll see right through me. The longer I can hold out on my secret, the better it is for me. She's going to hound me, pressure me into going out with him, and I can't.

"I don't get it. If your mom is feeling well, why aren't you sleeping? Oh, it's because you're watching *Livid*?"

No, I wish it were, but unfortunately because of you, my best friend, I'm on the phone while it's airing, and I haven't upgraded my cable to include a digital video recorder.

"That's not why, either." I'm starting to like this game. I'm wondering how long I can go until I break and tell her why I'm so tired.

I hit print on my computer, and the paper schedule spits out so I can look it over before posting it. Stella takes a donut out of the box and starts munching away, her eyes unfocused as she tries to figure out what is going on in my life. It's sweet, really, how much she cares, but it's not all that complicated. For her, the fact that I have stopped dating to care for my mother boggles her mind. Add that to my rule of never dating an athlete, and she's completely beside herself. I'm just not as carefree with my heart as she is.

"Welp, I'm officially confused," she says, tossing the donut box onto my desk. I give her the stink eye, but to no avail. She isn't buying my act, and honestly, it's getting harder to keep everything bottled in. "I give up. Why are you so tired?"

I calmly fold my hands over my stack of papers and look at her as if she's being reprimanded. "I've been on the phone for the past three nights with Cooper Bailey."

Her eyes go wide, and her mouth drops open, but I slowly shake my head back and forth. "Before you start planning my wedding, there is nothing going on between us, and I am still not going out with him."

"Then why's he calling?" The confusion is back. I guess it's too much to accept that a single man and woman can be friends and not lovers these days.

"At first I thought it was to ask me out, but I told him no before he could even get the words out, and we started talking. One night has turned into three, but after last night, I think we're done chatting."

"Why?" she asks, leaning forward.

"All he does is ask me questions about Fort Myers, and I think he knows it all by now."

"But?"

"But what?"

"Do you like him?"

Sighing, I push away from my desk and take the schedule over to my corkboard so I can look it over. "It doesn't matter if I do, Stella. It's never going to happen."

"How do you know if you won't give him a chance?"

I turn and face her. "Because he lives in Boston and I live here. And I'm not looking for a relationship that ends in April. And moving out of the state is out of the question." I throw my hands up in the air. "*All* of this is out of the question. I'm not going on a date with Cooper Bailey."

"Ainsley?" my intercom beeps with my secretary interrupting us.

"Yes, Edna."

"There's a Mister Bailey on the line for you."

Stella smirks and crosses her legs. She's making it clear that she has no intention of leaving my office. My ass falls into my chair as I thank Edna for letting me know.

"You better say yes."

Shaking my head. "I won't."

The phone feels like it weighs a hundred pounds in my hand while my throat feels as if it has shrunk, leaving me barely enough space to swallow.

"He...hello," I say after clearing my throat. I don't know why he's calling me at work when he has my cell number.

"I'm sorry to bother you at work, Ainsley."

"It's not a bother. What can I do for you, Cooper?"

"I was wondering if you'd like to go to lunch with me?"

"Ainsley?" Stella says, tugging on my arm. I look up at her and catch a glimpse of Cooper standing in my doorway with a bouquet of flowers in his hand. They're my favorites, too, sunflowers and roses. Stella takes the phone from my hand and hangs up for me.

I'm caught off guard by how handsome he is and how the pictures online don't do him justice, even the ones where he's dirty from playing baseball, and my mind races with images of sponge baths and long showers. I admit that, after we spoke the other night, I looked up him up on the web. I find him attractive, but that doesn't alleviate my fear about athletes. It shouldn't matter that I can see myself tracing the outline of his jaw or that I want to feel his stubble scratch against my fingertips or that I need to see a picture of him without a hat on so I can imagine what it'd be like to run my fingers through dirty blond hair. From my experience, athletes aren't honest people, and they easily forget their personal commitments when something else comes along. I've been down that road before, and it's not something I want to experience again. I don't care how cute he is in his khaki shorts, deck shoes, and Boston Renegades polo. I'm not going to let it faze me that, when he smiles, it's slightly crooked, and I've imagined what it would be like to be held in his arms.

"Sorry to barge in, but I was in the neighborhood."

In the neighborhood that's a forty-five-minute drive from where you live? The words are on the tip of my tongue, but I hold them back. The man I've been trying to avoid, even if I haven't been very successful in my attempt, is standing in my doorway with flowers in his hand.

"I wanted to thank you in person for all the help you've given me this week, and I'm wondering if you'd like to go out to lunch?"

"Cooper—"

"Of course she would."

Stella comes behind me and pushes me toward him, leaving me with two choices. I can go and let him down gently after lunch, or I can be an epic bitch and tell him that I'll never go anywhere with him. Option two sounds the best right now, but people are staring, and that would be incredibly unprofessional of me.

Cooper hands me the flowers, which are already in a vase, making it easy for me to set them on my desk. They're beautiful—purple roses and bright yellow sunflowers—and they not only brighten my office but also my mood. It's only lunch. Lunch can't hurt, can it?

"They're beautiful. Thank you."

"You're welcome, Ainsley." I pretend to inhale the fragrance of the roses, but I'm really fighting off the emotion I feel when he says my name. It happens when he's on the phone with me, and each time I find myself pausing when he says it. It's the way my name rolls off his tongue, making my name sound softer than it is.

Cooper motions for me to walk ahead of him. I don't glance at

Edna and whomever may be lingering near her desk, but I hear the whispers and know I'll be water cooler gossip and subject to a barrage of questions when I return.

He's a gentleman, that much I can say. Cooper opens the door of his car for me, waits until I'm seated, then he shuts it and gives me just enough viewing pleasure when he runs around to the other side.

"Pull yourself together," I berate myself. I shouldn't be here.

"I found this little café not far from here. I thought we could go there."

"You never asked me about Naples, only Fort Myers. How did you find the café?"

Cooper smiles, causing my insides to stir. I hate that it takes one look from him and my resolve begins to chip away.

"The web," he says winking before he pulls into traffic, leaving me speechless. He used me for three days to give him information on Fort Myers but used the web to find us a place to eat. I think I've been duped.

And I think I like it.

# NINE

## Cooper

When I found out we were having a night practice, I started to panic. The last three nights have been spent sitting in my car, parked in the lot, talking to Ainsley. Little by little, I've been getting to know her, only to discover that my initial feelings toward her were spot-on. Her laugh, the way she says my name, and even the way she sighs all make me feel different. They make me feel like I've known her for years, even though we've just met.

I knew it was a long shot, showing up at her office. If she had said no, I would've just left it at that and moved on, but she didn't. Not that she had a chance to, considering her friend all but pushed her out the door. Flowers, chocolates, or whatever her friend likes must be sent to thank her for helping me with Ainsley: first her number and now this. Clearly she sees something in me that she likes for her friend.

Now Ainsley's in my car and I can smell her perfume. The scent, whatever it is, works for her. If I weren't already interested in her, I would be, simply because of the way she smells.

"Thanks for coming to lunch with me."

"I didn't have a choice," she reminds me. I play it off, as if it's no big deal that she was forced to go with me. My goal, by the end of the day, is to have her agreeing to another date, and hopefully another one after that.

Thankfully, traffic is light and navigating the roads in Naples is fairly easy.

"How is it that you know where to go here, but don't in Fort Myers?"

I can feel her gaze on me, and I try not to smile, but I'm grinning like a damn fool. This woman, she does things to me that I can't even begin to describe. It's not just her looks but also her being. I feel like I need to be around her.

"Uh…a recommendation from Branch Singleton," I tell her. It's not far from the truth. He is the one who encouraged me to surprise her at her office after he warned me that players have to watch out for the cleat-chasers because they're not always chasing for the right reasons.

His comment left me confused until Davenport filled me in about his situation. Seems Branch has a child that he never gets to see, and that doesn't sit well with him. I can't blame him, really. I'd give anything to have my mom back, even if it were just for a minute.

After I put the car in park, I take a chance and look at Ainsley just to see her, to memorize what she looks like in my car. I turn slightly and catch her staring, and I can't help but stare back. Her eyes wander over me, and when she finally reaches my face, her hazel orbs bore into my brown ones. There's something in the air; it's a mixture of her perfume, my cologne, and the lust I'm feeling for her. If this were any other time, I'd make a move, but not with her. I can't. The timing has to be impeccable.

After getting out of the car, I run around the side to let her out, making sure I avoid looking at her through the front window. I don't want to know if she's watching me or not, and I'm afraid to look. I'm afraid that I will trip and fall on my face. She'll laugh. I'll think it's funny, until I'm home nursing some wound that I have to hide from the skipper.

"Are you always this polite?"

My hand is on the small of her back while I guide her into the restaurant, holding the door open so she can pass through first. Her question catches me off guard, giving me pause. Aren't all men like this? That is the one thing my father was strict about: manners.

"I am," I tell her truthfully. "It's the way I was brought up."

"Two for Bailey," I tell the hostess, still making sure that Ainsley is in front of me as we follow the hostess to our table.

"Well, your mother did it right," she says, sitting down and taking the menu from the hostess.

"It was my father. My mother died when I was young. I honestly have very few memories of her, and what I do remember, sometimes I wonder if I made them up."

Her eyes peer over the menu, and I see sadness. "How do you mean?"

I shrug, setting my menu down. "I'll look at a picture of her, and I think of the day it was taken. What the weather was like, how she smelled, what we did that afternoon. It's moments like those that make me wonder if it's real or if I want them to be real."

"How long did it take for the memories to start fading?"

I look at her questioningly, wondering why she'd ask something like this. "I don't know, maybe a year or so. I didn't have a lot of memories of her to begin with, so it's hard to say."

"Do you miss her?"

I ponder her question for a moment, unsure of how to respond. I miss her because, at one point, she was in my life, but I've been told that I do. I don't know if it's a feeling I have deep inside of me or if it's because that is what people expect of me. I don't think about her, not like I think about my dad and wonder what he's doing, so it's hard for me to say whether I miss her or not.

The waitress saves me from answering by arriving at our table to take our order. Ainsley orders first, choosing the alfredo, while I select the spaghetti and meatballs. Only after I place my order do I realize that Italian probably isn't the best first date place.

"Uh, sorry about the restaurant. I wasn't thinking about the sauce."

"It's okay. I promise not to be messy." She winks, setting me at ease.

"Phew." I wipe my forehead, causing her to laugh. It's a sweet sound, and one I enjoy listening to over and over again, and the sound is so much better when she's doing it in person and not over the phone.

"So, Ms. Burke, what do you do in your free time?"

"Try to avoid eager baseball players like yourself."

I fall back into the booth with my hand on my chest. "You break my heart."

"I'm sure you'll survive." She drinks from her glass of water, never taking her eyes from mine.

"What if I don't? Will you nurse me back to health?"

Ainsley leans forward, the ends of her strawberry blond ponytail falling over her shoulder. "You're not very subtle."

I match her position and reply, "Not when I know what I want."

"And what's that?"

"To see you again. To take you on a proper date."

She sits back and begins to fiddle with her napkin. "I don't date athletes."

As if she has impeccable timing for awkward situations, the waitress returns with our drinks and a basket of bread, giving me a moment to formulate a witty response.

"Bread?" I ask, tipping the basket toward her. We each take a mini roll, add butter, and eat quietly.

"I'm sitting here trying to fathom why you don't date athletes, and I think I've come up with a list."

"You have? I can't wait to hear this," she says, setting her bread aside and leaning toward me.

"Right, my first thought is because some of us are freaking ugly. I mean, have you seen some of the linebackers for Miami? Those guys have some seriously big heads, and I'm sorry, but I can't picture you with a guy like that." She smiles, giving me hope.

"But that only covers football. Basketball players are probably too tall for you, and hockey players have missing teeth. That leads us to baseball, and the only reason I can come up with is that you think we smell." I start to lift my arm to check and see if I do in fact smell, but she stops me.

Ainsley's hand lingers longer than would be deemed friendly. When she finally pulls away, the smile she had is now gone and the pensive look is back. I haven't been in many relationships in my life, but I can tell that her aversion to athletes has to do with someone hurting her. People don't normally swear off an entire class of men without good reason.

Before I can ask, our food arrives. I thank the waitress and place my napkin in my lap. It's a damn good thing my shirt is red or I'd be walking out with visible stains by the look at the heaping amount of pasta, red sauce, and meatballs.

"Did you want to explain what you said?"

She shakes her head no. "There's no explanation needed. I just don't date athletes."

"I get it. Whatever happened, it must've been bad."

Ainsley sets her fork down and places her hands in her lap. She looks at me wearily, opening and closing her mouth. Each time I think she's about to say something, she changes her mind, only to try again.

She finally shakes her head and fiddles with the end of her fork. "I think that when you're lied to repeatedly by someone you love, you lump everyone into one category. For me, that's athletes." Ainsley speaks without making eye contact.

I reach my hand across the table and place it on hers. It's a bold move and one that will likely get me kicked in the nuts. "I like to pride myself on being different, better than the other guys out there. I don't know if I should plead my case or not, but I don't frequent the bars or pick up random chicks. I dated briefly in college but have focused mostly on my craft. I know you don't want to give me a chance to prove differently, and I probably can't sweet-talk you into it, but know…" My words trail off because I don't know what I want her to know. I'm sure she can figure out that I like her. Hell, I've only asked her out three times now, and the only reason she's here is because I bombarded her. I call her nightly, but it's only to talk about Fort Myers and the places that I need to visit. I'm trying, but maybe I need to stop.

Ainsley stares down at her food, moving her fork around absentmindedly. Removing my hand from hers, I go back to eating. The conversation has ended, as there isn't much to say anymore. I'm trying to bring down the barricade between us, and she seems intent on keeping it up.

Once people get it in their minds they don't like something, or in this case someone, it's hard to change their thought process. It sucks for me because I really think she's beautiful, and I want to get to know her while I'm here in Florida.

I can stomach only a few more bites before I push my plate away and call for the check. Honestly, I want to get up and just leave her here, but that's not how I was raised.

"You ready?"

She nods as I toss down a few twenties to cover the tab and wait for her to walk by me, following her out just as I followed her in. And even though she wants nothing to do with me, I open the car door for her and wait until she's inside before shutting it. This time, I don't run to the other side or even walk briskly. Each step I take is harder than the last because all I want to do is pull her out of the car and ask why. Why does she have to lump me in with her notion that we're all liars? She doesn't even know me well enough to say something like that.

But I don't. Instead I get behind the wheel and drive her back to the zoo. And this time, I don't get out to open the door for her. I continue to look ahead, waiting for her to say something.

"Thanks for lunch."

"Sure, take care, Ainsley."

She doesn't have to tell me again that she's not interested. The message has been sent and received. I'm pulling away before she even has a chance to shut the door, leaving her in the parking lot to watch me drive away. This isn't how I expected the day to go, not even close. At best, I would've called her later, before practice, with some dumb excuse for directions just so I could hear her voice, but that won't happen now, not ever again.

I can't believe I thought I could change her mind by showing up at her job. That seriously was dumb thinking on my part.

The drive back to the training facility is quick, because I exceed the speed limit and traffic is light. When I get inside, I change quickly and head for the batting cages. It's time to get some aggression out. I don't know what the asshole looked like that hurt her, but his face is going to be on the ball that's going to meet my bat repeatedly.

Way to ruin it for me, buddy.

# TEN

## Ainsley

Instead of going back into my office, I slip into my car, where I let the tears flow freely. They're a mixture of anger, hatred, and plain stupidity. I want a redo. I want to go back to the moment when Cooper walked into my office with those beautiful flowers so I can let my heart dictate what I'm going to say and do instead of my brain, because my heart wants to like him even though it goes against everything I was told from the time I started dating.

"No athletes."

It's not only my rule, but my mother's as well. She was more specific early on, preaching that baseball players were nothing but trouble and to stay far away, so I did and went for football instead. That turned out to be disastrous. And after witnessing many of my high school friends in precarious situations, I started following my mother's advice wholeheartedly.

And just when I think that I can finally let Cooper in a little, to maybe get to know him and start hanging out, he tells me about his mother and sends my head into a tailspin. Cooper devastated me when he told me that his mother died and his memories of her have all but faded.

That's the reality that I'm facing now, and my biggest fear is that I won't remember my mother in the years to come. Sure, I can buy her brand of perfume so that I can smell the scent she's worn all my life, but what about other little things? What about the way her eyes light up when she has good news or how she dances when she's cooking? I can't capture those moments now, and to try to record them would be futile anyway. Now my mother never has good news, and she stopped cooking long ago.

Already my memories are hazy, and I'm often reminded of a moment when she's holding my hand and says "remember when," only I don't, but I still play along. I should write them down, but the thought of letting go of her hand while she tells me a story pains me. So I stay there, trying to burn every single word into memory so that someday, when I have a son or daughter, I can share the stories.

Thoughts of Cooper filter into my mind. I blink hard, trying to send them away, but it's no use, he's already found his way into my mind with his crooked little smile and beautiful brown eyes.

Even during lunch, I had to fight to maintain my resolve. I'm attracted to him, and I can't deny it. Knowing that there are flowers on my desk from him makes me giddy. I should be sitting in my office and smelling the fragrant roses, remembering the look on his face when he came through my door. Instead, I'm wallowing, and we all know that a self-inflicted pity party will get you nowhere in life.

I contemplate going back into the office but know that I would be tempted to call Cooper, especially with his flowers sitting on my desk, and apologize for messing up what could have been a perfectly enjoyable lunch. Or instead I could go home.

I opt for home. I want to talk to my mother, maybe go for a walk. It's time that she tells me why she swore off baseball players. Maybe her story will help me once and for all with Cooper and give the reasoning behind my words a little more power. He sees right through me, and that honestly scares the living daylights out of me. Most men take what I say and leave, but not Cooper. He wants the reasons, the facts behind my stance.

My drive home is usually done on autopilot, but this time I find myself wondering what Cooper is doing. Where does he live? What does he do in his free time? These are all questions I should've asked earlier, but I put up a wall that his gallant efforts couldn't break down. I know he's frustrated. I could see it on his face, and I don't blame him. I'd be angry too if the tables were turned.

Driving through the development to my mother's condo, I wave at the few people who are walking. It's a gorgeous day out, and my mom needs to be outside, getting some fresh air. The challenge will be getting her out of her rocking chair. She likes to sit there, with an afghan on her lap, and stare at the pond. I swear she's waiting for a gator to rise from the water. Mom has mentioned a few times that she's been waiting her whole life to see one.

"I'm home," I yell, making sure she can hear me upstairs. When she got sick, I moved out of my apartment and into her place so I could take care of her. My independent life changed drastically. My social calendar ceased, and my friends suddenly didn't have time for me. Stella is the only one who is still around, but I've known her for years. She grew up knowing my mom and has been trying to take some of the burden off of me. But it's my burden to bear. I'm her daughter, and it's my job to take care of her.

I climb the stairs and stop in her room. She's exactly as I thought she would be, sitting in her rocker with a cream-colored afghan draped over her lap. Today, her scarf is light purple with violets on it.

"Do you want to go outside?" I ask her as I sit on her rented hospital bed. "It's warm, the flowers are all blooming, and the birds are chattering away."

"No, I'm fine here." That's her canned answer. I've asked her to fight for her life, for the life that we have planned, but I know in my heart she's given up. The chemo makes her sick for weeks on end; she's frail and can't walk unless assisted by a walker. Her life isn't as it was just a year ago, and I have a feeling it's hard for her to remember those days.

I sigh, letting the frustration set in. I don't know what else I can do to help her get over this funk.

"What's wrong, sweetie?"

Oh, Mother, where do I even begin? I shake my head, not knowing the answer. "I don't even know, Mom. So much is going on that I can't wrap my head around everything."

"You need to find a nice man. Someone who is going to take care of you when I'm gone."

"Will you stop saying that?" I crouch down in front of her so she can see the agony on my face. "You're too young to leave this realm, Mom. You can fight the cancer. You can get up and start living your life instead of sitting in this chair, waiting to die."

A single tear falls from her eye. I wipe it away gently, knowing that her skin is sensitive.

"Have you thought about looking online for a man?"

Exasperated, I stand and go back to her bed. "I met a guy. In fact, we went to lunch today."

"Is he nice?"

"I think so," I say, shrugging. "I didn't give him much of a chance because I made the mistake of complimenting his mother on his manners, and he corrected me, saying his mother had died when he was younger. My heart hurts for him."

I move around her room, checking her pitcher of water and making sure she took her meds.

"Death is a part of life, Ainsley. Some of us just go sooner than expected."

"Yeah, but you can fight this, and you're choosing not to."

"I am fighting. You just don't want to see it. You expect me to go out and play golf or take the boat out with my friends. I'm weak, Ainsley. It hurts to walk. I wouldn't be able to swing my club, let alone climb over the edge of a boat to get in, and I don't want anyone to help me. Don't let my situation mess up something that could be important to you."

"Doesn't matter." Sitting on the small stool in front of her, I gaze out the window staring at the same nothingness she looks at all day.

"Why do you say that?"

"Because he's a professional athlete. I met him a couple of days ago when the Boston Renegades came to the zoo to hang out with some underprivileged children."

I don't need to look at my mother to know what she's thinking or to know that her hands are gripping the arms of her rocker.

"You know how I feel about athletes. They're nothing but trouble, every last one of them."

"I know, but you've never told me why, so I'm asking now. Seconds ago, you tell me not to let what's going on here mess things up, but as soon as I mention athletes, you avoid the subject. Mom, I need to know, because I have a feeling that I'm chasing away a really great guy. All my life, you've told me to stay away from them, but never why." I take her hand and place it in mine, resting it against my cheek.

"Remember that time you dated what's-his-face—"

"Mom, I don't want to remember my relationship with Mark. I thought he was different and he wasn't, but what if this man is and I'm not being fair to him?"

She sighs and runs her free hand over my ponytail. "Ainsley, I want you to be happy."

"I know."

"Love can be such a fragile thing in our lives, and I've let something that happened to me so many years ago affect you, and I'm sorry. I only wanted to protect you from my own heartache."

"I know," I say again. "I think I like this guy."

"Is he the one you've been speaking with at night?"

I nod and look at her questioningly. She cracks a smile, one that I haven't seen in a long time. "I'm your mother. I know everything."

Laughter quickly fills the room, changing how I feel at the moment. I gently rest my head on her lap, letting her stroke my hair until I'm almost asleep. It'll be these moments that I miss.

"Ainsley, do me a favor."

"Anything, Mom." I raise my head and look into her eyes.

Her hand softly cups my cheek. "Don't be like me and wait for love to find you. Go out and grab it by the horns, or baseball bat if that is what your heart desires."

"Do you think I should?" I ask, trying to fight back the grin that's forming. I don't want her to see how eager I am.

"Of course."

"I'm going to go for a walk. Do you want to come? Maybe we could go watch his practice, and you can help me decide if I should tell him how sorry I am for being an epic B to him?"

She laughs again, but shakes her head. I knew she would say no, but it was worth a shot to get her out of the house. I lightly kiss her on the cheek and check the nurse's schedule before I leave to make sure someone will be here to cook dinner later.

I opt to drive instead of walk over to the park. I've only ever driven by the Renegades training facility, so I follow the people in front of me, hoping they know where to go. Chairs are lined up in the grass, watching the Renegades practice. I find an open space and sit as close to the fence as I can get.

The viewpoint from here isn't that great, but the atmosphere is nice. I listen in on conversations around me; the fans talk about the upcoming season, what they have to do to win, and who is going to shine for the BoRes. When Cooper's name is dropped, I try to listen a bit harder due to the noise to hear what the people are saying. Phrases like "Rookie of the Year" and "too much hype" causes small rifts between people, making me wonder what Cooper thinks of all of this.

I'm sure he, along with the other guys, has been trained to ignore what is being said about him, although I don't know how he could. I think it would bug me to know that people are always talking about my performance and analyzing everything that I did.

The ball is hit into center field and easily caught. The name Bainbridge is used, and my heart drops. It's easy to admit that I came here in hopes of seeing Cooper, but if he's not playing, there's no reason to be here.

"Cooper Bailey."

His name is announced over the loudspeaker, and I lean forward trying to peer through the cyclone fence for a look at him.

"If his team is in the field, why is he batting?" I ask the older gentleman next to me.

"This is their first nighttime scrimmage under the lights. They're announcing names to audition a new announcer."

"Oh. I gotcha." I nod along. I suppose it makes sense that this would be the time for on-the-job interviews to happen.

The sound of the ball cracking against the bat has everyone standing up, including me. The right fielder has turned around, watching the ball over his shoulder. He leaps, trying to catch it, but it sails over his glove and into the mitt of a little kid who seems ecstatic. The announcer yells "home run," and on instinct, I place two fingers in my mouth and whistle.

"Sweetie, if you're going to whistle like that during these games, don't sit by me, okay? My hearing aids can't take it." He laughs as he sits back down and starts jawing at his friend about how Bailey is going to be a shoe-in for Rookie of the Year.

When the guys switch, Cooper runs out to center field and throws the ball back and forth with the right fielder. From what I can see, he's laughing. He should be. He's doing what he's always dreamed of, according to his bio.

The game continues for about an hour until everyone disappears into the dugout. Everyone packs up, chatting about the first spring training game in a few days, while I continue to lean up against the fence. I'm in no rush to go home, and the solitude is nice. There's a peaceful feeling in the park that somehow seems to make everything okay in my life, even when I know it's not.

By the time I get to the well-lit parking lot, there are a handful of cars left, and mine is the farthest away. As I pass by a few of them, the guys call out, but I ignore them and hurry past.

The sound of shoes slapping against the pavement behind me has me walking faster. I can't believe I'd be so stupid as to park this far away from the entrance.

"Ainsley, wait up."

I freeze at the sound of Cooper's voice and stop, turning around quickly, only to have him run smack-dab into me. We both let out an *oomph* as he catches me, keeping me from falling to the ground.

"Are you okay?" he asks, leaving his hands around my waist.

"You scared me."

He looks over his shoulder at the guys behind us, who are making comments, and shakes his head. "Ignore them."

"I plan on it."

Cooper steps back, putting some distance between us. "What are you doing here?"

I look at the ground, wondering if I can just be honest with him and—if so—at what cost? "I need to apologize for earlier," I start off with. "I was a bitch to you, and you didn't deserve that. I'm going through some health stuff with my mom, and your story about your mother really hit home."

"And the fact that you don't want to date me."

I laugh because the look on his face is priceless. He's mocking himself at my expense.

"There is that little factoid."

"But you're here?"

"I am. I thought I'd go for a walk earlier this evening and heard a baseball game, so I drove over to check you guys out."

"What'd you think?"

"It was fun. You hit a home run."

His face lights up, and that alone makes this conversation worth it.

There's pride in his features, and the fact that I saw his accomplishment clearly means something to him. "Can we go somewhere and talk?"

My mother's words echo in my mind. She wants me to be happy. I'm not saying Cooper is the one who will do that, but maybe he is. There is only one way to find out. "Yeah, I'd like that."

He walks me to my car, keeping his hand on the small of my back the whole time. He gives me his address and asks me to meet him there, and I agree to, knowing that once I do, there is no going back.

# ELEVEN

## Cooper

"Let's go," I tell my two roommates.

"Hot date?" Brock Wilder asks. I shake my head, climbing into my car.

"She's a fine-looking woman," Frankie Guerra adds. "Is that the chick from the zoo?"

"Yeah," I say, pulling out of the parking lot and into traffic. Of course because I'm in a hurry, everyone in front of me is moving slowly, and I'm unable to pass.

"Damn, rookie, you're not wasting any time hooking up with the locals," Wilder states. And even though he's a rookie, too, the guys on the team have taken to calling me "rookie," and it's stuck.

"It's not like that." Even as I say the words, I know it's not true. I want to spend time with Ainsley, even date her, but what happens when it's time to leave? Does this become a long-distance relationship where she comes to visit me or I live in Florida in the off-season? Honestly, I'd take Florida over the cold Massachusetts winter anytime, but what about during the season?

I clear my mind of all those thoughts when I pull into the complex and see that Ainsley is waiting outside her car. I tell the guys I'll be up later, hoping they get the idea that I want to be alone with her, and now isn't the time to get friendly.

As soon as I'm out of the car, she's pushing off her Jeep Wrangler to meet me halfway. I'm happy that she's making an effort to see me. The only thing that can make my night any better is if I'm pulling her into my arms and kissing her. And as much as I want to do that, especially in this moment, it has to wait. I need the green light from her. She's made her position on *us* very clear, and I'm not about to cross the line.

"You're here," I state, pointing out the obvious.

"I said I would be."

That she did.

I look around the complex, trying to find a location where we can go and talk, but our options are limited. My apartment would be ideal, but I don't want the guys saying shit about her or teasing her. As far as I can tell, she doesn't give a shit about sports, much less baseball. "Now that I have you here, I don't know where to go to talk."

"I know a place," she says. "Get in, I'll drive." She leaves me speechless as she heads back toward her car. I'm dumbfounded by her change in attitude toward me, but I'm not willing to question it. I'm going to ride this wave as long as I can. I quickly rush to the passenger side and get in.

"Where are we going?" I ask. I turn my ball cap around to prevent it from flying away since her top is down and it looks like we're heading toward the parkway.

"I thought we'd go to the beach."

"Isn't that like thirty minutes away?"

She glances at me quickly before turning back and focusing on the road. "Do you have a curfew or something?"

I shake my head. "Nope, drive on." I may not have a curfew, but six a.m. comes very early, and it's our last practice before we start pre-season play. I suppose, since I went without much sleep in college, one night now isn't going to hurt me. Besides, it's for a good cause. I'm into Ainsley, and if she wants to take me to the beach, I'm going to let her.

She turns up the radio and starts singing along to the song. I know it as well so I join in, and before I know it, we're having our own kara-oke party while we're cruising down the road. When we hit a stoplight, I expect her to stop singing, but she doesn't, and the people pulled up along the side of us start singing, too.

Before I know it, we're at the beach. The car is shut off, the music has stopped, and the only thing we can hear are the waves crashing onto the shore.

"Coming here at night affords me the ability to sit and think with-out too many people around."

"Is it safe?"

"I don't know. I never thought about that. I suppose in some aspects it's not, but there are always a few other people around, so..." She gets out of her car before finishing her sentence. She shouldn't walk the beach alone at night, but who am I to tell her so? I quickly follow her, catching up with her in the sand.

We walk side by side until the dry sand turns wet, and then we both sit down.

"When I was little, my mom used to bring me here all the time. I'd swim and play while she read her book, or she'd come into the water with me. It's funny, when you're a kid, you have no worries in life, but the minute you become an adult, everything changes."

I wish I could relate. "My life was the opposite. I've always had the pressure to succeed in baseball on my shoulders. My dad, he was strict about everything. In fact, if he knew I was out here now and not sleeping, he'd have something to say about that."

"That's sad."

Shrugging, I slip off my socks and sneakers, burying my toes into the cold sand. "It is, but I wouldn't be where I am today without that kind of structure."

"Do you like playing baseball?" Ainsley slips off her shoes and pulls her legs to her chest, wrapping her arms around them tightly.

"I love it. I love everything about the game."

"Do you ever wish you had done something else?"

I think about her question and wonder what else I could've done. If my dad and I hadn't turned to tossing the ball in the backyard, where would we be? For us, it was therapeutic and a way for me to express how angry and hurt I was that my mom had died. The harder I threw, the better I felt. The more my dad cringed when he caught the ball, the more satisfying it was that he was hurting as much as I was.

"I don't know what else I would've done, honestly. Baseball is what I know. My dad used it as a tool to help me cope with my mom's passing, and before I knew it, I was trying out for these elite baseball clubs and making all-star teams. College and major league scouts would come watch my games in high school, and I thought, 'Wow, this could be a career for me.' I was drafted out of high school but chose to go to college first. I wanted something to fall back on in case baseball didn't work out."

"What's your degree in?" She turns and looks at me. The moon is casting enough of a glow that I can make out her facial features. Now would be the perfect time to lean over and kiss her, but I have to keep reminding myself that it's not what she wants from me.

"Well, the only thing that made sense."

Ainsley holds her hand up. "Don't tell me, it's something to do with sports."

I nod, holding back laughter. "Yeah, broadcasting. I figure I can become a commentator or something when I retire."

"Interesting," she says, turning back toward the ocean.

I lean into her, bumping her with my shoulder. "Don't be like that."

"Like what?"

"Like I took the easy way out with my degree, or my career isn't the same as a doctor or whatever."

"Is it, though?"

"Baseball is America's game. It doesn't know social class, race, or any other classification. It's a game every one can play and afford to participate in. You don't have to have straight A's to go to college to play ball. Hell, most players come to the majors right out of high school. It's a game for everyone."

"A game that you make millions of dollars at."

"It's no different than being an actor. We bring entertainment to people." I counter her claim.

She seems to ponder this before nodding. "The ticket prices for your games are outrageous."

"That's on the owners, not me. The players don't set those prices."

Ainsley turns to face me. "But you do. You get paid millions of dollars to play the game you all agree that you love, and people can't afford to go to your games. If you didn't make so much, more people would be able to go watch you."

"True, but the same could be said about doctors. If they didn't charge so much, or insurance companies, for that matter, more people would be able to get treatment."

She doesn't know that my mom couldn't get the treatment needed because we couldn't afford the more expensive drugs, or the specialists. The insurance my father had simply wouldn't cover the expenses.

"I don't like this argument," she says.

"Me neither. I think we should talk about something else."

"Like what?" she asks.

Taking her hand in mind, I kiss the top of it before meeting her gaze. "Like you going out with me."

She shakes her head.

"I know, you don't date athletes, so think of me as a sports broadcaster." I waggle my eyebrows at her, and she laughs.

"You're hard to resist, Cooper Bailey."

With those words, I pull her closer. "Then stop resisting me, Ainsley." This is my chance, and I take it. My lips brush against hers lightly, testing her resolve. She's either going to punch me, push me away, or let me continue to kiss her.

# BOSTON RENEGADES

The winter was long, but thankfully we had very little snow, and now the day that we've all been waiting for has arrived.

The smell of hot dogs, freshly popped popcorn, and the sweet sounds of baseball are in the air as the BoRes open their spring training play this afternoon against Minnesota.

Skipper Cal Diamond is starting rookie center fielder Cooper Bailey after what he called a strong showing during training. Diamond went on to say that it's too early to determine who will be starting when the season officially kicks off in April.

Other reports out of training camp indicate that Branch Singleton will be sitting out as designated hitter today to nurse a sore hamstring, and the recently acquired Michael Cashman will be taking the pitches from Hawk Sinclair to start things off with the BoRes.

Aside from the above changes, the lineup is expected to be the same as last year's for today's game.

# GOSSIP WIRE

Lisa Bainbridge has filed for divorce from center fielder Steve Bainbridge. This does not come as a shock to the BoRe faithful as she's made her plight front-page news. The timing, however, could've been better, in our opinion. It'll be interesting to see just how the ironclad prenup comes into play and whether Bainbridge will have to pay her.

Former catcher Jasper Jacobson, who has been rumored to be a key player in the Bainbridge divorce, was seen in Boston when he should've been at spring training! It makes you wonder what exactly is going on.

Catcher Jose Gonzalez, who is fighting for a starting spot in the lineup, recently announced via social media that he's looking for a wife. Seems Gonzalez needs to take some much-needed media lessons like Ethan Davenport had to. Anyone remember when Davenport sent out his address?

The BoRe Blogger

# TWELVE

## Ainsley

You remember your first kiss. It doesn't matter how old or how young you are when it happens, you remember. The same can be said each time you experience a first kiss with someone new.

The night Cooper kissed me, I felt like it was my very first kiss all over again. I hadn't expected it, and when it happened, I felt a surge of desire and longing. The butterflies that I've ignored fluttered freely, and I wanted to crawl into his arms and have him hold me, but I held back. He's everything that my mother warned me about.

Still, even sitting on the beach, I thought being friends with him wouldn't be such a bad thing to have in my life. Except all that changed when we drove back to his apartment; he held my hand the whole drive, and all I could think about was the kiss and how I wanted more. Was it good? Yeah, it was. His lips were soft, and the kiss tender. The way the back of his fingers brushed against my cheek had me leaning into him even more, but I was too ashamed of my earlier behavior to make my own move.

When we arrived at his apartment, I didn't expect to be kissed again, but I was, and as much as I hate to admit it, I liked it a lot. There was no lead-in. No conversation that would gradually bring him closer to me. Cooper leaned over the second I had my Wrangler in park and held me captive under his lustful gaze. I have no doubt he's used to women falling at his feet when he wants something, but that's not going to be me.

He licked his lips, and I knew I was left with two choices: turn away or meet him in the middle. I chose the latter and brought my lips to his. The softness of the kiss turned hot and desperate quickly as his tongue traced the outline of my lower lip. With lips parted, I let him in. The warmth of his tongue, the feel of his hand on the back of my neck, and the smell of peppermint lingering from his gum spurred my body into wanting more. My small whimper was enough to tell Cooper that I was enjoying every second of this kiss. And I was, immensely.

Now I find myself watching the clock on my computer tick down, minute by minute. The old adage "a watched pot never boils" doesn't hold a stick to a watched clock. I swear, each time I look up, only a minute or two has passed.

"Where do you want to grab lunch?" Stella asks as she comes into my office. I look up from the file I'm reading and shake my head.

"I'm sorry, I can't today."

"Why not?"

Aside from the other day when I went with Cooper, Stella and I always go to lunch together. It's usually somewhere on the grounds, but there are times when we'll order in or head to a restaurant.

I look at the clock once more, seeing that I have about thirty minutes before I have to leave. "I'm going to Cooper's game. It's opening day."

Stella's mouth drops open before morphing into a huge grin. "You're doing what now?" she asks, even though we both know she heard me loud and clear.

Up until now, I've been able to keep a straight face, but there's no denying that I'm grinning like a love-struck fool, except I'm not in love. I'm very much "in like." The love thing won't happen. I refuse to open my heart up that much to him, knowing he's leaving in a month.

"You're ditching me for the hottie?"

"I'm not ditching you. I'm taking half the day off to go watch a baseball game."

"You like him, don't you?"

I attempt to ignore her and look busy by shuffling papers around, but I give up. I throw my hands up in the air and nod. "I do, and I hate myself for it. I have one month with him, and I can already tell it's not going to be enough."

Stella comes around my desk and pulls me into her arms. "It's going to be fine. He'll have the money to fly you to Boston, or come and visit you."

"No, it's not going to be like that," I say, shaking my head. "You know I can't leave my mom, and their schedule is crazy. I already looked. I mean they get like five days off total. I'm not going to ask him to choose me over baseball. This is his career."

This is the same pep talk I've had with myself since we kissed. Most people would say it's just a kiss, something you can do with anyone, but for me it was different. He's different. He's kind. His hands rough and calloused. I thought they'd feel hard against my skin, but I found his touch to be soft, and he knows what he wants. Cooper pursued me, staying front and center in my life even when I denied him, all because he wants me.

"I'm sure, if he wants to be in your life, he'll do whatever needs to be done." Stella makes everything seem so cut and dried.

"He has a career that isn't in Florida, but fifteen hundred miles away—"

"How do you know?" she asks, interrupting me.

"I looked it up," I reply, embarrassed.

Stella laughs. "Of course you did, because you like him."

"I do, Stella, and I don't want to. My heart is a freaking traitor, and Cooper is just chipping away at the façade so easily."

"How so?" She pulls the chair from the front of my desk around to where I am and sits.

"It's stupid, really, but there are little things that I've noticed. Like when we're together, he's always looking at me. His eyes aren't wandering around but completely focused on me. The way he smiles, it makes me wonder what he's thinking every single time, but it's also the intrigue and the love he has for his job. The passion behind his words reminds me of how I feel working here."

"You're in love," she says, drawing out the word *love*.

"I am not. I barely know him. We've been on one disastrous date and spend most of our time talking on the phone. Love isn't even in my vocabulary."

"Whatever you say. Give me details later. I'm off to grab some lunch."

I look at the clock, and my eyes go wide. "Shit, I gotta go." I kiss her on the cheek as I scramble to grab my bag. I'm changing my clothes before I get to the park so I'm more comfortable.

"Hey, maybe next time you can take your best friend?"

"Yeah, I'll ask Cooper. He got me the ticket."

Stella waves and leaves my office, shutting the door behind her so I can change. I tell my secretary to call only if it's an emergency and book it to my car. One privilege of holding the position that I do is that my car is close. If I were still with the giraffes, I'd have an almost thirty-minute walk back through the parking lot.

The atmosphere at the ballpark is energizing. From the retirement community to the kids, everyone is here to enjoy the first baseball game of the season. I check in at will call, giving my name to the lady behind the tempered glass.

"Oh, you're Cooper's guest for the day," she says, sliding an envelope under window. I step aside and open the envelope, revealing my ticket and a note.

> *Ainsley,*
>
> *To say I'm excited that you're watching me play today is an understatement. Thank you for saying yes! Please read all the notes.*
>
> *I'll see you after the game.*
>
> *Cooper Bailey #25*
>
> *P.S. I'm counting this as a date* ☺

I reread the note before tucking it into my pocket. He also gave me vouchers for food, which I find comical, but I guess if this is a date to him, then he's paying for my food, and there's a note saying that I have something waiting for me at the gift shop.

My ticket is scanned, and once I step inside the concourse, I can finally grasp what Cooper is saying about the smells of the ballpark. The hot dogs, popcorn, and pretzels invite you in, welcoming you to enjoy the day. I make my way to the gift shop and present the coupon that Cooper left for me. The lady behind the counter smiles and hands me a bag.

"Enjoy the game," she says.

"Thank you."

Finding a spot along the wall, I peek inside the bag. There's a hat and a T-shirt with *Bailey 25* stenciled on the back. I like the thought, but I'm not sure I want to wear it, until I see a group of younger girls all wearing his shirt. Finding the nearest bathroom, I quickly change and then make sure I have my hot dog, popcorn, and lemonade before locating my seat.

Before I take my seat, I smile at the man who is sitting next to me. Both teams are warming up, and it takes me a minute to spot Cooper. Deep down I'm hoping he sees me.

People file in all around me, excited for the game. I am, too, as this is my first professional game, spring training or not.

The National Anthem is sung, and the starting lineups announced. The Boston faithful cheer for everyone, and I make sure to whistle for Cooper when his name is called. I do it again when he runs out to center field.

Watching him jog gives me the perfect opportunity to stare at him. There's something about a uniform, be it sports or otherwise, that really makes a man look fantastic. I try to snap a few pictures of him, but they're blurry, and I realize that, if I'm going to come to any more games, I need binoculars so I can fully pay attention to him while he's in the outfield.

Loud music plays as the first player comes up to bat. The first pitch and he's swinging, and Cooper is moving into position. He catches the ball, easily from what I can gather, and everyone goes crazy. The announcers say a few nice things about Cooper, all of which I happen to agree with.

It's the third inning before Cooper gets his turn to bat. The man next to me has a few choice things to say about him while he's standing there. Every pitch sparks a new comment, and he writes down a note. I hadn't seen him do that for anyone except Cooper.

When Cooper strikes out, he grumbles a long line of expletives and writes a few more notes down.

"I take it you're not happy?" I say jokingly.

He glares at me and shakes his head. "No, I'm not. He didn't waste years of training to strike out to this pitcher. He's not focused on the game."

"Do you know Cooper?"

This time he looks at me, the scowl meaner than before. "I'm his father."

I slink back in my seat and focus on the game. It's probably a bad time to introduce myself as Cooper's friend, and by his attitude, I'm not sure there will ever be a good time.

# THIRTEEN

## Cooper

Everything in my life was lining up perfectly until I got the call from my dad. Things with Ainsley are moving along nicely, and Diamond informed me that I was starting the first game. These are two very important and hard-earned moments in my life. I never took into consideration that my father would head to Fort Myers to watch me play. Honestly, the idea never even occurred to me that this would so important to him that he'd take time off from work. I figured he'd wait until I was in Boston before he came to watch. That was an error on my part. He was coming to town, and I couldn't very well tell him not to show up.

I can't stomach the thought of him meeting Ainsley, because he won't approve of her. To this day, I have yet to bring a girlfriend around because his thoughts are always the same: They either want me for my money or they're a distraction. He can't see that they want to be with me for me. He only sees that they're around me because of my career. And that's not how I see Ainsley.

I don't believe she's the type to be with anyone for money. She certainly didn't even want to go out with me, but I whittled her down with my charm. I'm not sure that will be enough, though, if my father said something to her.

When I come in from warming up, my stomach drops instantly when I see Ainsley sitting next to my dad. I was tempted to call her and ask her not to come, but I don't think that would've gone over very well. The last thing I want to do is give her an excuse to stop seeing me. It's my plan to see as much of her as I can before we head back to Boston. After that, it'll be a mutual decision on how to proceed.

I had every intention of making sure Ainsley knew I saw her in the stands until my dad showed up. I can't put her through his wrath. It would be unfair, and I need time to talk to her about him.

Throughout the game, I struggled. I struck out three times and hit into a double play. This isn't the time for me not to be at my best when I'm up to bat. Having a nonexistent batting average to start my season isn't exactly how I want things to go. The only aspect of my game that didn't suck tonight was my fielding. No one could get anything by me, and I saved two home runs. Unfortunately, we lost four to seven, and Hawk Sinclair is pissed.

The clubhouse looks like a war zone with stools in locations they shouldn't be, the laundry bucket is tipped over, and there is a lot of yelling coming from Diamond's office. Sinclair was upset when Diamond took him out of the game. Since it's our first preseason game, Sinclair needs to save his arm for when our games count. He's already in the rotation as a starter. He has nothing to prove. Where I have everything.

By all accounts, we should've beaten Minnesota. We have the better team on paper and should be a contender for the American League title this year. We can't lose games. Come out strong and finish stronger: That should be our motto. I know I need to do my part as well.

"Hey, rookie, we're going out tonight. You in?" Travis Kidd asks as he walks by buck-ass naked.

"Nah, man. Thanks, though."

"You sure? Guerra and Wilder are coming."

An empty apartment sounds like bliss. "My dad is here. I need to hang with him."

"Suit yourself."

There could be ramifications for not going out. Not from the organization, but the players. I don't want to be seen as someone who doesn't like to have a good time. I'd love to go out, bond some more with the guys, but I have a pressing issue to take care of. We all have someone overbearing in our lives; mine just happens to be my father.

I shower and change, preparing to face the inevitable. I have to choose between Ainsley and my dad, at least for tonight. With my cell phone in my hand, I text my dad.

I'll meet you for breakfast. I'm hitting the batting cages.

And rattle one off to Ainsley.

Can you meet me at my apartment?

Ainsley is the first one to respond with "sure," putting me somewhat at ease that she won't have a run-in with my father if they were both waiting for me. The guys say goodbye, asking again if I want to go to the bar. Right now, I'd love to hit the bar and knock back a few to numb my thoughts on tonight's game. It seems like the best way to look forward to tomorrow. Hell, I'm not even looking forward to five minutes from now.

I stall in the clubhouse as long as possible, waiting for my father to text back, until I have no choice but to head out and face the music. I know the speech well as I've heard it a time or two. Thing is, I don't want to hear it now, nor do I need to. I'm playing at a professional level and have coaches to help me figure things out. I can't say that to my dad, though. He'd find it to be an insult and I'll never live it down.

Before I turn the corner that will bring me face to face with my dad, my phone chimes. His name flashes on my screen with a new message.

That's good to hear. You need it. I wasn't impressed.

I pocket my phone, knowing that it's not going to matter what I have to say. Besides, some things are better left unsaid. I'll deal with him tomorrow morning before practice so he can tell me everything I'm doing wrong. Until then, my mind is focused on Ainsley.

The drive to my apartment seems to take forever, and as soon as I pull into my complex, Ainsley's Wrangler comes into sight. She hops out as soon as I park my car, coming over to meet me.

"Hey," she says as soon as I'm out of my car.

I respond by pulling her into a kiss. She doesn't hesitate, silently telling me it's okay to go further. Pushing her against her car and holding her face in my hands, we make out like two horny teenagers until headlights flash in our direction.

"Do you want to come up? The guys are at the bar so it'll just be us."

"Yeah."

Her hand feels good in mine, like it belongs there. I guide her through the courtyard, and she follows behind as we climb the steps to my apartment.

"It's a mess," I tell her as I unlock the door. "But we can hang out in my room." I open the door and flip on the light, illuminating the bachelor pad. All three of us are to blame. Had I known Ainsley was coming over, I would've cleaned up this morning. Leading her down the hall, I turn on the light for my bedroom, which is surprisingly clean considering the state of the rest of the place is like a pit.

"Are you guys always this sloppy?"

"Sort of." I shrug, tossing my keys on to my dresser and kicking my sneakers into my closet. I fall onto my bed and sigh, rubbing my hands over my face. The frustration of the day is starting to build.

"Where'd you say everyone is?"

"At the bar."

"What? It's only like four in the afternoon." I feel the bed dip and realize I'm being a horrible host. She removes one of my hands from my face and curls up into my side.

"I like this," I tell her.

"Me too."

"I played like shit."

Ainsley sits up on her elbow and looks at me. "It's only the first game."

"Doesn't matter. I have expectations. I know I'm better than Bainbridge, but if I don't prove it now, I won't get much of a chance once the regular season starts. I only have a month to wow the coaches."

"Well, it only took you a few days to wow me."

I roll over onto my side and face her. She leans forward and kisses me.

"Are you saying you're finally wowed?"

She ponders my question playfully before answering, "I am officially wowed. I had fun today. Thank you for inviting me."

"You have a ticket anytime you want one, Ainsley. You just have to let me know."

"I wish your games weren't in the afternoon."

"Yeah, but it still gets dark early, and the lights take a lot of electricity to run."

"That makes sense. I can come on Saturday. Maybe Stella will come with me."

"Just say the word and I'll leave tickets for you at will call." I try to kiss her again, but she pushes me away. She's grinning from ear to ear so it can't be because I smell.

"Thank you for the shirt and hat."

"Oh yeah, let me see." I attempt to turn her around, but she does it for me while pulling her hair to the side. I trace the letters of my name and number, down and up, as I move closer to her. When I get back to the top, my fingers rest on the neck of the T-shirt. I pull it slightly and place my lips there, testing her.

I continue to kiss where the neckline is, moving it as I go along my path. Ainsley rolls her neck, giving me a better angle with each kiss. Seeing her in a shirt that bears my name, a shirt I picked out for her, turns me on. Hell, she turns me on just by allowing me to be in her presence. I've never felt this way about anyone before. Women in the past, they were something to pass the time during the off-season and never someone I could see a future with. Ainsley is different. I don't care that I've only known her for a week. I want to be with her.

I maneuver myself to sit against my headboard and bring her into my lap to give her a massage. Ainsley's head moves back and forth as my fingers press into her muscles. I know she's under a lot of stress and I can feel the tension in her shoulders.

"Wait a second," she says, leaning away from me. She pulls the hem of her shirt over her head, exposing her bra and back to me.

"Shit," I mutter as I feel myself starting to get hard. When she leans back into me, my erection grows. "Sorry," I tell her. Poking her in the back with my dick isn't something I want to be doing.

"For what?"

"Um ..." I clear my throat and avoid answering her. If she can't feel the protrusion, I'm not going to bring it to her attention. I'd rather die from humiliation at this point. I go back to work on her shoulders, switching between kneading and feather-light touches. Every pass, I pause and kiss her neck before continuing with her massage. Now that she's let me do it once, I don't want to stop.

When my hands get to her bra straps, I falter, wondering what she's going to say if I move them. The only way to find out is to try. I slide my fingers under the straps and push them off her shoulders, watching as her skin pebbles with goose bumps. Her hands reach behind, unclasping her bra.

"Ainsley, what are you doing?" I ask huskily. She's toeing a line I'm not sure she wants to cross. I'm so attracted to her that I've imagined myself with her many times, but never in my wildest dreams did this happen.

She turns in my lap, facing me with her beautiful breasts on full display. I swallow hard and try to peel my eyes away from them.

"What does it look like?"

"Um..." Once again words are lost as I try to focus on her and not her breasts. "I don't know. I'm a guy staring at a beautiful woman who has suddenly taken off her shirt and shown me a glimpse of herself."

"Do you like what you see?"

Looking down at my crotch, I smirk. "I think the evidence speaks for itself."

Ainsley brings herself forward, straddling my lap. "I know that I made things difficult when we first met because I'm afraid of getting my heart broken."

"I'm not going to break your heart, Ainsley. From the moment I saw you at the zoo, I knew I wanted to get to know you."

"Me too. I've just been fighting the truth this whole time."

The tension between us changes. It's as if we both know what's coming next. I pull her onto my lap and bring my lips to her skin. Each kiss leads me to the gift she's offering. My fingers roll her taut nipples, causing her to grind against me. Reaching down to taste her, my tongue laps over her sensitive flesh. Ainsley arches into me, pushing her breasts into my face and rubbing her core against my erection.

Her hands are everywhere, lifting and tugging at my shirt. I slip it off for her and bask in the way her hands feel against my skin. Her lips are on my neck, teeth nibbling my skin, causing a fire to burn within me. Sliding her off my lap, I lay her down and caress her breasts as her hand slides down my shorts, digging her fingers into my ass.

"Ainsley, what are we doing?"

"What do you want to do?" she asks breathlessly as she flexes her hips into me. I fight the groan that is building, afraid of what her reaction might be.

"I want it all," I tell her truthfully. "I've wanted you from the night at the beach. I can't get you out of my mind, but know if we do this, there's no turning back."

"It's what I want, too, Cooper."

# FOURTEEN

## Ainsley

Cooper hovers above me. The strain of his muscles is evident in his arms, and the torment in his eyes is clear. I've been so hot and cold with him he's probably expecting me to roll out from under him and bail. I can't blame him, really. My standoffish attitude and defiant nature are probably worse than any curveball he's faced in the batter's box.

But I want this and I want it with him. Call it female intuition or hormones, but something deep inside is telling me that things with Cooper are going to be different. He's going to show me that love exists and that not all men are pigs when it comes to other women. He chased me, and I've finally been caught, despite trying to run from him.

Cooper slowly realigns himself and sits back on his knees, his gaze roaming over my body as my chest heaves. The prospect of what is about to happen excites me. I take in his tempting, attractive physique, from his broad chest, to his devilishly handsome face, to his growing erection. The stare-off we're having is intense. Heat fills my body as he examines only half of what I'm offering him.

His hand moves over his arousal, never breaking eye contact with me.

"You're teasing me," I tell him, reaching for him to come closer. The prolonged anticipation is almost unbearable.

Cooper leans forward on his powerful arms and blazes a trail of openmouthed kisses down the center of my body, bypassing my eager breasts. He licks a path above the waistband of my shorts, pulling them down little by little until I feel the cool air mix with his warm breath above my mound. Instinctively, I arch my hips as he tugs my shorts off, leaving me in nothing but my underwear.

My heart beats loudly as his hands roam over the lace of my panties. Each brush along my core sends shivers up my spine. I lift my hips again, showing him that I want to go further.

Slowly, he peels the remaining undergarment from my body, his eyes smoldering with desire as he looks at me. "Are you sure?" he asks, his voice strong and confident.

"Without a doubt." I peer at him with intense urgency. The sexual magnetism in the room is about to combust, or I will, if he doesn't touch me soon.

"You're so beautiful, Ainsley. You have no idea how much I want you." He lingers over me, his arms creating a bridge to keep him from lying on top of me.

"Show me," I demand, confidently using my feet to push down his shorts. To my surprise, he's gone commando, causing me to gasp at the site of his manhood. His fully erect penis bobs against his stomach. Without pause, my hand wraps around his shaft, pumping lightly. I'm awarded with a throaty groan and a searing kiss as his lips claim mine.

His kisses are hungry, needy, as he nips at my lips, making love to my mouth. One arm steadies him while his calloused hand massages, pinches, and rubs my breasts, making the ache between my legs increase.

The strong hardness of his lips is now on my breasts as he moves down my body, removing himself from my grip. I call out in displeasure, earning a chuckle from him. My hand delves into his hair, massaging as he teases me.

He returns to kissing me, but only briefly, before he's making his way down my body. Before I know what's happening, I'm being pulled to the end of the bed with my legs never touching the ground. I raise my head slightly to see my legs are over his shoulders and he's smiling at me.

My head drops to his bed, and my back arches off the comforter when he licks my already wet pussy. He does it again with his thumb adding pressure to my swollen clit. Cooper sucks greedily at my core, taking everything that I'm offering him. My fingers dig into his blanket as my body temperature rises, thanks to the way he's making me feel.

"Fuck, you taste divine, Ainsley. My fingers beg to touch you, to feel inside of you, but my cock demands that your sweet pussy feel him first."

"Sounds like you have a dilemma," I say, pushing my hips toward him. He stands, stroking his erection while I gawk at him. I lick my lips, letting him know that I'll take him in my mouth, but he shakes his head no.

Cooper reaches for the drawer in his bedside table and pulls out a box of condoms. He tears one open, sliding it over his shaft.

"I bought these this morning," he tells me, as he motions for me to move up the bed. He crawls between my legs, causing the ache to return with a mighty force. "I had hoped after the beach..." He trails off as he centers himself. I trust him. I trust that he's telling the truth and isn't a man-whore.

Cooper sits back on his knees, with me on my elbows, as I watch him enter me. My eyes roll back as my body adjusts to his size. He pulls out, and my insides ache, waiting to be filled again.

"Cooper, don't tease me."

He enters me, fully sheathing himself. I cry out and fall against the mattress. Another thrust and my nails are digging into his thighs as our eyes meet. His hands move down my sides until they're firmly gripping my hips. Using them as leverage, he pumps into me, slowly, watching each time he enters my body.

"This is so fucking hot," he says as he disconnects from my body, only to push himself back in. I rise up and watch as he enters my core each time.

I gasp in sweet agony as the pressure quickly builds. I've never been fucked slowly. I've never been with a man who takes his time to bask in the emotion of what we're doing. Even as his hips move faster, he watches us connect, either with body parts or with our eyes.

Cooper's hands roam over my body, seizing my breasts while my hips meet his thrusts. His fingers pinch my taut nipples, causing me to scream out. He moves forward, his body partially covering mine, changing our position. My legs rise over his hips, allowing him to go deeper.

"Yes, yes, Cooper. Oh shit," I say breathlessly. He groans in between kisses, as our bodies become a frenzy of desire. He moves faster, pumping into my body as if I've been made for him.

"Fuck, Ainsley. Fucking magic," he says, thrusting faster.

My legs start to quiver as the intense sensation of my orgasm starts. "Don't stop," I beg him. "I'm so close, Cooper, please don't stop." I cup his face with my hands and kiss him deeply, giving him every moan and whimper I can as my walls clench down around him.

He pulls away, grunting out his release even through the aftershocks. Our bodies are slick with sweat as he collapses on top of me, and our breathing is labored. I hold him to me with my fingers playing with the back of his hair, causing him to sigh.

Cooper kisses my neck until he finds my lips. This kiss is different, hungrier, if that is even possible. When he slides off me, I feel a loss I've never felt before. In past relationships, I've never had the desire to be locked in someone's embrace, but that is what I'm feeling now. I reach over and touch him. He smiles and holds my hand.

Rolling onto his side, he brushes my damp hair out of my face. "I feel like I should thank you."

"For what?" I chuckle.

He shrugs. "That was the most intense love-fucking I've ever done."

"Make love?" I question, rolling onto my side to match him. He places his hand on my hip and leans down to kiss the valley of my breasts.

"I don't want to scare you by saying the wrong thing," he says in between kisses.

When he finally looks at me, I smile, hoping to convey that I'm more than okay with everything right now. "I love that you're so sensitive, Cooper. It's endearing."

"Don't tell the guys, okay?"

I laugh, and he pulls me into him. We start to make out until he pushes me away.

"I need to dispose of this condom." He slides off his bed and disappears from his room as naked as the day he was born. It's a good thing his roommates aren't home, although if they were, I don't know if we would've done what we just did.

Cooper returns with two glasses of ice water, handing me one. "Thank you."

"You're welcome."

His phone starts to ring. It must be a designated ring tone, and by the look on his face, whoever is on the other end is someone he doesn't want to talk to right now.

"Hello," he says as he sits down on the bed, placing his glass of water on his nightstand so he can put his hand on my leg.

"Yeah, I did."

"Fine."

"Yes, I know, Dad." He sighs heavily.

"I said tomorrow."

"No, I can't right now."

"I just can't. Tomorrow."

"Yeah, bye."

Cooper throws his phone onto the chair in the corner and leans back on his bed, covering his face. I'm sure that was a conversation he didn't want me to hear, and because I'm nosy, I'm going to ask him about it. "Everything okay?"

"You're here, everything is perfect." He pulls me to him, and my body molds to his. His words don't match his body language, and even though I know better, I press on.

"Do you want to talk about it?"

He shakes his head. "That was my dad. He's in town, and he's pissed about my performance today." Seeing what a conversation with his dad does to Cooper gives me mixed feelings. When I sat next to him earlier, I thought we'd have a friendly bonding moment over our admiration of Cooper. It took only one inning for me to realize that his father is on the extreme level of parenting. I know I should mention something to Cooper but don't want to worsen his mood.

"Well, the performance I just witnessed was a home run," I say, winking at him. He smiles, but it doesn't reach his eyes. "I'm sorry, Cooper."

"It's not your battle. I've been trying to cut the cord, so to speak, for a while, but short of me telling him to get lost, he doesn't get it. He said

I'm distracted, not focused, and if I'm lucky, they'll send me back to Triple-A."

I don't have a clue as to what any of that means, so I don't ask. So what if he didn't get a hit today? There was a bunch of other players that performed the same as he did. "It was one game. You have thirty more to prove that you are where you belong."

He looks at me quizzically. "How do you know how many games we have left?"

I look away sheepishly, realizing I've been caught. He tickles my sides until I find myself under him again. "Tell me."

I roll my eyes and pretend like I don't care. I do, but he doesn't need to know. "I looked you up."

"You did? Before or after we met?"

Totally beforehand. "After."

"Hmm, and?" He waggles his eyebrows at me.

"Cooper Bailey, are you fishing for compliments?"

"I am if you've got them."

"And nothing. I already had your program, so I thought I'd look to see what you're doing socially since you were calling. I was pleasantly surprised to see you don't act like a douche, unlike some of the players."

"I'm not a douche."

"That's good to know, since we've just had sex."

"We love-fucked, Ainsley, and we're about to do it again." He leans over to the nightstand and grabs another condom. "Roll over," he commands, and I do, getting up on my knees.

He slaps my ass and groans. "You better hang on, Ainsley."

# FIFTEEN

## Cooper

Waking up with Ainsley beside me wasn't something I had planned on. Before we knew it, the afternoon had turned to night and Guerra and Wilder came home. The last thing I wanted to do was parade her in front of them. Knowing them the way I do, I knew they'd be disrespectful, but in a playful way, and I have no doubt Ainsley would have played along, but I wasn't in the mood. It was fairly obvious to me that she was content staying when she had slid underneath my blankets and closed her eyes.

But I didn't. Each time I closed my eyes, I thought she was going to disappear. I watched her until my eyes couldn't stay open any longer. I'd startle awake when she'd move, fearful that she was trying to sneak out. I didn't want the night to end and knew, once the sun rose, we'd be in that awkward stage of "did she really mean to give herself to me," and that wasn't something I was looking forward to.

Shit, just thinking about being with her last night has my body zinging. Never in a million years did I expect her to be so forward, so willing. The way her body reacted to my touch, that alone was enough to make me hard. Every moment of us being together is seared into my mind. Images of her, when she was the most vulnerable, replay over and over, reminding me of what we shared. And what I hope to share again.

What I didn't bank on is her waking up at four a.m. to tell me she was leaving. I wanted her to stay wrapped in my arms, where I knew she belonged, but she was insistent that she had to get home. I know her mom isn't well, and she was probably worried about her.

Instead of heading back to bed, I decide that this is the perfect time to get some batting practice in. I'd wake Wilder and Guerra, but the likelihood of them wanting to go to the park so early is nil. They're dedicated, but not like I am.

The drive over to the park is quick, and when I pull into the parking lot, the field lights are already on. Which is a bonus for me since I won't have to wait for them now. As soon as I step out of my car, the sound of the bat cracking against the ball gets my blood flowing. Someone is here, thinking the same thing I am—more practice. I stop in the clubhouse to slip on my cleats and grab my mitt before heading out.

When I get to the top of the concrete stairs, I freeze. Putting balls into the pitching machine is one of the grounds crew. In the batter's box is Steve Bainbridge. Part of me wants to turn around and head back home, since the animosity between us is brewing. The other part of me wants to take my swings, too. If he's here practicing, then I should be as well.

The crunch of the gravel under my cleats gets his attention. He holds up his hand and tells the guy to stop feeding him the balls.

"What're you doing here?" he asks with his bat resting on his shoulder. Bainbridge is an intimidating guy, but I stand tall next to him.

"I need some practice," I tell him honestly. He knows that I'm gunning for his starting spot. It's no secret. Even the organization expects it. Bainbridge is close to retirement, and I'm young, eager, and better when there's a side-by-side comparison.

"All right, rookie."

Bainbridge drops the bat and heads over to the pitching machine. He exchanges words with the guy who was helping him and takes his place behind the net. I pick up a practice bat and swing it a few times to warm up before stepping up to the plate.

"What do you want to work on?"

"Fast balls," I tell him. Bainbridge shows me the ball before dropping it into the machine. This isn't like taking batting practice from your coach, where you can time your swing with his pitching motion. These balls are coming in hard and fast whether you're ready or not.

The first one I foul off, followed by the next four.

"Fuck," I mutter, digging my feet into the dirt. I stand in the box, waiting for the next pitch. It comes, I swing, and it's another foul.

"Do you want some advice?"

The competitor in me says no, but the baseball fan says yes. If Steve Bainbridge is willing to offer me some advice, who am I to say no? "Yeah, please," I say, stepping out of the batter's box.

He turns off the machine and brings the bucket of balls over to me.

"Face the fence," he says, kneeling down. "Let's go back to the basics of keeping your eye on the ball. I know you're some big shot down in Triple-A, but the pitching here is different. These guys can put a ninety-eighter by you before you even have the chance to blink. Your reflexes are slow. And I'm willing to bet people pitched to you because they were afraid of you.

"Not to mention you see the same guys more in the minors than you will in the majors, so you can't mentally adjust to their technique."

I stand there listening to everything he has to say and realize that he's right. Thinking back to yesterday's game, my swing was too slow, and I was always behind the ball.

"Did you ever do this when you were younger?"

"Yeah, I did. This is how I learned how to bat."

"No, it's how you learned to keep your eye on the ball and not memorize where it's going to be."

Bainbridge sets up just outside my bat's reach and kneels down with the bucket of balls next to him. I ready myself as if I'm in the batter's box and take his first toss. The ball smacks into the fence, ricocheting off and landing on the warning track.

"King told you to rotate your hips more. You need to power through your swing and use the momentum to move the ball."

I do as Bainbridge says and recall what Mickey King had said about swinging through with my hips. Ball after ball, my swing feels more natural, much like it used to last year.

"Okay, let's try the machine again."

By now, the sun is rising, and the lights are starting to get shut off. The crewmember who was helping Bainbridge earlier shagged all the balls from the outfield and has brought them back for us.

Stepping back into the batter's box, Bainbridge turns the machine on and shows me the ball before sending it through the chamber. By the time I register the sound it makes coming out of the chute, the ball is soaring toward me. Putting my weight on my back leg, I step into my swing and watch the yellow ball hit against the belly of my bat. I grunt as I swing through and watch the ball sail over the center field wall.

Bainbridge is watching it, too, and when he looks back at me, he's smiling. "Again," he says, showing me the ball.

We continue like this until my arm is sore. As we go around picking up the balls, I ask, "Your turn?"

"Nah. I have stuff to do before practice, but I'll be here tomorrow, same time." He walks off the field with two buckets of balls, leaving two for me to carry. He didn't exactly invite me, but it sounds like I'm welcome if I want to show up in the morning. I think he knows I'll be here. Baseball is in my blood and any chance to practice, especially with Bainbridge, I'm going to take it.

After a quick shower, I head over to my father's hotel. I've been down this road with him before, the one where he's upset with how I'm playing. I usually just sit and listen—sometimes I'll take notes—but I always work on the things he points out. He's not a professional, but he is my dad, and he's all I've got.

I text him, letting him know I'm at the hotel, and he gives me his room number. When I get to this floor, the door to his room is already ajar so I go in.

"Hey," I say as I enter the room. This is your average hotel with two beds, the standard television set, a table with two chairs, and a nice, large window that gives you a view of nothing.

"What's wrong with your arm?"

I look at him questioningly, and he points to my shoulder. I shake my head, wondering how he knows I'm sore.

"Batting practice this morning with Bainbridge."

"Getting to know your enemy. That's a good strategy."

Except he's not my enemy, he's my teammate, regardless of the situation.

"Anyway, do you want to go get breakfast?"

He stands and grabs his Renegades hat, slipping it onto his head. We walk back to my car in silence, which is perfect for me. I have enough thoughts running through my head as is; I don't need to add his as well. As soon as we're in the car, I turn the radio up, hoping he catches my drift that I don't feel like talking just yet.

"The food is supposed to be good here," I tell him as we pull into a diner not far from his hotel.

"Who told you this? Bennett, Mackenzie? Or was it Branch? I've always liked his game."

What does someone's game have to do with where they eat breakfast? I leave his stupid comment alone and enter the diner. As luck would have it, Kidd and Davenport are here. They wave at me, which gets my dad's attention.

"Introduce me," he says, forgetting that he's my father and not some fan. I reluctantly walk over with my dad following behind. I'm afraid to look back for fear that I'll see his tongue dragging on the floor like an overzealous puppy.

"Travis Kidd, Ethan Davenport, this is my father, Roy Bailey."

They shake hands while I stand by awkwardly. My dad starts in on their stats from last season while the guys sit there letting their breakfasts get cold. The guys listen to everything he has to say, being good sports. I don't know if it's that I don't have the patience for this or I just don't have the patience for my dad at all right now.

The waitress signals that she has a table for us, and I nod, acknowledging her.

"Come on, Dad."

"It was great to meet you guys," he says, shaking both their hands again. He follows me to the table, sliding into the booth. "You could've let me talk to them longer."

"The restaurant is busy, and it was our turn to sit."

"Your friends are going to think you're rude." He opens the menu and starts reading. I glance over at Kidd and Davenport. They seem happy and content, even after our loss. That is how I want to feel, except I don't. My nerves are frayed, I'm on edge, and I'm about to snap at my father for being so inconsiderate to my teammates.

"What's good?" he asks, breaking my train of thought.

"I don't know. Ainsley says she likes the pancakes." As soon as her name slips past my lips, I cringe. I study the menu, hoping that he didn't notice.

"Who's Ainsley?"

"She's a friend."

"Where did you meet her?"

"Media day at the zoo," I say, flipping the menu to the next page. Anything I can do to keep from looking at him.

"Coffee?" The waitress appears in the nick of time. I turn my cup over and watch her pour the black liquid into my cup, watching as the steam rises. She pours some for my dad as well before heading to the next table.

"You met her at media day and talked about pancakes?"

*Sure, why not? It's an ordinary conversation to have with someone.* I roll my neck, preparing for the argument that I'm sure is going to happen.

My silence speaks volumes, which only pisses him off.

"So you're getting some on the side, huh?"

"She's a friend, Dad. There isn't anything wrong with having a friend."

"You know women are a distraction, and clearly you've been spending too much time with her already. That was evident by your shitty batting performance yesterday. I'm hoping today is better."

He sighs and takes a drink of his coffee. "Women have demands that you're not going to be able to meet, expectations. They won't understand your hours, the training you put your body through, and the mindset of being a professional athlete."

I set my menu down and look at him. "Why not? Davenport is married. Said it's the best decision he's ever made, and he's younger than I am. You know, I'm not a kid anymore. I made the decision to finish college so I have something to fall back on when baseball is over, and I spent a year in the minors getting ready."

"Davenport didn't."

"You're right, he didn't. He also won the College World Series and fucked up big time as a rookie. I keep track of people just like you do."

This seems to shut him up long enough for us to order. Breakfast is anything but pleasant; the tension in the air is thicker than the smell of bacon grease. I know my father means well, but it's about time he lets me grow up and make my own decisions, my own mistakes.

# SIXTEEN

## Ainsley

I study myself in the mirror, looking at the same colored shirt and shorts that I wear five days a week. My hair is pulled back with a few wispy strands shadowing my face. My makeup is minimal, the color neutral and warm. I rarely notice a difference in my appearance, especially since my mother became ill. Your life changes when the one person you've counted on your whole life now has to count on you. You forget the simple things, like some blush to rosy up your cheeks or that new shade of lipstick you saw a commercial for but can't remember the name of when you're picking up a prescription. You learn to get by with the basics because you're too exhausted to do anything else.

And that is when people, mostly men, stop noticing you. You pretend not to let it bother you. It does, but you're too busy with life to let it take hold of you until you're lonely.

Cooper likes me like this. He likes the Ainsley who is tired at the end of the day, who hardly wears makeup and never does her hair because putting it up in a bun means I get ten more minutes of sleep.

Cooper likes the woman staring back at me in the mirror, the one who originally brushed him off and told him no repeatedly. I know that bothered him, because it bothered me, too, but he stayed. He kept coming around, even after I'd rejected him. It showed me his strength and character, showed me that maybe he's not the person I had pegged him to be.

Last night that all changed, and this morning I'm tired, and my cheeks are naturally rosy from just thinking about the attention he gave me. My lips are plumper, pinker, from the sensual kisses that still linger in my mind. And my body—I may be exhausted and achy, but it's well worth it.

Still, the athlete thing plagues my mind. Growing up, it's all I've heard and witnessed. I have friends who have been dubbed cleat-chasers because every season they're looking for some unsuspecting fool to sweep them off their feet.

Now I guess I can be put into that category. A man whom I didn't want to have anything to do with was persistent and has swept me off my feet. Guarding my heart is going to be a challenge, though, because I can already see him taking a piece of it when he leaves.

Now that I'm looking at myself in the mirror, I see a woman who is happy. I see the Ainsley I used to be, long before death started knocking on our door.

"You didn't come home last night." My mother appears in my doorway. Her bald head is uncovered, showing small tufts of hair that haven't fallen out yet.

When I was little, I used to love to play with her hair. She kept it long and would let me brush, braid, and even curl it. Growing up, I was a momma's girl and she was my best friend.

Now she's a shell of who she used to be, and it's not fair. The cancer that she carries inside is eating her alive. I know she doesn't feel well and is probably tired of me nagging her about getting out of the house

HOME RUN

to enjoy life—because, believe it or not, she still can have one—but she refuses. She's given up before the battle has breached the front line.

"I was out with a friend and didn't want to wake you." Part lie, part truth.

"What's his name?" she asks, as she comes in and sits on my bed.

I hesitate with my answer because I don't want to lie to her about what Cooper does. I hate not telling her the truth, but she should be happy for me. That is all I want—a little bit of happiness—and Cooper is providing that for me at the moment.

"Ainsley?"

Taking a deep breath in, I look at my mom with her expectant eyes and spill. "His name is Cooper. He's the one I mentioned the other day."

"The baseball player?"

The smile on my face is unpreventable. Just thinking about Cooper and what he may be doing right now makes me feel alive with excitement.

"Is my warning falling on deaf ears?"

"It's not, Mom." I sit down next to her and bring her hand into mine. "For years, I've listened to the warning, and for the most part, I've followed. I'll never forget the pain I went through back in college. Sometimes it's still fresh in my mind, but I can't let that fear guide me forever."

"But—"

I hold up my hand, letting her know that I'm not finished.

"All my life you have steered me away from athletes, which is funny considering where we live, and I've never asked you to tell me why. I've accepted that you had a bad experience and are trying to protect me. I love you for that, Mom, but I can't live my life that way. Cooper is different. Besides, you should see him, Mom. He's so handsome that he can have any woman he wants, and he *chose* me. Cooper chose me, and it feels really nice to be chased."

There's a tear that escapes and falls down her cheek. I wipe it away and bring her into my arms. We stay like this for a few minutes until she pulls away from me.

"I don't want you to get hurt."

"I know. Believe me, that is the last thing I want, and I honestly think Cooper isn't going to hurt me."

"Ainsley, you know he's not staying here."

I nod, and my chest grows tight. I don't want to think about Cooper leaving at the end of the month. I've already looked up his schedule and know that I'll see him a few times a year when he's down here, but any quality time can all be forgotten until October at the earliest.

"Long distance can work, but that's beside the point," I tell her. "We're friends, and we're having fun, enjoying each other's company."

She nods, but the worry is still on her face. Someday I'm going to have to sit her down and ask her to share her story because, whatever it is that happened to her, it really did a number on her views when it comes to athletes.

When I pull into the parking lot at the zoo, Stella is just getting out of her car. I check myself in the mirror before shutting off the engine and getting out.

"Morning," I say, not hiding my enthusiasm. She eyes me cautiously before she falls in step next to me.

"Is your phone broke?"

"What? No, why would you ask that?" I fish it out of my bag and show it to her. She snatches it out of my hand and hits the home button.

There's a list of text messages and missed phone calls. Most are from her, but the most recent one is from Cooper.

I reach for my phone, but she pulls it away before I can get it.

"What were you doing? Or should I say *who* were you doing that you couldn't call me back?"

I revert to my teenage years and roll my eyes. "I don't kiss and tell, you know this."

"Since when? We tell each other everything."

"Since…" I survey the parking lot and make sure there isn't anyone around who can hear me. Or hear Stella, for that matter, because I have a feeling her reaction might be a little over the top.

"Start dishing. I can see it in your eyes, you're freaking dying on the inside with juicy gossip."

"I was with Cooper until four this morning." I bite my lip to keep myself calm.

"Holy shit, you did not!"

I nod vigorously, knowing what she's implying.

"You little minx, you. Give me the deets."

"I'm not giving you any details, Stella." I reach for my phone, and this time she gives it back. I'm tempted to see what Cooper wants but don't want to interrupt my time with Stella. She's important to me. And she's going to be the one to nurse my broken heart when Cooper leaves.

"Was he good? Did he know what he was doing?"

In an instant, my cheeks warm, and she's clapping her hands.

"Holy shit, Ains, you got laid!"

"Uh huh."

"How many… you know?" She wiggles her eyebrows in excitement.

Once again I find myself looking around the area to make sure we're alone.

"I didn't count."

"Liar. I'm calling you out on your bullshit right now, Ainsley Burke. How many times did that hot piece of ass make you come?"

"I lost count, Stel. Like legit lost count because he was insatiable. You know how your first time can be awkward and you don't really know what to do when you're done?"

She nods.

"We didn't have any of that. He held me, kissed me, and didn't ask if I wanted to do it again. He just told me to roll over. And you want to know the best part?"

"Duh!"

"*I* seduced *him*. Everything felt right about being with him. He wasn't pressuring me. All he did was kiss me back. I don't know, Stella. I can't describe how I was feeling when I was in his room with him."

"Are you falling for him?"

I shake my head and start walking toward the employee entrance. "I'm going to have fun and put aside all the warnings. I know he's leaving, but right now I'm letting my hair down. I'm going enjoy the attention that he wants to give me."

"Well, I think you deserve all the attention. So I say go for it. Do what makes you happy."

When I get in, I greet the rest of the staff members and open the door to my office. On my desk is a large bouquet of roses that makes Stella gasp.

"I bet they're from your lover," she singsongs.

"He's not my lover. He's my love-fuck buddy."

"Excuse me, what?" she laughs.

I shrug. "Cooper called it love-fucking because it was intense, but so damn hot and romantic, but we're not together, so what we did would totally be classified as fucking."

"And now he's sending you roses? That's it, I'm finding me a base-ball player. Do you think any of his friends are single?"

I ignore her question and pull the card from the roses. The hand-writing is masculine, and I'm assuming it's his.

> Ainsley,
>> *Yesterday meant everything.*
>>> *#25*

"I'm officially jealous."

"Don't be. It's not what you think." I don't know if those words are for her or more for me. I have to remind myself often that this is only temporary.

"So what about one of his teammates?"

"Most of their bios tell you if they're married. Why don't you go shopping for one and I'll ask Cooper, or you can on Saturday when we go to his game."

"Oh, man, you're already planning to go to more of his games?"

"And wearing his number. Let's not forget my level of insanity. I've gone from hating the male athletic population to sleeping with one and parading myself around in his shirt."

"You're a goner. He showed you the goods, and now you're a cleat-chaser."

I'm not a cleat-chaser. This isn't something I plan to do again next year. Dating someone like Cooper is a one-time thing. The last thing I wanted to do was fall for him, and that is exactly what I've done. I thought I could ignore him, but Cooper was determined to break down my wall.

# BOSTON RENEGADES

Dear Renegades,

    The fans have high hopes for the season so yesterday's game really isn't sitting well with us!

    With that said, the Renegades lost their first spring training game. Such a loss isn't a big thing, but it still sets the tone in the clubhouse.

    Cal Diamond shocked no one when center fielder Cooper Bailey got the start. It's been pretty clear that Bailey is being groomed to take over for Bainbridge. It's unfortunate that Bailey's batting average stayed in the zeros in his first game. We'll chalk it up to jitters.

    The highlights of the day were the fast bats of Ethan Davenport, Branch Singleton, and Preston Meyers, all batting in runs and trying to put the BoRes ahead. Unfortunately, it wasn't enough to overcome the deficit, and the Renegades earned their first L of the year with a 7–4 loss.

# GOSSIP WIRE

Divorces are ugly and none more so than the Bainbridges'. A judge ordered Lisa Bainbridge to bring their minor children to Fort Myers so their father can see them. After a very public ranting session on the steps of the courthouse, Lisa boarded a plane (not a private jet, which she had requested) and flew to Florida. Rumor has it that Lisa was none too thrilled to be flying commercial.

Speaking of center fielders, it seems Cooper Bailey has taken interest in one of the staff members from the zoo. According to my sources, she met his father at the game, making Day One a family affair.

Bryce Mackenzie has called off his engagement to Gabby Nolan, citing time and distance as the cause. We're sure it couldn't be because Ms. Nolan was seen entering the home of pro tennis player Ralph Amato, who was once rumored to be having an affair with the model turned designer.

Easton Bennett has been seen with a young blonde while out and about in Florida, which continues to spur rumors that he's not the father of his on-and-off-again girlfriend's child. Maybe Bennett is housing Anna and her son until she can get back on her feet?

Don't forget, the BoRes will have some charity events coming up, plus a chance to run the bases with your favorite Renegade!

The countdown begins until our Renegades are back in Boston where they belong...freezing with the rest of us!

The BoRe Blogger

# SEVENTEEN

## Cooper

Sending Ainsley the roses was probably the cheesiest thing I've ever done, but I had to show her that she was on my mind. The last thing I wanted her to think was that the night before hadn't meant anything to me. It meant everything to me, and I want to show her properly.

After dropping my father off at the hotel, I made my way to the park to get ready for our road game. We're traveling a whole twenty miles down the road to play Minnesota again. Today's outcome will be different if I have anything to say about it. My workout with Bainbridge opened my mind, not only with my batting but with him as well.

He's my teammate, but I want the starting spot. Cal Diamond could move me to another position in the outfield, but Kidd and Meyers are both stellar players, and the only way I'm taking one of their spots is if they're getting a night off.

Maybe I should seek a trade. My agent can easily work a deal that gives the Renegades some draft picks, except this is where I want to play.

In the clubhouse, the guys are loud, and when I walk in they all say hi, everyone except Bainbridge.

"Rookie, we missed you yesterday." Kidd slaps my back as he walks by. "Today, though, no excuse."

"I can't. I have to be up early," I tell him. I don't mention that I'm hoping Ainsley calls and I end up seeing her tonight. I also don't want to tell Kidd that I'm planning on meeting Bainbridge here in the morning to work out. Jesus, just thinking about him helping me, and the fact that I want his starting spot, makes me feel like a fucking douche. It's the nature of the beast, though. Bainbridge is my team-mate, and that's what we do for each other. I know that I have a lot to learn from him, but if the roles were reversed, I don't think I'd be willing to help someone.

As soon as we're dressed, we're on a bus heading crosstown to Century Link for our game. I'm ready to avenge the loss from yesterday and show the coaches what I can really do. The Cooper Bailey that they were witness to is not who I am when I'm up to bat. I'm usually focused and steady, and I know what pitches are for me.

The drive to the stadium is short, and when we get off the bus, the fans are waiting by the fence for autographs. I drop my gear and head over, taking the lead, and start signing everything from balls, to bats, to programs and baseball mitts.

"Thanks for coming out," I say as I sign my name. The first time I signed my name was the first game I played in college. Kids were lined up after the game eager for my autograph. They thanked me for a great game. That is when I realized that watching baseball was their entertainment, and I was responsible for getting the job done.

I never felt any pressure to get the job done in college or in the minors. Everything flowed naturally. I never felt uncomfortable up at bat or nervous in the outfield. Yesterday's jitters could easily be chalked up to it being my first game, and with the added pressure, I freaked myself out.

I continue down the line, making sure to get every single person in line. Even adults are lined up, pushing their merchandise toward me for an autograph.

"Are you excited to finally be a Renegade?" an older man asks, catching me off guard. In my mind, I've always been a Renegade. It was just a matter of being called up. When they drafted me, I knew I was pegged as Bainbridge's replacement, so waiting a year in the minors wasn't going to be an issue. I was able to excel there and pretty much forced their hand into either bringing me into the fold or trading me.

"I'm happy to be playing ball," I tell him. Playing baseball is all I've ever wanted to do. It's really all I've known. It's what I love. I've said this before. If I'm not playing for the Renegades, I'm playing for some other team.

"Can I have a picture?" a young girl asks as she leans over the fence.

"Sure thing." I crouch down and get into the viewing space of her camera. She fumbles with her phone, trying to get us both in.

"Here, let me do it. My arms are a little bit longer." I take her phone from her and snap our picture a few times, even giving her a silly-faced one.

"Thank you," she says, giggling, as I hand her phone back. She huddles with her friends as they look through the photos.

"They like you," Bainbridge says as we near the end of the line.

"I need fans if I'm going to compete with you," I tell him honestly. He pauses and grabs my arm, halting my steps.

"We're not in a competition, Bailey. We're teammates, and that means we have each other's back, regardless of who is out on the field playing."

"That's easy for you to say, Bainbridge. You have the starting spot that I want. I have goals that can only be achieved by playing. If we're rotating, or I'm playing every third or fourth game, those goals will never be reached."

He shakes his head. "You're young; the accolades will come. Develop your game first, get a feel for what you have to do to better yourself. Most importantly, love the game *and* your team. We're a family, and it's not meant to be dysfunctional."

Bainbridge walks away, shaking his head. A hard pat on my shoulder has me looking to see who's next to me.

"He's been around a long time," Davenport says. "He came into the league at eighteen and had a rough few years. From what I've heard, he was hazed and treated like shit, so he tries to make sure that doesn't happen to anyone else."

"I'm not being hazed."

"No, I guess you're not, but maybe he feels like you're hazing him."

"What do you mean?" I ask Davenport, unsure why he would say something like that.

"We've all been there—trying to fit in and make a name for yourself—but there are ways to go about it, and from what I see, you're trying to keep Bainbridge at arm's length."

"He was supposed to retire," I remind him. "Last year, that is what I was told, and when I got the call, I thought the retirement announcement was coming. And here I am, vying for a position against one of the best outfielders in the league. The pressure is building."

"Dude, it's our second game. Go out and have some fun. Give yourself until the middle of the month to start freaking out. We're rusty. Most of us sat on the beach all winter."

"Speak for yourself," I mutter to myself as Davenport walks away.

I replay his words over in my head, wondering what sort of attitude I'm projecting when I'm out there. Thing is, until someone points it out, I don't know what to fix. Telling me that I'm being an ass isn't exactly showing me that I am one.

Bainbridge gets the start, and as I stand in the dugout, I look at the grandstands and easily spot my father. Thankfully, I can't see the scowl I know is on his face from where I am. I know he's part of my problem. He's so hell-bent on me being perfect that it's what I expect of myself. There's never any room for error and definitely never a learning curve.

The Twins take the field, and the warm-up pitches are sent across home plate. Kayden Cross, our first baseman, steps up to the plate and takes the first pitch, a ball that looked high and outside. The second is delivered, and he sends it soaring down the third base line for a fair ball.

"Yeah, that's the way to get us started, Cross," Kidd yells as we clap. The fans behind us boo. "They're a bunch of tit wipes," he says, causing me to choke on my water.

"You come up with the best one-liners."

"It's his way of coping with his epic douchiness," Easton Bennett, our shortstop, says in reply to my statement.

"You're such a nut beater, Bennett," Kidd says in retaliation, causing the rest of us to laugh.

"Now batting for the Renegades, right fielder Preston Meyers."

"Let's go, Meyers," I yell out.

"Remember, you'll get farther being a teammate," Davenport says before he climbs the steps and heads to the on-deck circle.

I try to ignore him, but he's right. Since I've been here, I've been worried about *me*. And *my* individual accolades. Baseball is a team effort: not a single person can do everything.

Meyers walks, putting two on for Davenport. The crowd cheers loudly for him when he gets up to bat. He takes the first two pitches before blasting a shot to deep left. We're all on our feet, yelling for him, Meyers, and Cross to run.

When all is said and done, Davenport is sliding into third for a triple with Cross and Meyers safely crossing home plate, giving us a two-run lead to start the game.

Branch Singleton is pumped and jumping around as he steps into the batter's box. He swings at the first pitch, missing. Same with the second. Our third base coach, Patrick Phelan, calls a time out to settle Branch down. He steps back into the batter's box and takes the next pitch, a ball. The fourth hurl has him swinging and missing.

"Fuck," he yells as he marches toward the dugout. No one really says anything because it's all stuff we've heard before, like "you'll get it next time." There's always a next time.

The skipper makes changes in the third, sending me to center field with the score tied at two apiece. I run out and start my warm-up with Kidd. We toss the ball back and forth while our pitcher warms up with five pitches to get the bottom half of the inning started.

Brian Dozier, the second baseman for the Twins, steps in and takes the first pitch before smacking the shit out of the ball and sending it between Kidd and me. Kidd is yelling that he has it, so I move into position to back him up in the event he drops it or it goes over his head.

"I go, I go," I yell once I have a better angle, but Kidd doesn't budge. I say it again, this time more forcefully, but Kidd continues to backpedal. I'm left with no choice but to move out of his way and let him catch the pop fly even though it should've been my catch.

He jumps at the last minute, snagging the ball before it goes over his head. There's a collective boo from the crowd and a large audible sigh from me.

"That was close," he says, laughing.

I'm not sure what's funny, so I head back toward my space and wait for the next batter.

We escaped the inning with no runs, still leaving the score tied. Heeding the words of both Bainbridge and Davenport, I try not to let the earlier situation with Kidd bother me. The ball was caught, giving us an out, and that is what's important.

"Up to bat for the Renegades, center fielder Cooper Bailey."

"Knock it out of the park." I hear my dad's call as I walk toward home plate. I had forgotten he was here, somehow blocking him out of my mind. Earlier at breakfast, he left a sour taste in my mouth, and his words aren't easily forgotten.

As I step in, I remember my early morning session with Bainbridge and how he helped me, reminding myself that he's a teammate and my success is his as well.

I take the first pitch. It's high and outside, and when I look over at the dugout, Bainbridge is leaning over the railing with his head turned in my direction.

The next pitch is low and called a ball.

"Wait for your pitch," someone yells, probably my dad. If it is, he needs to remember I'm in the majors. I don't have to be told to wait. I already know.

The third pitch looks good, and I start my swing, only to hold off as the ball sails high and out of my strike zone.

"Fucker got lucky," the catcher says, trying to throw me off my game.

I dig in and square my hips. "Maybe you can have him send me a meatball instead of this shit."

"Yeah, rookie."

My next pitch is exactly what I want. It's fast, down the middle, and prime for the taking. I swing, connecting with the ball. It sails toward the right field line, meaning I was behind on my swing. I lean toward the left, willing my ball to stay fair. If it does, it's a home run. When it hits the stands, I drop my bat and start running toward first base amidst the cheers from my teammates.

"Foul ball," the ump yells, causing Diamond to come out of the dugout and me to falter in my steps. I turn around and throw my hands up.

"That was on the left side of the line," I say, pointing in the direction of the ball. There are a few fans also voicing their displeasure with the call.

"Bill, what the hell? That ball is clearly fair," Diamond says when he reaches the umpire.

He shakes his head. "I saw it go right."

"That's fucking bullshit, and you know it." The words are out of my mouth before I can stop them.

"You're outta here," he says, tossing me out of the game. I stand there, shocked at what just happened, while Diamond is up in his face. Coach Phelan and our first base coach, Shawn Smith, step in between Diamond and the ump, separating them.

Diamond grabs my arm and drags me to the dugout, pushing me toward the long hallway that leads to the clubhouse.

Once inside, I throw a few chairs across the room until Diamond appears in the doorway.

"What the fuck was that?"

"Sorry."

"You're sorry? Your job is to play the game. That is it. If it's a foul ball, you get your fucking ass back in the batter's box and wait for the next pitch. I'll do the dirty work."

I nod, knowing he's right. He slams his hand against the wall and sighs.

"This is your second game, Bailey. Being ejected does not look good and will not bode well."

"I know."

He doesn't say anything else, leaving me with my thoughts. It's only day two, and I've fucked up royally.

# EIGHTEEN

## Ainsley

"Cooper Bailey has just been ejected from the game."

"Steve, I don't understand what just happened but the young rookie has been ejected from the game, and Cal Diamond doesn't look happy."

"You're right, Larry. I think this is the first time Diamond has ever had to come out of the dugout this early in the season."

"And neither does Bailey. Being ejected from a spring training game isn't going to sit very well with management."

I can't believe what I'm hearing, and now they're onto the next batter. Moving on as if nothing has just happened. I sit back in my chair with my eyes focused on the radio, willing the reporters to give me an update on Cooper.

"What the…"

I shake my head. "I don't even know, Stella."

We decided to take a late lunch today so we could listen to the game, and now I'm wishing I didn't, because I'm not sure how to process this information. Cooper doesn't seem like the type to get ejected. He loves the game, and all he wants to do is play, so this seems out of character.

I turn the radio off and look at Stella. "Wow," she says, sitting back. "Yeah, I don't know what to think."

"No, I'm referring to the fact that you turned off the radio when we were listening to the game. I thought you were a fan."

I roll my eyes at her and stand, taking my walkie talkie off the base. "I need some fresh air," I tell her as I leave my office. I tell my secretary that I'll be wandering around if they need me, flashing my radio so they know I'm reachable.

As soon as I step out, the warmth of the sun fills me, making me long for the scorching summer days that are ahead. I've never been a fan of the cold, opting for hot days and warm nights.

The zoo is busy for midweek with lots of day cares bringing their children out for some springtime fun. In a few days, Jambo's calf will be on display, and we're expecting a surge of visitors.

The reticulated giraffe exhibit is bustling with activity when I arrive. There are young kids feeding our family of giraffes. To me, they're the gentlest animals, aside from the elephants, and they love to interact with their visitors. I think about heading into their exhibit but don't want to distract them from the children, so I move on to the next, all while thinking about Cooper.

He doesn't strike me as a hotheaded person, and yet being thrown out of a game seems to be a result of his temper. Granted, I don't know him that well, nor do I know the game, but I can't imagine something being so bad that you're asked to leave.

Halfway through my tour, Stella catches up with me.

"They won," she says, falling in stride with me.

"That's good at least."

"Yeah... what are you going to say to him?"

I stop and lean over the railing, looking over the lion sanctuary. The train for visitors rumbles nearby and laughter fills the air. This is my happy place.

"I don't know. I think I'll wait until he brings it up."

"Has he ever been violent with you?" she asks, and I shake my head. When we're together he's sweet, caring and gentle. I would've never thought that this would happen to him, especially since he's trying to earn a starting spot on the team.

"If he was, you know I wouldn't give him the time of day."

"True," Stella says, sighing. "Maybe he's a chameleon."

"Or maybe he's human and had a bad day," I suggest. "We all have them, and until he tells me what happened, there's no point in speculating. I'm sure he'll call me later."

We continue to walk through the park, checking each exhibit and stopping to chat with a few of the people who have yearly memberships. By the time I'm back in my office, the zoo is an hour away from closing, and the entrance is being locked down. I pull my phone out of my desk drawer, hopeful that Cooper has called, but find that only my mother has phoned.

"Hi, Mom," I say as soon as she answers.

"Are you busy?"

"Never too busy for you. What's up?"

"I decided to listen to the game today."

I close my eyes and hang my head. Of course she did. Why, of all times, does she suddenly take an interest in baseball?

"Ainsley?"

"I'm here, Mom."

"He seems to have a temper."

"Let's not judge, okay? We don't know what happened or what was said. When I talk to him, I'll ask him. So until then, let's forget what you heard today."

Mom lets out a rattling breath, making my insides tighten. I don't care that her doctors think she'll get better. Her last scan was not positive, and I think she's getting worse.

"What time will you be home?" she asks, changing the subject. I have no doubt she'll bring it up again, but hopefully I will have spoken to Cooper by that time.

"I'm about to leave now. What would you like for dinner?"

"I think I'd like to go out tonight."

That idea brings a smile to my face. "That's great. I'll be home in about a half hour."

We say our goodbyes and hang up. I'm tempted to call Cooper, but figure that he'll call when he's ready. I can be patient while he works out whatever is bothering him. I take one last look at my flowers, wishing I could bring them home, but I don't want my mom asking any more questions than she already has, and honestly, I want to leave my relationship with Cooper between us. Keeping my lives separate will allow me to decompress when I need to . . . from both of them.

I'm lucky and make it home in thirty minutes. When I walk in, my mom is dressed and sitting in a chair in our living room.

"You look nice," I tell her as I kiss her on the cheek. She's dressed in a blue flowered dress with matching scarf. The color gives her ashen skin some vibrancy. "Give me five minutes to change."

I don't give her a chance to say anything before I disappear down the hall and into my room. I change quickly and readjust my ponytail before I'm back in the living room. "Where do you want to go?"

"I was thinking I want pie for dinner."

I stifle a laugh and nod. "Sounds good, even though I should tell you no. Don't you remember me asking for dessert for dinner when I was younger?"

"Yes," she says, taking my arm so she can stand. "But I'm your mother and you have to follow my rules." She winks, making me wish I could capture this moment on film. These days are few and far between, and I need more of them.

Once I have her situated in her car, I take the long way to the restaurant that serves her favorite peach pie. I'd love to take her for a ride in my Wrangler, but I don't think she's strong enough to climb in, and I can't lift her.

"Oh, it looks like they're busy," she says as I pull in. Indeed, there's a tour bus in the parking lot, which means most of the seats will be filled. The diner has been here for years, since back when my grandparents were teenagers. They used to hang out here after school, drinking fountain sodas and listening to their music. My mom came here as a child, and both she and my grandparents brought me here. The diner has been owned by the same family for generations and makes the best dessert around.

"Do you want to go somewhere else?"

She shakes her head. "We can wait for a table if we have to."

I knew that would be her answer, so I shut off the car and run over to help her out. She walks gingerly to the door. Her steps are slow and calculated.

"Mom, are you sure you're feeling okay?"

"I'm feeling great, just tired."

Tired is how she's always feeling. I know the chemo is supposed to weaken your system, but at what point does your body start rebuilding?

Surprisingly when we enter, only half the restaurant is filled, and we're seated right away.

"You'll have to excuse the noise," the waitress says as she sets down our menus. "The Boston Renegades are here celebrating their win."

I look at her quickly and then my mom, whose eyes narrow. The pull to go see Cooper is strong, knowing he's a few feet away from me, but I know my mother would rather tie me to the chair than let me get up and go see him. Even using the bathroom as an excuse won't work since we're closer to the restroom than he is. Truthfully, though, I wouldn't go over because that would likely embarrass him.

Instead of trying to catch his eye, I open the menu and pretend to look over my options. I already know what I'm getting—apple pie with ice cream—because I get it every single time I come here.

When the waitress comes back, we place our orders, and an awkward silence falls between us. I fiddle with my napkin while my mom sips on her coffee.

"You don't have much to say?"

"Just thinking," I tell her.

"About what?"

Cooper and how he made me feel last night.

"Work. The new calf was born a few nights ago, and he's about to make his grand debut to the visitors."

"And that concerns you?"

No, not really, but I can't tell her what's actually on my mind, so I fake it. "It's always a risk, putting a newborn out in the open, but the Board of Trustees want him seen. I'm nervous is all, for him."

"Why wouldn't you be?" she asks, completely unaware that I had to change my job around to accommodate the cancer taking over her body.

"I'm sure he'll be fine," I say, just as the waitress brings our pie over. "Thank you," I tell her as she puts down the delicious concoction in front of me. My stomach growls with anticipation, and my mother laughs.

"Didn't you eat lunch?"

"Yes, but I firmly believe that your stomach holds a special place just for dessert. Because while I ate a late lunch, I'm starving for dessert."

I take the first bite, and the warmth of the apple pie mixing with the cold of the ice cream feels like heaven inside my mouth.

"Why did you take a late lunch?"

"Um..." I look up at the sound of rowdy laughter and smile. It's good that they're enjoying each other's time and making the best of it. I'm still concerned with Cooper, though, and how he's coping with what happened today. "I wanted to listen to the game."

"I see."

I wish I had the confidence to ask her exactly what the issue is. Shouldn't *my* happiness be on the forefront of her mind? It shouldn't matter if the guy that I like is white, black, or yellow, drives a truck, lives in the slums, or plays baseball. She should be happy that I found someone that I want to spend my time with.

"Are you ready to tell me your story?" I ask her. It's probably not the best time to say something, but I want to know.

"What story?" She doesn't look up when she answers, and I can't tell if she's being coy or not.

"Your aversion to athletes? It started long before I started dating Mark and grew exponentially when he cheated on me. But not all athletes are like that."

She sets her fork down and wipes her mouth on her napkin. "There are better people in the world that I'd like to see you with."

"That doesn't answer my question. You have a specific hatred toward athletes, and I want to know why. I deserve to know why."

I cross my arms over my chest and wait for her to respond. She doesn't at first, instead choosing to take another bite of her pie.

"Mom?"

She sighs and sets her fork down again. "I've known a few in my life, and none of them turned out be admirable. It's not uncommon for a mother to want someone different for her daughter. Date a doctor or a businessman. Date someone who comes home to you every night and doesn't spend half his time on the road where temptation will get the best of him."

"Who is it that you dated? Is it my father that made you this way?"

"No, it's not. Now finish your ice cream before it melts."

She returns to eating, but the eerie feeling I have in the pit of my stomach leads me to think that my father is someone famous, or was. I've never known him, not even his name, and she's never hidden the fact that he left before I was born. Deep down I know I have to get the information from her before it's too late. If he's out there, I at least want to know who he is.

**BOSTON RENEGADES**

It seems that the young rookie has a temper! We've all seen it in baseball, especially during the regular season when tempers flare, but never during spring training.

What is Cooper Bailey thinking?

What is Cal Diamond thinking?

If this isn't evidence of a future problem, I don't know what is.

The Renegades pulled out the victory, despite the ejection of Bailey, over what was a disputed foul call. Bailey is going to have learn to pick and choose his battles and remember that Diamond is the one paid to get in the ump's face.

Tomorrow, the Tampa Bay Rays will be at Jet Blue Park. The Rays are rumored to be moving to Montreal if they can't strike a deal for a new stadium in Tampa Bay. Of course, some of the commingling that went on with their current facility probably isn't sitting well with the city officials. Montreal has expressed its desire to have a Major League team return to its city, and they prefer the American League and are promising the Rays organization a brand-new state-of-the-art stadium.

# GOSSIP WIRE

Not much happening in Fort Myers...yet, but give the
guys time. The rookies always make for great fodder!

The BoRe Blogger

# NINETEEN

## Cooper

We won, and I missed it. I had to watch from the clubhouse while my teammates celebrated the victory on the field. Even when they came in, they were jovial while I sulked on my stool, ready to leave. Except the team had other plans, which consisted of a team dinner. It's a tradition after our first win. The organization charters us to the same diner they've been going to for a few years and buys us dinner. The guys tell me that this restaurant makes the "best damn pie" ever, and by the way this place smells, I'm already in agreement without having tasted a piece yet.

"Cheer up, rookie," Davenport says, sitting down next to me. It's easier said than done, but he's right. I can't dwell on what I can't fix. I do need to get my head straight, though, because whatever I have going on right now isn't working for me.

"I'm not making a good impression."

"On who? Diamond or Stone? They both know what you can do, so stop stressing about it and just play ball. It's spring training. Who gives a shit if you play well? We're all rusty. Don't be so damn hard on yourself."

*I* care and probably too much. I need to relax and find my groove.

"What'd you say out there anyway?" Davenport asks.

"I said the call was fucking bullshit."

"Seriously?" he asks, shaking his head. "Bill must be having some serious issues going on right now. I've said worse than that, and he's never said a thing to me."

"I've never even lost my temper before. I think I was so stoked that I connected with the ball that I needed it to be fair."

"It was fair," Bainbridge adds as he sits down on my other side.

"That's what I thought," I say in agreement.

"Next time, let Diamond do your fighting. When it comes to season play, you're the most important player when you're up to bat. That is where your focus needs to be."

I nod, accepting his advice. Thing is, I know all of this, but have seemed to forget everything I've learned over the years.

Diamond greets the waitress when he sees her. Kidd cracks some off-handed joke, making us laugh. Everyone cheers when she tells us that they have extra pie baking just for us.

"So, rookie, are you using a batting glove?" Kidd asks. I look at him questioningly, wondering why he'd ask me something like that. The guys around us laugh, but Kidd keeps a straight face.

"Um...I use two."

He tries to hold back a laugh, but to no avail. I shake my head, quickly realizing that it's another one of his sexual innuendos. I throw the paper from my straw at him. "Are you ever fucking serious? You act like an eighteen-year-old."

"I gotta keep shit from getting too serious here," he says. I choose not to ask him what the innuendo is, because I don't want to know. For all I know, I've just insulted Ainsley.

Speaking of whom, I pull out my phone hoping to see a text from her. I don't know if she listened to the game today. Though I actually hope she didn't. Getting ejected isn't exactly a glowing recommendation when I'm trying to start a relationship with her. Instead, I find the slew of missed calls from my dad and an equal number of texts from him, berating me for my actions, each text message angrier than the previous one. I knew he'd be pissed, and I could've probably headed some of these messages off if I had answered his first call.

After dinner and dessert, we drag our tired asses back to the bus and head back to the stadium. Once I'm in my car, I text Ainsley while Guerra and Wilder get in and situated.

Do you want to come over?

I don't really want her there while Guerra and Wilder are there. However, I want to see her, be with her. But I also have to be up early. After today I'm going to work even harder to figure out what's going on with my game. I can't tell if it's mental or what, but something has to change. This is my dream, and the last thing I want is for it to slip away because of my inability to perform at this level.

I'll meet you there!

Relief washes through me, except there's a nagging voice in the back of my head that the guys aren't going to take this lightly.

"So my friend is coming over tonight," I say as I pull out into traffic. As I suspected, they start saying stupid shit that I'd be saying if the roles were reversed. I'm starting to think baseball players never grow the fuck up.

"She's hot," Wilder says, and Guerra echoes the sentiment.

"Yeah, and she's nice, so don't be douches when she gets there."

"Well, hopefully you won't be getting laid," Wilder says. My brows furrow at his comment, but I leave it alone. Most bros are slaphappy if their friends are getting laid. Maybe he's afraid he'll hear us. I'll turn on some music to drown out the noises.

Neither of them make any promises about leaving Ainsley alone when she gets there, which scares the shit out of me. For all I know, they'll start running around the apartment in their jockstraps, scarring Ainsley for life, or making her laugh. Sooner or later, she's going to end up spending time with them, just not now. Tonight, I want her all to myself.

She's waiting in the parking lot when I pull in, and as soon as I'm parked and out of the car, I'm walking toward her. My steps are eager, and my heart is pounding. I've never felt this emotion before or the desire to be in someone's presence as much as I do with her.

"Hey," she says, as a smile plays on her lips. Just being with her makes me feel better.

I collapse into her, wrapping my arms around her. She melts into me, nestling into the crook of my neck while her fingers play with the hair that is visible outside of my hat.

"Rough day?"

"You have no idea," I mumble into her skin. "But this is making it better."

She laughs, and her breasts shake against my chest, making me stir in my shorts. I can't hide how attracted I am to her. "Sorry," I say, backing away, but she doesn't let me go far.

"I like that I can do that to you." She looks down at my crotch and back at me with a wicked glint in her eye.

"I don't want you to think I asked you over here to get laid."

Ainsley steps into my space, placing her hands on my hips. I have to look down at her, and when I do, her gaze intensifies. This woman... she has to be what the romantics refer to as "the one." I never thought about that soul mate shit or true love, but if this how it feels, then I'm game. I don't care that my mind is constantly wondering what she's doing. From the second I laid eyes on her, I knew she was meant to be in my life.

"If I didn't want to be with you, I wouldn't come over."

My hand slides down her arm until our fingers are locked together. I give her a slight tug and nod my head toward the stairs that lead to my apartment.

"It's still a mess, but this time Frank and Brock are home. If they're crass, I apologize now. When you spend as much time as we do in clubhouses and on the road, we tend to lose all the manners we were taught growing up." I laugh, hoping to defuse any potential comments that they may blurt out when she meets them.

"I'm sure they'll be fine."

I shake my head. "We're athletes; it's in our nature to be pigs," I say as my hand rests on the doorknob. She gives my hand a light squeeze, and I open the door, surprised when I find neither of them in the living room, making our getaway to my bedroom that much easier.

Once inside, I shut and lock the door, watching as Ainsley looks around. Can't say anything in my room has changed from yesterday or even earlier this morning, but she's still looking like everything is new to her.

Is she nervous? The more I think about it, I am, and I can't explain why.

"Do you want to talk about today?"

I toss my keys onto my dresser and kick off my shoes. "I'm guessing you listened to the game?"

She nods, and I sigh as I take off my baseball cap. Ainsley giggles, and I immediately try to tame the crazy mess my hair must look like after being under my cap for so long.

"I'll talk, but only because you asked me."

"Fair enough. Do you have something I can wear?" She starts

unbuttoning her shorts and lifts her shirt over her head, exposing her pink lace bra. I swallow hard and only lose sight of her when her shirt lands on my head, covering my face.

"Sorry," I say from behind the fabric, earning a chuckle from her. I try not to stare when I pull her shirt away, but to no avail. She's so damn beautiful that I can't get enough of her.

I hand her one of my T-shirts. It's just a plain white one that is fairly comfortable. She slips it over her head, covering herself before dropping her shorts to the floor.

I quickly follow suit and shed my clothes, leaving myself in my boxers. Ainsley crawls into my bed, even though it's still early. Plugging my phone into the portable speaker, I turn on some music as background noise and hopefully to prevent the guys from hearing us.

"Today was the worst." I lie on my side to face her, pulling her close so our legs intertwine with each other's.

"I'm sorry." Her fingers softly move through my hair, soothing me. "Has this ever happened to you before?"

Closing my eyes, I shake my head slowly and bask in the feeling of the light massage she's giving me, helping to ease some tension. I love that she's concerned about my game, but it shouldn't be her worry. However, leaving the game on the field isn't something I've ever been able to do, especially since it's always been a topic of conversation for my father and me. My life has revolved around baseball and nothing else.

"I don't have a bad temper, and my comment wasn't anything that I haven't said before. Davenport thinks the ump was just in a foul mood and took it out on me."

"Will you get in trouble?"

"Not really. Diamond will probably ride my ass for a few days, but that doesn't worry me."

"What does?" Ainsley leans up on her elbow, bringing her lips into perfect kissing position. I lick mine and fight the urge to ignore her question and just kiss her.

"That I'm past my prime for the big leagues. When I was drafted I chose college first, and a lot of people have said I made the wrong decision. In my heart, I know it was right, but now I'm competing with guys five to six years younger than I am and coming right out of high school to play. Their bodies haven't taken the beatings mine has."

"I happen to think your body is just perfect."

I open my mouth to disagree with her, but her eyes tell me otherwise. Of course, if I were paying attention to her and not hosting my own pity party, I would've felt her fingers trailing through the patch of hair leading to my quickly hardening dick.

"I think I should stop talking."

"I think you should kiss me."

My thumb brushes against her lips, causing them to part. Her hand sneaks under the waistband of my boxers, enticing me even more. Once our lips touch, she moans, sending waves of pleasure right to my crotch. This is different from our first time. There's no exploration, no getting to know your partner. Everything now is eager, and each kiss, each groping and pass of a hand—mine over her breasts or hers along my shaft—increases the intensity between us.

I bunch my shirt—the one she's wearing—and lift it over her head so I can taste her peaked nipple through the lace of her bra. My nimble fingers work to release her breasts from their captor, and once free, my hands are massaging while my mouth suckles them.

She strokes me, increasing the fire that is burning inside of me. I lay her down and hover over her, relishing the way her hand feels wrapped around my hard-on. Ainsley pushes my boxers off of me, exposing my erection.

I curl my fingers around her panties and pull them down her legs, breaking the hold she had on me, and kick my boxers off. Ainsley is impatient and pulls me on top of her, my cock jumping the moment he feels her wet core.

I kiss her and move my body along hers, teasing her warm flesh. Nails dig into my ass and her hips rise up, trying to create the friction we both need. I'm startled when she grips my dick and guides me to her entrance.

"I need a condom," I tell her between kisses, forcing myself to leave her so I can grab one. I blindly reach for the drawer, opening it to reach for the box. Only I don't find it.

"What the fuck?" I say, climbing off of her so I can get a closer look. "Son of a bitch." It dawns on me now why Wilder made that comment in the car about getting laid—the fucker has taken my condoms.

"What's wrong?"

I flop on the bed and will my erection to go away. "My roommate took my condoms," I mumble into the bed while picturing every disgusting thing I can. Ainsley doesn't help matters when she starts kissing my back, my neck, and finally pulling on my earlobe.

"I'm on the pill," she whispers seductively into my ear. My head pops up, and I look at her. She presses her lips to mine, and maneuvers to pull me on top of her. I go willingly because I want to feel connected to her.

"Are you sure?" I ask, needing to know she has no doubts about us.

"I am." She hitches her leg over my hip, and when I push into her, I almost come immediately. The sensation of being bare and feeling her take me in is indescribable. I have a feeling Ainsley Burke is going to be my doom. That is if I don't destroy myself first.

# TWENTY

## Ainsley

I will not fall in love with him.

I will not fall in love with him.

I say those words repeatedly as I look at myself in the mirror. The red marks on my neck, a result of his scruff rubbing against my heated flesh as he moved inside of me last night, are a reminder of what I've done.

Never in my life have I had unprotected sex until last night. I don't know what came over me, but it can't happen again. But how do you tell the person that you've made a mistake? How do you look someone in the eye and say that you now want him to wear a condom without hurting his feelings, or ego, for that matter? I was horny and stupid, and now have to find a way to tell Cooper that we can't continue to have unprotected sex. He just has to understand that this is a personal decision and not because I don't trust him.

A loud bang shakes me from my reverie. I pause for a second before that voice in the back of my head tells me that something is wrong. Opening the door, I stall, listening for any sort of sound that may alert me as to what that noise was. Down the hall, I peek into my mother's room only to find she's not there. A few more steps and I am at the top of the stairs looking down at my mother, in a heap.

"Mom," I scream as I rush down. "Mom, can you hear me?"

She doesn't answer, and panic starts to set in. I search for her pulse. It's faint but there, and as I reach for my cell phone, I realize it's in the bathroom because I was contemplating sending Cooper a picture before I took a good look at myself in the mirror.

"Shit," I mutter as I scramble to the kitchen to call for help. After dialing, I tell the operator that I believe my mother fell down the stairs, and she is unconscious but has a faint pulse. They ask me to stay on the line, but our phone is older and is still attached to the wall.

This is karma coming back to bite me in the ass. If I had just listened to my mother about dating Cooper, I wouldn't have been in the bathroom trying to take a fucking selfie of my tits for him, and she wouldn't have fallen.

"Help is on the way," I tell my mom. I want to straighten her out and fix her clothing, but I don't know if she's broken anything, and I don't want to make things worse for her.

"Ainsley…" Her voice is groggy, and as she tries to reach for me, I clasp my hand around hers.

"It's okay, Mom. Help is on the way."

"What happened?"

"I don't know. I was in the bathroom." Doing shit I shouldn't be.

The sound of sirens is a welcome relief, and as much as I hate letting go of her hand, I have to in order to let the medics in.

They come in, one asking me a barrage of questions while the other tends to my mother. These are the same questions the operator asked me, but I suppose they need to ask again. I have no doubt I'll be asked once more when we get to the emergency room.

"What's your name, ma'am?" I hear the medic ask my mother. Her response is mumbled so I blurt out, "Janice Burke."

"Okay, Janice, can you tell me what happened?" the medic asks. I feel helpless as I look on, watching them work on my mother.

"I found her like that," I say, pointing to her. "I heard a loud bang, and when I came out of the bathroom, she was at the bottom of the stairs. I felt for a pulse but didn't want to move her."

"Does this hurt?" The medic presses and moves her arms and legs, checking to see if anything is broken.

My mom only moans, and the tears I've been holding back fall freely. They work to load her onto the stretcher and ask me to meet them at the hospital. It takes me a moment to realize that they're gone before my brain kicks my ass into gear and I'm grabbing her list of medications and my purse and running out the door.

I'm only seconds behind the ambulance and am there when they put her into a room. The hard orange chair is an unwelcome friend, and my body groans. I've spent far too many hours in a chair identical to this one and foresee many more hours, if not days, that I'll be here. I sit down and wait for them to finish transferring her to the hospital bed, along with hooking up the machines. I sigh as the sounds from the monitors fill the room, letting me know her heart is beating and she's breathing.

"Ms. Burke."

"Hi, Dr. Sanchez."

"Hello, Janice. Can you tell me what happened?" He writes in her chart, even though she's not answering him. She's been in and out of consciousness since I found her.

He turns to me. "Do you know what happened?"

I shake my head. "I came out of the bathroom and found her at the bottom of the stairs. I had heard the crash and went looking for her. She asked me what had happened so I'm guessing she doesn't remember anything."

"We're going to take her down for a CAT scan and get some X-rays to make sure nothing is broken."

Dr. Sanchez nods toward the orderlies who unhook the machines from their stands and attach them to her bed.

"We'll rush the results so we know what we're dealing with," he says, pulling up another one of the orange chairs. "Tell me how things have been at home."

I fill him in on how she usually doesn't ever want to leave, but also tell him about our dessert date the other night and how I felt like that was a turning point for her. But this fall is definitely a setback.

"I know her last scan didn't show a lot of promise, but I'm confident in her treatment. I'm hoping this fall is just that—a fall. People who have a weakened system sometimes lose their balance and take a tumble, and it's nothing to worry about." He places his hand on my knee and smiles. "I'll let you know soon."

With that, he takes his exit, leaving me in a sterile, empty room while the emergency room staff bustles around outside the walls. I don't want to know what's going on out there because I've been on that side before with the tears falling, my heart breaking, and my world crashing down around me. I hate this place just as much as I hate the cancer that is stealing my mother from me. Even if she's winning the battle, it's taking her spirit, and I don't know if she'll ever bounce back from it.

The sound of squeaking tires and soft mumbles startles me awake. The orderlies are back and hooking my mother up to the machines. I stretch and close my eyes as my muscles rebel against me. They're sore and achy, and my neck has a kink it in from falling asleep in the chair.

"How's my mother?" I ask when the nurse walks in.

"She's fine but is sleeping. She should wake up soon."

The nurse doesn't say anything else before exiting the room. I know Dr. Sanchez will be back in to give me the results, but it's the waiting that is going to kill me.

Taking my chair, I set it down beside her bed and hold her hand in mine. She's clammy and probably in need of another blanket, but I can't move. Since she's been battling cancer, she has aged, and it hasn't been gracefully. Her beauty has been eaten away by the amount of chemicals being pumped into her body. Her plump cheeks, full lips, and brilliant eyes no longer exist. Her clothes hang from her body as if she can't afford new ones, and she no longer walks with purpose but shuffles her feet along until she can find a place to sit and rest.

"Ahem."

I raise my head and wipe my tears when Dr. Sanchez enters the room. He looks somber, and my stomach twists in a knot.

"I'm going to just be blunt."

"It's what I expect," I remind him. There's no need to sugarcoat anything for me. Even though I would love for him to come out and say she's perfect, I know better.

"She has a broken ankle."

"That's easy to fix, right?" My hopes start to soar.

"It is, but we can't."

"Why not?"

He pulls the stupid orange chair close to me and sits down. Tears prickle my eyes, but I fight them back.

"The cancer has spread, Ainsley, and there isn't anything we can do. It's everywhere now, lungs, kidneys, and liver."

"What does that mean?" My voice breaks, and I have to cover my mouth to hold back a sob. Deep inside, I know what it means, but he has to tell me. I have to hear the words come out of his mouth.

"She has weeks, maybe a month or so left. She's too weak for chemo or radiation, and we can't do surgery—there's just too much cancer—and whatever we do try and remove, I have a feeling more clusters will take their place. Her immune system is already compromised, and opening her up will only cause her more harm than good."

"Is she in pain?"

He shakes his head. "No, we've started her on liquid Roxanol and will administer the dosage through her IVs. She'll be in and out of consciousness for the most part, and some days will be better than others, depending on her pain tolerance."

"Okay," I say, looking over at my mother, who seems to be frailer now than she was minutes before he walked in.

"I'm sorry, Ainsley. I wish my news was better."

I wipe away the tears and turn back toward her, giving her all my attention.

"The nurse will call for hospice care, and they'll be here to pick her up. It's two floors above, and I'll still be able to check on her."

"Can't I take her home?" Once the words are out of my mouth, I want to take them back. I already know the answer. My mother will never see the inside of her condo again.

"She needs twenty-four-hour care, and her insurance won't pay for a live-in nurse. We can send her to hospice or keep her here. It's your choice."

I nod, tuning him out. I don't want to think about what tomorrow, the next day, or even next week will be like.

I gently lay my head on her stomach and watch the rise and fall of her chest. I knew this time would come, but I never expected it to arrive so soon. I don't care how much faith you carry within yourself, once you hear the word *cancer* you fear the end. Even the most positive people, like my mother, accept the reality of the situation. It's a horrible disease that rips families apart, both emotionally and physically. And right now it's killing me inside.

My mom stirs. I'm by her side so she can see me.

"Ainsley."

"Hi, Momma," I say, reverting back to when I was a child and called her that. Sometimes I wish I had never had grown up and stopped using that form of mother, because right now it sounds perfect and has brought a smile to her face.

"I'm ready to go home."

Her statement isn't lost on me. While I'm thinking of her condo, I know she's thinking of another home where she's no longer in pain, her hair is back, and she's happy. Unfortunately for me, what's going to make her happy is going to break my heart.

# TWENTY-ONE

## Cooper

It's been a few days since I've seen or even spoken to Ainsley. We've texted, but she's been too busy to get together. Truth is, so have I, but that doesn't stop me from counting down the days until our one day off this month so I can take her on a proper date. The last thing I need is for her to feel like she's a booty call or that I don't want anyone to know we're dating. Hiding out in my bedroom is probably the last thing she wants to do.

Her seat remains empty in the stands. I don't want to give it to someone in case she can make it, but on the other hand, I'm thankful that she hasn't been at the games, because I don't want her anywhere near my father.

The tongue-lashing I received from him the morning after my ejection was enough motivation to keep Ainsley away from him. The last thing I want is for her to be on the receiving end of his tirades. He only sees me for baseball, nothing else. Women are a distraction, and that's what he'll tell Ainsley. I want to think that losing my mother really did a number on his romantic side. There has to be a nice guy buried somewhere deep inside.

We're riding a two-game winning streak and facing the Twins for the fourth time this month. I've racked up a whopping two RBIs, and both just happened to be on sacrifice flies. I've yet to reach base, and we're already eight games in. To make matters worse, my average shows a string of zeros when I'm up to bat. Never in my baseball career have I had a batting average of nothing.

When I see my father's name appear on the screen of my phone, I think about sending him to voice mail, which honestly will only complicate matters. He's all I have in this world, aside from the team and Ainsley, and whether I like it or not I still need him.

"Hey, Dad."

"Morning. I'm outside your apartment. Let's grab breakfast."

I look over my shoulder and sigh, wishing Ainsley were here so she'd be my excuse not to have to deal with him today. "I'll be down in a second." I hang up without saying goodbye and pocket my phone.

When I get outside, he's standing next to a cherry-red convertible with a shit-eating grin on his face. He tosses me the keys, which I catch easily.

"You drive," he says, pushing himself off the car and walking over to the passenger side. The weather is still somewhat mild here so the leather seats aren't an issue when I slide into the driver's seat.

"Where'd you get this?"

"I'm test driving it for a few days. I think I might move down here. The weather agrees with me."

I laugh. "Wait until a tropical storm rolls in. You'll find yourself buying a kayak instead."

He laughs. I can see him living down here, though. The warm weather will agree with him.

I start the car up and listen to the motor purr. I've always said that once I hit it big, I'll treat myself to something nice, but right now my check is sitting in my bank account just in case the organization changes its mind about me. They have every right to, since I feel like I'm not living up to their expectations.

Once I hit the road, with the wind blowing in our faces, I decide that we don't need breakfast but instead a nice drive along the coastline.

"You're distracted," he says once we're away from the city noise.

"I'll be fine." Those are the same words that Diamond says to me over and over again. I'm trying to believe him, but I'm not so sure.

"Your focus is wrong. Pull off up here," he tells me as he points to a lookout spot. I do as he says and shut off the car.

"I know I've been hard on you, but I've seen your potential since high school and only want the best for you. This is your chance, and your mind is elsewhere."

"It's on baseball."

"Maybe part of it is, but the other part is on that woman you've been seeing. You're distracted, and it's because of her."

I fight the urge to turn and glare at him. Instead I remain facing forward, unwilling to give him an ounce of satisfaction that he may be right. I wouldn't go so far as to call Ainsley a distraction, but she's definitely on my mind more than baseball is.

"When did you meet her again?"

I sigh and rub my hand over the leather steering wheel as I try to come up with some way to change the subject. Thing is, he already knows the answer, so ignoring his question will only anger him.

"It was before the season started, right? I was hoping it was just a quick thing, but I'm gathering I'm wrong?"

I nod, unable to say the words.

"That's what I thought." He pauses. "I'm not trying to be a hard-ass, but you worked too hard for this opportunity, and now you're letting it all slip away. You're not giving the Renegades a reason to keep you. Hell, right now you're not even Triple-A material, and you're going to find yourself in the singles."

"It's not that bad," I mutter, even though I don't believe my own words.

"It *is* that bad." He hands me my stat sheet, along with a list of the other rookies in the league who are all vying for spots on their teams. I'm dead last. If any prospective team is looking at this to make a trade, I wouldn't even be considered.

"I've been working on skills every morning with Bainbridge," I say, holding my hand up so I can finish talking. "As much as I want his starting spot, he's not my enemy. He's my teammate. We've been taking batting practice every morning, but for some reason, I can't connect with the ball during the game."

"That's because your mind is elsewhere. If I see it, Cooper, so do your coaches. Your eyes are wandering the stands looking for your friend, even though she hasn't shown up since the first day. And I've noticed, when you come up to bat, you look at me and frown. That tells me your mind is on her when it needs to be on the game."

I'll never admit that he's right, even when he might be. Ainsley's not the problem, though, I am, and I need to fix it.

I stare out the window, taking in the scenery. Something has to change or I'm going to find myself without a stable job. I suppose that I saw this coming, and that is why I chose school over the game four years ago.

"You need to save your career."

"I know," I respond automatically.

"You need to break things off with her."

I shake my head, unwilling to do that. I want to be with her.

"Is she worth your career?"

His question gives me pause. Is she? I haven't known her long enough to make a life-altering decision like that. If I were Bainbridge and going through what he is, maybe the choice would be simple. He chose baseball over his wife. Lisa asked him to retire and move back to their home state and started having an affair at some point, according to the guys in the clubhouse, but ultimately he could've chosen her.

Baseball is what I know. It's been my passion, my dream for as long as I could remember. And Ainsley...she's fun. I love being with her and already know that she means something to me, but is it enough?

"Is she?" he asks again. I shake my head, unable to get the words out of my mouth. Instead, I start the car and head back to my apartment. Before I make any decision, I need to see her. I need to talk to her, because part of me feels like she could be worth it.

After my father drops me off, I get in my car and head to the zoo. I tried to call Ainsley, but each call went to voice mail and she's not returning any of my text messages. Hell, maybe I'm worried about nothing, and she's as freaked out as I am.

When I walk into her office, her secretary smiles.

"Is Ainsley here?" I ask.

I should've known by the look on her face that the news she was about to deliver wasn't going to be good. "No, I'm sorry. She's taken a leave of absence."

My hands clutch the rim of the counter, and I nod, exiting before I can let my emotions get the better of me.

"Cooper!" I hear my name being yelled from behind, causing me to stop.

"Hey," her friend says when she catches up to me. "What are you doing here?"

"I came to see Ainsley, but I guess she's not working." My tone is sarcastic. I'm fucking pissed that she'd do something like this. I know we're not official, but this is something you tell the guy you're fucking.

"She didn't tell you?" She looks shocked when she asks her question. "Wow."

"Do you know where she is?" I ask, knowing that her friend will help me out. She pulls out a notepad and scribbles something down.

"Her mom is sick and in the hospital, but I figured she told you. Anyway, this is where you'll find her."

I take the piece of paper and thank her, rushing to my car. Instant guilt washes over me for thinking Ainsley did something malicious. Once the address is in my GPS, I'm speeding toward the location. She's going through something and likely needs my support, and here I am being a dick.

It's funny that I can't remember much about my mom except when she was in the hospital. Those days are crystal clear and come rushing back as soon as I step past the sliding glass doors and into the antiseptic-smelling halls.

With one last look at the note to verify I'm at the right door, I take a deep breath and knock before pushing it open.

Ainsley's eyes meet mine. If I was expecting happiness, I'm sorely mistaken. To say she's shocked that I'm here would be an understatement. She looks downright angry.

"What are you doing here?" she seethes, as she pushes me out of the room and into the hallway.

"I needed to talk to you."

"So you tracked me down? Why didn't you call?"

"I did, you sent me to voice mail." I reach for her hand, but she recoils. "Ainsley?"

She shakes her head and looks away. "You shouldn't be here, Cooper."

"Look, if you're trying to protect me—"

"Protect you? My mother is dying and you think this is about you?"

I step back and put some space between us. "I just thought..." My words fall flat as she shakes her head. Tears fall, and as much as I want to comfort her, I'm not a stupid man. I know when I'm not needed... or wanted, for that matter.

"You need to go," she says coldly.

I let her words sink in, refusing to believe they mean anything other than what she's saying, despite her demeanor. My whole reason for needing to see her today has changed, and I don't like it. Seeing her today was supposed to remind me that she's worth the fight. That what we have can grow into something deeper for the both of us.

"Ainsley? What's going on?"

"I don't have time for you right now, Cooper. I need to focus my attention elsewhere."

She says all of this without making eye contact with me. I look around to find people staring, even though they're trying to look busy. A few of them have their phones out, and I can only imagine what they're saying to their friends or posting online. Whatever, I don't give a shit right now.

I step forward and place my lips to her forehead. She sighs but makes no other move to touch me.

"I'm sorry, Ainsley," I say, before turning to walk away. I fight every urge I have to turn around and go back to her, to go back and demand she fight for us, but for what reason? Realistically, things wouldn't have worked once spring training was over. I'd be in Boston, and she'd still be here, taking care of her mother. I'd see her when the Renegades came to town, and that's it. Long-distance relationships rarely work out, and it's not like I can just fly down on the weekends. It was two weeks of fun, and now it's over. We both got what we needed from each other.

# TWENTY-TWO

## Ainsley

Watching Cooper walk away was one of the hardest things I've ever had to do, but it's for the best. I don't want his pity where my mother is concerned and I don't want him to relive everything he went through when his own mother died. I know he has very few memories left, but death is something you'll never forget.

People linger around me; a few whisper and maybe even point fingers, but I don't care. It had to be done. I can't deal with the text messages telling me that he's missing me or that he wants to see me. This will mean no more voice mails and no more nights in his arms. It's for the best. He can move on and forget I ever existed.

I wipe away the tears angrily, pissed at myself for letting karma win. My mom told me to stay away from athletes, and if I had listened, maybe she wouldn't be withering away to nothing in a hospital bed.

Going back into her room, I find the static sound of beeps oddly comforting. This is my life now, watching my mom give what little fight she has left in her until she flat-out gives up. I don't want her to, but it'd be one hell of a miracle if she were able to pull through this.

The morning-shift nurse comes in to check my mother's vitals. She smiles softly at me, but I can see the judgment in her eyes. I'm not stupid. Cooper is famous around here. His face is known. To these die-hard baseball fans, I just did the unthinkable.

Once she closes the door behind her, I break down and muffle my cries with a pillow. I let the tears flow as I scream out my anger and frustrations. I knew the end for Cooper and me was close, but I thought I'd be able to hang on for a few more weeks.

"Ainsley," my mother's weak voice calls out and has me rushing to her bedside.

"I'm here."

"Okay, sweetheart. I missed you."

There are moments of lucidity for her, and then there are times like this when she doesn't make any sense.

"I didn't go anywhere," I kindly remind her, but my words fall on deaf ears. Each day, even hour, she's slipping away from me, and there isn't anything I can do about it.

"Hey." The sound of Stella's voice grabs my attention. She rushes in and pulls me into her arms. "How's Mom?"

I shrug. I don't know how to answer a question like that anymore. I can't say she's doing well, because the cancer is eating her body up. Where's the positive in that?

"You've been crying?"

"Cooper came by," I say, which doesn't seem to surprise her. "You told him where I was?"

She nods and pulls me over to the cot that I've been sleeping on. "He came to work, Ains. He was asking for you."

"You had no right."

She blanches at my words. "So ignoring him was the way to go?

The man came to your office to see you, thinking you'd be there. Why didn't you just tell him what was going on?"

I turn my gaze back to my mother and shrug. "I don't want his pity or to hear about what his mother went through. Our situations are different."

"And what if he didn't do that? What if he just held you and let you cry on his shoulder?"

"He can't. Baseball comes first, it always will, and I don't want to burden him with this. It's for the best. I need to focus on my mother and prepare myself for what I'm about to face alone."

"Just because you don't have a father or a stepfather to lean on doesn't make you alone. I'm here. I've always been here, and I'm not going anywhere."

I go back to my orange chair and rest my head next to my mother's leg. Every day I notice subtle changes in her, and each one brings her closer to the end. Her breathing is no longer what I'd consider normal, and I find myself comparing my intakes of air to hers. Her skin is no longer white but bluish in color, and her eyes are lifeless.

"Let me sit with Mom for awhile. You go freshen up, maybe call Cooper."

"Cooper and I are done, Stella. I told him today that things are over."

"Why would you do that?"

I stand to face her with tears in my eyes. "Because he's leaving in a few weeks and he'll want to see me as much as possible. I'm not leaving this hospital while she's here," I say, pointing to my mom. "So what's the point, huh? Should I lead him on so when I want to get laid I can go over to his place?"

"Ainsley." She reaches for me, but I bat her arm away.

"You don't get it, Stella. My mother is dying, and Cooper doesn't fit in my world. He never did. I should've stayed away from him like Mom warned me, but I didn't, and now here I am paying the price."

"Do you really think this is your fault?"

I look back at my mom, a shell of the woman she used to be, and nod. "It is."

Stella scoffs and throws her hands up in the air. The silence between us is tense, and if we speak, words will have been exchanged that neither of us will forget.

"Go take a walk. I'll stay with your mom."

Stella doesn't wait for me to agree. She takes the orange chair and sits down, instantly putting her hand on my mom's.

I hesitate for a moment, wondering if I should go or stay here in case something happens. What if my mother needs me again and I'm not here?

When Stella picks up the book that is sitting on the foot of my mother's bed and starts reading it aloud, I know she's in good hands. Stella isn't going to let anything bad happen to her, and if something goes wrong, she'll have me paged.

Downstairs in the cafeteria, the Renegades game is on. I glance at the clock and realize that Cooper was here minutes before his game started. He put me first, and I brushed him off as if he were yesterday's news.

Pulling out one of the chairs, I sit down and focus on the game. The Renegades are already down by five runs, and I can't help but think this is more karma coming back to bite me in the ass.

Before I know it, the game is over, and they've lost, scoring only two runs. While I was watching the game, Cooper never made an appearance at the plate, nor did they show him in the outfield.

I pull out my phone to call him, but seeing his name on my screen twists the knife deeper in my heart. My call goes to voice mail as I suspected it would. It's stupid to think he'll call me back after the way I treated him.

I grab something to eat, only to realize that I'm not hungry. Stella is still reading to her, even though my mom is sleeping when I enter. She sets the book down and looks at me quizzically.

"What'd you do?"

"Nothing, why?"

"Because you look ... funny?"

I sigh heavily and pull my phone out of my pocket to see if Cooper has messaged me.

"I think I made a mistake with Cooper."

"Duh, but you never listen to me, so why the sudden change of heart?"

I motion for her to follow me over to my cot and fill her in on the baseball game and how Cooper was here right before game time, putting me before his career.

"Ainsley, that man is in love with you."

I brush her off. He likes me, but love is unlikely. "I don't believe that for one second."

"Believe what you want, but no man is going to put a contract worth millions of dollars on the line to go after someone he only likes."

The thought that he could lose money because of me turns my stomach into knots. I know he's struggling to fit in and show the organization what he can do. So if I've ruined his chances with the team, that'll make me the biggest bitch in the world.

"I'm trying to fix it," I tell Stella. "I've called him and asked him to call me."

"Good luck," she says, and while the sentiment is good, I have a feeling she's being sarcastic. I wouldn't be in this position if I had thought before I opened my mouth.

Stella stays for another hour or so, splitting her time between my mother and me. She wishes me luck again before she leaves, and I promise to call her as soon as I hear from Cooper.

As the hours go by, I start to pace, both in my mother's room and outside of it so I don't disturb her. My phone hasn't left my hand since I called him, and I've even gone as far as dialing out to make sure it's still working. Waiting for him to call is making me feel like a teenager again, when I sat by the phone and waited for the phone to ring.

If I were Cooper, I wouldn't call me back, especially after what I said to him. He doesn't owe me anything and doesn't need the stress of my piss-poor attitude.

But I need to talk to him. I need to apologize and let him know how sorry I am for acting the way I did earlier. Even if he doesn't want to listen to me, I'll have no choice but to blurt everything out and pray that he's paying attention to what I'm saying.

As the day turns to night, my hand is starting to cramp from holding onto my phone for so long. I risk another call and pray that he answers.

"Hello?" I pull the phone away from my ear and make sure it says Cooper's name, because the voice that answered is female.

"Um . . . is Cooper there?"

"Yeah, hang on," she says, giggling. The noise in the background indicates that he's at a party, which means he finally took the guys up on the invite to the bar. I know he's been telling them no to spend time with me.

"'Sup," he says into the phone. His voice is loud and somewhat slurred.

"It's Ainsley."

Silence.

"Cooper?"

"What do you want?"

I close my eyes and tell myself that I deserve the hostility in his voice.

"I want to talk about today."

"There's nothing to talk about," he says.

"I have some things I need to say—" Before I can finish, his name is called by a female voice, and he tells her that he'll be right there. My heart drops, realizing that my mom was right all along.

"Look, Ainsley, I gotta go."

"Are you with someone right now?" I ask, knowing the answer is going to kill me.

"What do you care?"

"I do, Cooper, that's why I'm calling."

He laughs. "We both knew how this was going to end. No need to drag it out for two more weeks. Thanks for the good time, Ainsley." He hangs up before I can say anything to him. Those words...they sting, but they're not him. He doesn't talk like that.

Unless he does and was only putting on an act in order to get me into bed.

"No," I say out loud shaking my head. "I refuse to believe it."

"Believe what?" one of the nurses asks, stopping in front of me. I've seen her around before, but she's not one of my mom's usual nurses.

"That my sort-of boyfriend used me for a good time."

"Yeah," she sighs. "That happens a lot around here. Women get starry-eyed when the players come to town. They turn stupid, really."

She goes back to work, leaving my mouth wide open in shock. Why did she assume I was dating a baseball player? Is that what all the single women do during the months of February and March?

Unsatisfied by my conversation with Cooper, I call him back, only to be sent right to voice mail. He's either quick with the ignore button or he's shut his phone off.

There's only one way to get through to him, and that is to go see him. I call Stella and ask her to come sit with mom so I can go fix things with Cooper. Face-to-face is the only way this will work. He needs to know that, come the end of the month, I'll still be here.

# BOSTON RENEGADES

HYPE!!!

Cooper Bailey is nothing but hype. And where the hell is he? Why isn't he playing? The fans would like to know what happened to the guy who was batting .393 last year in Pawtucket? Did he suddenly forget how to play?

I'm sorry, Mr. Bailey, the fans are expecting big things from you and you're not producing.

Management may need to rethink Bailey as Bainbridge's replacement because batting barely .100 is not going to suffice in the majors, even with his stellar defensive abilities.

Many have pointed out his lackluster performance could be because of his recent breakup with his girlfriend, but honestly, this has been going on from the beginning of spring training.

We're not sure what Diamond is thinking, but let's hope things change when the Renegades return to Boston.

The city of Boston will be holding a parade from downtown to Lowery Field on Sunday, celebrating the return of our team. Lowery Field will be open for free tours. It's highly suggested you book now.

The autograph session starts at three—line up early!

The season officially kicks off when the Indians come to town. It should be noted that first pitch is at 4:10 p.m.

Welcome home, Renegades!

## GOSSIP WIRE

With the return of the Renegades, the Gossip Wire will be heating up. Unfortunately for us, Travis Kidd decided to take a break from his antics while in Florida, but we're sure he'll be adding a lot of fodder to our column. Let's just hope he knows that we love him dearly and enjoy his dating habits.

The BoRe Blogger

# TWENTY-THREE

## Cooper

The Renegades are winning. It'd be nice to say that I'm part of that, but the truth is ... I'm riding the pine. In fact, my ass is starting to hurt, and I think I might have a sliver or two from sitting on the wood so much.

But this is my fate. I earned this because I had my head in the clouds during spring training and didn't focus on the prize in front of me. At the time, I thought I was invincible, that my talent from Triple-A would carry over, and I could easily take the starting spot from a veteran player like Steve Bainbridge. I know that I'm wrong now, and, sadly, it's taken me too long to realize the error of my ways. At best, each game gives me hope that I'll see some field time, and if I don't, I'm there cheering on my teammates because that is what I'm supposed to do.

Accepting that I may have fucked up my career hasn't curbed the longing I feel for Ainsley or the memory of how she looked when I last saw her. That day in the hospital will forever be one of my worst. I thought that it was going to be the last time I ever saw her until she showed up at my apartment that night. Not an hour after she called and I blew her off. The look on her face, the sadness and shock in her eyes—I knew I had hurt her—even though I didn't do anything wrong.

I had never been told not to suit up before for a game until that encounter with Ainsley. When I arrived at the clubhouse, I had missed our mandatory meeting, and Diamond pulled me into his office. He never raised his voice when he told me how disappointed he was in me and asked if I even wanted to play baseball anymore. My answer was an automatic yes, but he didn't believe me and suggested I take a day or so to truly think about what I want out of life. It took me all of five minutes of watching from the dugout to realize that baseball is my life and it's what I want to do.

It didn't take the guys long to figure out that something went down with Ainsley. Kidd was the first one to bring it up, along with something about having a party later. As much as I balked at the idea, I had no choice once Wilder and Guerra invited everyone over to our apartment. To make matters worse, I was tagged by the women at the party as the guy with a broken heart. It's crazy to think about all the women who wanted to listen to my story, offer a shoulder to cry on, and even cook me some meals to help mend my broken heart.

I took one woman up on her offer to listen, and that's when all hell broke loose. Ainsley showed up, assuming the worst when she saw me in the kitchen talking with another woman, and stormed out of my apartment yelling that her mother was right and all athletes are pigs.

And I didn't chase her when she left, which is probably one of my biggest mistakes. I wanted to, but something held me back. Maybe it's knowing that nothing was going to change. The fact is I am leaving in a few weeks, so I let her go and part of me still regrets it every day, but the other half of me knows it was the right decision for both of us.

Getting dumped by Ainsley sent me into a tailspin. My numbers didn't improve, I started committing fielding errors, and my bat was all but nonexistent. I was a guaranteed out when I stepped up to the plate. Each time I heard another skipper say something to his pitcher, my love for the game died a little bit more. They were right, though. My timing was off, I couldn't see the ball, and when I did, I watched it land right into the catcher's glove. During spring training, I was nothing but a liability.

Each day I waited with bated breath for Diamond to call me into his office to deliver the words that would send me back to the minors, but they never came. Instead, I received nothing but encouragement from him, spurring me to add more practice time and to work harder. All of this despite my father's nagging voice demanding that I ask to be traded because I wasn't playing. I couldn't tell him that I was content with where I was at right now because I still had a job. Being sent back to the minors, without an injury, would be a slap in the face, and that was something I wasn't ready for.

The only saving grace about leaving Florida is that my dad is still there. He's cozied himself up in a nice apartment on the ocean, far away from me. It would be nice to have family around, but I need a break from him. I know he means well, but I just don't think I'll ever get over his ill feelings toward Ainsley. I don't know if she was the reason for my poor performance at the start of the preseason, but she was definitely the cause during the last half.

Another thing I'm getting accustomed to: the BoRe blogger, who apparently used to be a fan of mine, now finds it comical to poke fun at me. I suppose it's not fun, per se, but whoever that person is has no qualms about pointing out how shitty I've been playing, or not playing, for that matter. I get it, I do. I'm a public person so nothing is off limits, but throw a guy a bone every now and again. Unfortunately for me, I spent hours combing over the blog posts, reading about how poorly I've performed since I was called up. As if I needed a reminder. I'm actually grateful for all the negative attention: It just makes me determined to prove them wrong. Luckily for me, though, I'm not the only Renegade subjected to the fodder—it's dished out equally—I'm just not in a position to change their views of me yet.

The clubhouse is empty when I arrive. It's not uncommon, but it's also nice to have a workout partner every now and again or at least someone to shoot the shit with. Branch Singleton told me the stadium is haunted, going so far as to scare the shit out of me one night. It's rookie hazing, and I'm the subject of a lot of it. Thankfully, the guys have stayed away from putting itching powder in my shorts or dye in my shampoo bottle. Wilder used to have dark hair and he's currently platinum blond.

From eight o'clock to five o'clock the stadium is bustling with activity from the office staff, and on game days, it's even crazier. Our trainers are usually here by midafternoon when most of us roll in, but on occasion, they'll be here early to catch up on injury reports and make sure everything is stocked.

We're eleven and nine and facing a National League team, the Atlanta Braves, this evening. We are home after being gone for five games, and every part of me wishes we were still down south. It's damn cold in Boston right now, and the weather is temperamental. One day, the sun is shining, and the next, it's snowing. This has to be the only drawback of playing on the East Coast; other than that, I love it, but I do miss the ocean views of Rhode Island, where I played Triple-A.

Traveling with the Renegades is a complete luxury, with our

chartered plane and custom coach buses. It's a definite perk of being in the majors. As much as I hate flying, I'd rather get there faster than sitting on a bus for hours, delayed in traffic or having to smell the stench from the toilet that your teammate clogged up.

I change quickly into my workout clothes, grab my headphones out of my gym bag, and head off to the weight room. Everything I'm doing today is to strengthen my core with sit-ups, push-ups, and wall squats because I didn't ask any of the guys if they'd want to come in early and spot for me. I figured since we just got home last night from our road trip that they'd want to spend time with their families. I know I would, if I had one waiting for me at home.

Working out keeps my mind off my life...and Ainsley, for the most part. I miss her, and the nights are the worst when I'm sitting alone in my apartment. When I need to hear her voice, I call her work number and wait for it to go to voice mail, only to hear the same recorded message over and over again: "You've reached the voice mail for Ainsley Burke. I'm currently on an extended leave of absence. Please press one to be connected with my assistant." There are times when I hang up and dial again, praying that she doesn't answer.

When I enter the gym, Davenport and Kidd are there with heavy-metal music blaring through the speakers and weights clanking against each other.

"What you guys doing here so early?" Even though Kidd is single, he's always romancing some lucky—or maybe unlucky, depending on how you look at it—lady. Coming in early to workout isn't really his cup of tea.

"Diamond asked us to come in and keep you company," Kidd says as he sets his weights down. Davenport punches him in the arm and rolls his eyes.

"I don't need a babysitter."

"He's not implying that," Davenport states. "He wants to make sure you don't get hurt lifting without a spotter."

"What's it matter if I get hurt? That'd be an easy way to put me on rehab assignment."

Davenport shakes his head while coming over to talk to me. He places his hand on my shoulder and looks me square in the eye. "Bainbridge is taking the next few nights off, and Diamond is giving you the start instead of putting Singleton out there. He wants you ready for tonight."

"Wh...what?" My tongue is tied as I say the word. I'm having a hard time comprehending what Davenport just told me.

"You heard me, rookie. You're starting."

"And we're actually here so you don't hurt yourself. Diamond doesn't want you overdoing it and pulling a muscle." Kidd slaps me on the back, pulling me back into reality. I'm starting tonight.

"I have to impress him," I say out loud for my benefit. It's my constant reminder that I'm always being watched, and now I'm being given the opportunity to show them what I can do.

Both Davenport and Kidd's expressions change from jovial to serious. They nod in agreement with me. "You're getting a chance to prove to him and Stone that you *can* play at this level. Don't blow it."

Davenport's parting words hit home. This is my chance, and I can't fuck it up. I stand there while they put their weights away and wait for me to join them on the cardio circuit. It's going to be an easy day and not one where I can take my aggression out on the dumbbells.

I slip my headphones on and join the guys on the indoor track. My pace is steady, staying behind Davenport and Kidd. After the second lap around, Singleton and Bennett have joined in. By the fifth lap, the starting lineup is running on the track, and most of the guys are surrounding me. I don't know if this is an attempt to keep me safe or a show of camaraderie. Either way, I'll take it.

After the workout, which consisted of every kind of "up" we could think of—push, pull, and sit—we're sitting down together for lunch.

"Do you guys do this every day?" I ask.

"Nah. I usually eat at home," Singleton says. His response is echoed by most of the players.

"So why are you all here?"

Hawk Sinclair, our starting pitcher tonight, sets his fork down and looks over at me. "Because we're a team, and sometimes one of us needs to feel like they're a part of the team."

Preston Meyers slaps me on the back. "Just make sure you're there to back me up tonight, right?"

I nod, appreciating that the guys are welcoming me... at least for this game.

**BOSTON RENEGADES**

He's arrived...finally!

Cooper Bailey showed us tonight what he's made of. With Bainbridge out for the week to attend a family funeral, the rookie got the call to fill the veteran's shoes, and boy, did he fill them by going three-for-three at the plate including a walk-off grand slam and throwing a sprinting Nick Markakis out at home on a tag-up.

Renegade fans—THIS is what we've been waiting for!

With tonight's win and the O's losing, that puts the Renegades two games back from first place at twelve and nine.

This could be our year, fans. This could be it.

Special note to Cal Diamond: Find a way to keep Bailey in the lineup.

## GOSSIP WIRE

As stated above, Bainbridge has taken some time off to attend a funeral. It's unknown who passed away, but Lisa did travel with her soon-to-be-former husband, adding some speculation that the couple could be headed toward a reconciliation . . . or it was her family member.

General Manager Ryan Stone and his wife, Hadley Carter, have announced that they're expecting their first child together. No timeline was given on when we can expect the newest member of the Stone family or if Ms. Carter will put touring aside to raise a family. Everyone at the BoRe Blogger wishes them many congratulations.

Cal Diamond was once again seen leaving the cancer clinic. A call to the front office confirms that Diamond is not sick but doing volunteer work. At this time, we're unable to confirm what work he's doing and why it wouldn't be done as a BoRe representative. Inquiring minds want to know!

# TWENTY-FOUR

## Ainsley

There comes a moment when you realize that your world is about to shift, and for me that moment is now.

"I left you," my mom says in a voice that is barely above a whisper. All week we've been talking about the end because we both know it's near. Any moments of lucidity that she has are spent going over details. From the day she entered the hospital, almost twelve weeks ago, we've been trying to nail down the specifics of her estate. Luckily, she has a will but there are a few odds and ends that we haven't discussed, like where she wants to be buried and the fact that she wants to be cremated.

"I'm right here, Mom." I don't correct her because there's no use. I'm in the same room I have been in since she was admitted. I rarely leave, sleep in an uncomfortable bed, and eat nothing but fast food. Even when Stella comes to visit, I never actually leave the hospital. I end up in the cafeteria or in the recreation room watching baseball.

People watch baseball for entertainment. I watch it for torture. Cooper has been doing very well for himself, and the Renegades are at the top of the division, leaving teams in their dust. I know he struggled for a long time to find his place on the team, and it seems like it's finally happened. I can't even begin to count how many times I picked up my phone to text or call him, to congratulate him on his success, but I never can seem to pull the trigger. That wound has since closed, and I'm not looking to open it up again. Even though there isn't a day that goes by that I don't think about him, it's better that we're each doing our own thing. Besides, the last thing I want to hear is how happy he is when I'm wallowing in self-pity while my mother dies a slow, painful death.

I'm surrounded by death. It's everywhere I look. I know it's part of being in hospice care, but for once, I'd love to see some happiness in my life. A couple of times, I've wandered down the hall only to find myself staring at the newborns through the large glass window. It's the only time I have faith in the world. Hearing a new baby cry brings a little bit of life back into me until I realize that, if and when I have children, they will never know their grandmother.

"I'm leaving you," she says this time while squeezing my hand. My tears are instant at the meaning of her words, and they fall rapidly down my face, splashing on my arm.

"It's okay, Momma." It's hard to be strong for someone else when you only want to fall at their feet and beg them to get better, plead with them not to die, but it's out of their control. It's what I hear almost every day when I ask if there is anything I should be doing for her: all I get is "Just be strong for her." But how does someone be strong against something so powerful as cancer? You can't be. All you can do is hope for the best, and even your best isn't enough sometimes.

"You'll be alone soon."

"I'll be okay. You just rest." I pat her arm, hoping to convey that we don't need to have this talk.

"I have a letter."

"For who?" I ask her, knowing that somewhere in her room there's a box of cards that she wrote out when she was first diagnosed. She wanted her friends to know what they meant to her. Most of them hung around until she starting shutting herself off from the outside world.

"You and him."

My heart drops, and excitement takes over. Is she referring to my father? Did she write about him? "What do you mean, him?"

She turns her head toward the wall, away from me. I get up and move to the other side of her bed and find that her eyes are closed. Gently, I run my fingers over her frail skin, hoping to wake her, but she refuses.

"Tell me, please," I whisper, begging for her to give me the answers I've been waiting my whole life for, but she doesn't budge. "Mom, please," I say again, only to jump when the door opens.

"Oh, my God, is she…" Stella covers her mouth with her hand and looks at me. I shake my head, wiping away my tears.

"She's still with us. She just dropped a bomb, though, and I'm not sure what to make of it."

I meet Stella at the foot of my mom's bed and give her a hug before retreating to my cot. During the day, I turn it into a makeshift couch with pillows that I've had Stella bring from home. It's the only way I can feel like I'm functioning and not spending all my time in the orange chair.

"What'd she say?" Stella pulls out tonight's dinner from her bag. It's roasted chicken and store-made potatoes.

"Well, I'm trying not to speculate, but I think she wrote a letter about my dad. I'm not sure, though. Lately it's been a few words here and there. Then she stops talking or she'll randomly talk about something she did when she was a kid."

"Wow, your dad?"

I nod before taking a bite of my food. "I'm not getting my hopes up, though."

"You've got to think that there has to be something in her room that gives you some direction, though."

"I don't know. With her, it's hard to tell. Whoever he is, he did a number on her, and she's not willing to forgive him."

"Maybe not him, but you deserve to know who he is, and if she's gone, she won't be around to tell you how you should feel or act toward him. And she won't have to witness it. I think a lot of her reasons for keeping him a secret is because she wanted you to love only her."

"That's selfish, Stella."

She shrugs. "Why else would she keep his identity a secret?"

I look over at my sleeping mom and wonder the same thing. Hell, I've been wondering who he is for as long as I could remember.

"I don't know, Stella." What I don't say is that he could've been married or maybe she never told him about me, fearful that he'd reject us. Or maybe he's the athlete, which would explain her aversion toward them. I believe the latter to be true because it would fit. I'm tempted to go home and start digging, but I can't leave her. Her end is getting close, and I promised her that I'd be here, holding her hand.

---

For weeks now I've survived on little sleep. Each time I'd close my eyes and start to drift, a nurse would come in to check on my mother. It seems that they know just the right time to open the door, much like when you're at a restaurant and the waitress comes by to ask how your meal is and your mouth is full of food so you can only nod, which is somewhat impolite.

Except tonight when the nurse comes in and checks on my mother, she leaves and returns immediately with another nurse. That's when I know her time on this earth is quickly coming to an end, and even though I'm distraught, I also breathe a sigh of relief, because soon she'll no longer be in pain.

"Ainsley?" I hear my name said softly, as if the nurse is trying not to wake my mom. I sit up and slide my legs out from under my blanket to face her. The soft glow from the muted light above my mom gives me enough light to see the features of the nurse's face, which is enough to confirm what my gut is telling me. "There isn't much time left."

I nod, understanding everything she's saying. The nurse returns to her duties, tending to my mother, while I sit there and look at her body, swollen with fluids and riddled with cancer. A single tear falls, the first of many to come, I'm sure, as I think about what tomorrow or the next day is going to be like.

Different. Everything is going to be different.

Picking up my pillow, I make my way over to the chair that I hate so much and sit down. My mom's hand is cold and clammy; she doesn't acknowledge that I'm holding it.

"How do you know?" I ask the nurse.

"It's her breathing. Her intakes of air are too far apart, and they're hard."

"Hard?" I question.

"Maybe hard isn't the right word," she says. "Her body is fighting for her last breath."

Glancing at my mom, I see exactly what the nurse is talking about, and that's when it hits me like a truck, square in my chest, and knocks the wind right out of me. I knew I'd cry, but the gut-wrenching sob that takes over my body is new and unexpected.

This is the last time I'm going to hold her hand, be able to see her, talk to her, and just be in the same space as her. All my life, she's all I've known. She's been my best friend, and even my enemy at times, but her love for me never wavered. I break the rules and crawl into bed with her, wrapping my arm around her as tightly as I can.

If the nurse has a problem with this, she doesn't say anything. I'm sure I'm not the only one who has done this, and I won't be the last.

"It's okay, Mom. I'm going to be okay," I tell her, letting her know she can go and I'll be fine. I've never wanted to say those words. I wanted to be selfish and demand she fight and stay here with me because I don't know how to do this thing called life without her. But I hate seeing her suffering. I hate that she's hanging on because she's afraid I'll be alone. I won't be. I'll have Stella and boxes full of memories to occupy my mind.

I rest my head in the crook of her neck. She doesn't smell like the mom I'm used to, but a mixture of soap and antiseptic. It's not something I want to remember, but I want her to feel me holding her, like she's held me so many times before.

"I love you, Momma." I gasp when she turns her head toward me, and I know that's her way of telling me, one last time, that she loves me, too.

---

It's been two weeks since my mother passed, and today she's finally being buried. I didn't want to put her to rest until everything was set, and now that her plaque is finally ready, she and I are taking the journey together to the cemetery.

I stand off to the side while the undertaker places the box containing her ashes into the chamber. He moves to allow me to put in the things I wanted her to have with her at all times. There's a letter from me, and one from Stella, a stuffed giraffe because, while they're my favorite, they were also hers and she loved coming to the zoo to feed them, and the necklace that my grandmother had given her. I thought about keeping it, but it was my mom's favorite and it should be with her. Once everything is inside, the chamber is sealed and her plaque set over the top. Her name shines brightly in brass with the words "Loving Mother" underneath them.

I arrange the flowers I brought and sit down next to her, taking a few moments for just her and me. These past few weeks have been difficult, harder than I thought they would be. I've hardly slept and barely eaten because I haven't felt very well, and I know the tasks before me are going to be daunting. I have yet to go into her bedroom because I'm not sure I can cope with not seeing her there.

"The peonies are in full bloom, and I'll bring you some every other day until I can't find them anymore," I tell her, running my fingers over her name. "I'm going to miss you so much, Mom. I don't know how I'm going to do this. Even when I didn't live at home, we spoke every day, and these past few weeks I've felt empty inside because you're no longer a physical presence in my life."

My biggest fear, one that she never knew about, is forgetting the littlest things about her. Her smell, her voice, and even the way she'd laugh or how she'd hold a book. It's been a year or longer since I've seen her dance in the kitchen, and while I used to laugh, I'd give anything to see her do it one more time just so I don't forget. Because right now, it's hard to remember. It's things like this that we take for granted and don't realize it until it's too late.

"Per your wishes, we didn't have a funeral, and I spread a few of your ashes at the zoo so you'll always be with me. Stella wrote you a letter. I didn't read it because I wanted her words to be kept between the two of you.

"And I know somewhere in your room there's a letter waiting for me, but I'm afraid to read it. I don't know if it's the fear that I'm going to hurt your feelings if I go looking for my father or my fear that he won't accept me. I'm not sure how much hurt I can take, so I'm going to hold off for now." A small gust of wind washes over me, and I know it's her.

"I love you, Mom. I'm sorry I didn't always show it the way you needed me to." I'm not sure how long I sit next to her marker while the sexton waits for me to be at peace with myself. When I finally start to stand, he's there to help me.

"I'll make sure she's fine before I leave."

For whatever reason, his words give me peace, and that is what I need right now.

# TWENTY-FIVE

## Cooper

My career is finally starting to take shape. Aside from not starting every game, I'm playing, and I couldn't be more thankful. After my rocky start, I thought for sure I was heading back to Pawtucket or, even worse, Double-A. But Diamond refused to listen to the naysayers and kept me on the bench.

We're playing the pesky O's today and are currently two games ahead of them in standings. I'm starting today and likely won't play the entire game unless my bat is on fire. If that's the case, Bainbridge will come in for Kidd or Meyers. Diamond has been messing around with our fielding spots to try to take advantage of the talent he has. Plus it allows the other guys to take a night off.

The Orioles are on the other side of the field, and Singleton is currently staring at them.

"Are you sizing up the competition?" I ask as I stand next to him. Singleton has about two inches on my six foot two frame and probably has me by ten or so pounds but can easily outrun me, and clocks the fastest base running in the league.

"Nah, just watching."

"They're a bunch of snot farmers," Kidd says as he joins us.

"Excuse me?" I choke as I try to hold back a chuckle while Singleton is bent over laughing.

Kidd shakes his head before nodding to the third base side.
"They've been whining to the local press about being in second place.
They're all fart munchers."

"Where do you even come up with these words?" I ask. I've been
the subject of a one-liner from him many times but haven't had the
balls to ask him where he gets them.

"He's a damn toddler, in case you haven't noticed," Bryce Mackenzie adds. He motions for us to start stretching, and I follow his lead.
Despite my rising batting average, I'm still a rookie and look up to
these guys—even Davenport, who is actually younger than I am.

"My life at home was shit," Kidd says when he catches up to us. "I
needed a way to cope so I started making jokes. It was easier to brush
off the bullshit from my dad."

"Sorry, man. I didn't mean to open any wounds."

"No worries, we all have that parent."

I know all too well what it's like to have an overbearing father. Thankfully, mine is watching games from the comfort of his beach house and
leaving me alone, although I do miss him. But having him a thousand
miles away affords me a life outside of baseball. He doesn't get to bitch at
me for staying out late or hitting a few clubs every now and again.

"My parents are awesome."

Kidd and I both push Davenport away when he says that. We've all
heard about how amazing and supportive his parents are, not to mention his hot-ass wife. It's funny, though, when he fucks up, because she
gets on him worse than Diamond does. We all joke that Daisy needs to
be on staff to keep us on the straight and narrow.

By the time we reach the warning track, the twenty-five-man team is in a row doing calisthenics. We laugh, joke, and razz each other no differently than what I'd imagine brothers would do.

We break off and start warming up with our groups. The infielders take grounders while the outfielders work on catching pop flies in the sun. After about an hour of this, we drag our asses back into the dugout to get the game underway.

As our names are announced, we step out and wave to the crowd before disappearing under our awning again. Diamond barks out for us to drink water and stay hydrated throughout the game before he sits back down in the corner where there's some shade.

"You okay, Skipper?" I ask, but he waves me off before telling me to get my ass out into center. I do as he says, jogging out after the National Anthem is played and some local kid yells for us to "play ball."

The first pitch is sent, and the crack of the bat has everyone yelling. I turn and run, watching over my shoulder as the ball sails toward me. My cleats touch the warning track, and I know I only have a few feet before the wall and I become close friends. The ball is high, and at the last moment I jump up, never taking my eyes off the ball, and squeeze my glove when I feel the hard rubber hit it.

When I land, the ball bobbles out of my mitt, but my other hand is there to snag it, and Kidd and Meyers are next to me, waiting to see if the ball drops. I raise my arm up high, and the umpire, who has come out to center field, signals an out. The crowd roars, and the guys slap me on the back.

"Good thing you caught that you tit twister," Kidd says as he jogs back to his position in left field.

"What the fuck, Kidd?"

He starts laughing and says something that I can't make out.

Max Tadashi gets the last two outs to end the inning. Justin Shaw, who happens to be Davenport's old teammate from college, is pitching for the O's today.

Kayden Cross is up to bat first and singles to right, barely beating out the throw. First base coach Shawn Smith is riding his ass about running harder, and I agree. When there's a chance you're going to be thrown out, you run your ass off.

Preston Meyers is up next and takes the first three pitches as balls. There's no way he's swinging at the next pitch, regardless if it's a meatball or not. We all watch as Shaw delivers the pitch for ball four, and Meyers flips his bat toward our dugout as he jogs to first.

"Hit away, Davenport," Diamond bellows from the dugout. He's still sitting in the shade and sweating profusely. I'm not sure if we should be worried about him or not, but it doesn't seem normal for a man who is resting.

Ethan steps into the batter's box and stares at his former college teammate. Right now, in this moment, they're enemies, but once the game is over, they'll be friends again.

"Swing the damn bat," Daisy Davenport yells from behind the dugout. We turn and look at her, only to be given the stink eye.

Davenport swings at the next pitch and sends it sailing toward the left field line. Cross and Meyers are running their asses off, and both score easily while Ethan is sliding into third untouched.

"Bring him home, Branch," multiple people in the crowd yell. When Branch steps up to the plate, I move into the on-deck circle and start my warm-up. I time my swing with Shaw's pitch, trying to get an idea of what he's throwing. This is my first time facing him, so the element of surprise is on both of us. Of course, it's always hit or miss and just depends on if it's going to be your day or the pitcher's. Right now, we're in his head so I'm banking on it being my day.

———————◆———————

Today wasn't my day offensively, but we came away with the win nonetheless. Shaw didn't get the better of me, but his fielders did. Prior to now, I've been hard on myself, tearing apart each action until I could make it better, but now I'm in the bar, sitting next to a very good-looking woman while she talks about interior design and how much she loves her job, and I'm asking myself, why can't I be more like Kidd and just sleep with any woman who comes my way?

Probably because I'm still somewhat hung up on Ainsley, even though I've stopped calling her. It wasn't doing me any good to hear her voice and the same message repeatedly. She's been hard to get over, and the few dates that I have been on haven't yielded anything promising.

I'm not sure if the woman next to me is the one for me, either, but I'm going to try. I angle my body toward her and open up to her. She continues to ramble about her business and starts listing off her clients.

I hold my hand up, and she stops talking. "I'm not looking for an interior designer yet. I still rent and can't see myself investing money into something I'm not keeping."

"Oh my, I feel like such a fool. I thought that's why you started talking to me."

I shake my head and try to hide the grin that is forming. She blushes and tries to hide behind her long, dark hair, a complete opposite of Ainsley.

"It's my fault. I started talking to you because I think you're pretty. I think that my pickup lines need some work, don't you?"

She covers her face, hiding even more of herself from me. I want to reach out and pull her hands away, but I'm not that forward. Slowly, she regains her composure.

"I'm sorry," she says, sticking her hand out toward me. I take her hand in mine and shake it. "I'm Carrie."

"Hi, Carrie. I'm Cooper."

"Oh that's funny, Carrie and Cooper." Once she finishes her sentence, her eyes go wide with terror, and she's covering her mouth again. "No, I didn't mean it like that."

"It's okay. I was thinking the same thing." I try to let her know that it's okay, and it was only a blunder. Hell, I've done it so many times.

I signal for the bartender and order us another round of drinks. She's making me laugh, and that is something I haven't done in a long time. Not since I was in Florida. It feels good to be like this again.

Carrie and I spend the rest of the night talking, sharing a small corner of the bar with the Davenports and a few of their friends. Not once does Carrie ask about baseball or what I do for work. Maybe she already knows, since everyone seems to know Ethan. It's nice to be able to sit and talk without the pressure of being on.

At the end of the night, I hail her a cab, not wanting her to drive home after drinking. Before she gets in, I give her my number and a lingering kiss on her cheek before she's being driven down the road.

Davenport yells my name from behind, and when I turn to look at him, I see nothing but fear.

"What's wrong?"

"It's Diamond. Stone just sent out a text that there's a press conference first thing in the morning. He's announcing his retirement effective immediately, and Stone will announce a replacement."

"What?" I pull out my phone and read exactly what Davenport just relayed to me. "This doesn't make any sense."

"I think he's been sick," Daisy says as she wraps her arms around Ethan's waist.

"Yeah, I read that over spring training, but he seemed fine."

"Something is definitely up. I mean, why is Stone bringing in someone new and not making Fisk or King the interim?"

"I don't know," I mumble while reading the words of the text message over again. Diamond has been my cheerleader from the get-go,
always there to remind me that I belong in the majors. I'm finally confident with my game play, but a new manager could want something
different.

"We're going to take off. I'll see you in the morning."

"Yeah, okay." I lean in and kiss Daisy on the cheek and watch them
walk arm-in-arm down the street. Both our places are close to the bar,
but in opposite directions. I pocket my phone and head toward my
apartment with my thoughts running rampant. I hate feeling insecure
about my future, and just when I thought I had it all figured out, a shit
storm starts to brew.

## BOSTON RENEGADES

After much speculation, Cal Diamond, our beloved skipper, announced his retirement effective immediately. As we've been reporting for the past year, this is health related, but Cal assured us this morning that it is not cancer. It is heart related, and he will be facing surgery in the upcoming months.

General manager Ryan Stone introduced Diamond's replacement, Wes Wilson. Wilson is best known for leading Team USA to an Olympic gold medal in our last games, as well as having a few NCAA titles under his belt. His recent stint in the minors adds to his résumé.

When asked why Stone didn't promote from within, he stated, "The job was offered to Cole Fisk, who turned it down, stating he was comfortable at the position of pitching coach."

Second baseman Bryce Mackenzie added, "I'm excited for Wilson to take the helm and saddened to see Diamond leave us. He's been a great manager and I'm going to miss him."

Wes Wilson was present at the press conference and added, "The Boston Renegades have a long-standing tradition of excellence, not only on the field but in the community. I have big shoes to fill in the wake of Diamond's departure and fully accept the challenges that face me. Right now, we have a winning organization, and I expect that to continue. Tonight's game will be no different. Cal and I have already sat down and gone over the roster. The fans should expect to see the same Renegades they've come to know and love."

First pitch is at 7:05 p.m. when the Renegades take on the Toronto Blue Jays.

Everyone at the BoRe Blogger would like to wish to Cal Diamond a speedy recovery and thank him for the wonderful years he's given us.

The BoRe Blogger

# TWENTY-SIX

## Ainsley

Her bedroom door mocks me every time I walk down the hall. Just when I think I'm ready, I can't twist the doorknob that will bring me face-to-face with everything she left behind. It doesn't matter that it's been a month. I can't do it. Dr. Sanchez suggested I donate all her clothes to a store that benefits cancer patients and their families, and while I think that's a wonderful idea, I don't know if I can part with her belongings.

Losing my mom has been hard. From the constant "I'm sorry" to the "It'll get better" comments, I've had enough. I don't want to be treated any differently or have people walk on eggshells around me. Her life should be celebrated. Laughter should fill her house, but as of now, it's only dread. I can't get out of my funk. My nights are sleepless, and I often find myself on the couch or staring out the back window. My days are lonely, and not even the television can keep my attention. Stella tries, but even her presence in my life seems to be forced lately.

Life needs to be normal again. My routine needs to go back to the way it was. I want to wake up to freshly brewed coffee, drive to work with the top down and the wind in my hair, and feed the animals. I want my job back working with the giraffes now that I don't need to be at home all the time. I've always been told it's there when I need it; I just don't know if I can pull the proverbial trigger and ask for it.

There's a knock on the door, and before I can bring myself to answer it, the door opens and in walks Stella. The smell of food makes me nauseated. I haven't felt well since my mother died, but I had hoped it would subside by now.

"I brought wine," she says, walking into the kitchen.

"Wine sounds good. What's in the bag, though? It's making my stomach roll."

"Really? It's just Caesar salads." Stella busies herself with opening the wine while I get the salads out. Whatever was bothering me a minute ago has seemed to subside. I empty the salads onto plates and set them on the table with Stella following quickly behind me with two glasses of wine.

"Hmm, this is good." It's been a while since I've had a glass of wine, probably since before my mother went into the hospital. Hanging out with Cooper... my thoughts falter as I think of him. Since my mother passed, I haven't paid attention to baseball, dismissing him completely from my mind. He hasn't called me, not that I expected him to.

"It is. I had it the other night with dinner." Stella pauses and catches my eye. For months, she's been eating dinner with me, and by the reddening of her cheeks I know she's been hiding something from me.

"Spill," I say as I set my glass down.

She slumps in her chair, almost as if she's been defeated. I know she's hiding her happiness from me and I get why, but she shouldn't have to.

"I met a guy," she states. "And I didn't want to tell you until I thought it might be serious."

"When did you meet him?"

"About two months ago."

"Jesus, Stella! You met someone two months ago and haven't told me?"

"You've been busy, Ains. Preoccupied with your mom, and I didn't want to burden you with my tales."

The fact that she thinks she's a burden to me causes me more heartache than I care to experience right now. She's my best friend, and if weren't for her, I'd be a pile of nothing trying to survive on crackers.

I reach across the table and take her hand in mine. "Stella, I love you, and I don't care what's going on in my life, yours is just as important, and I don't want you to feel like you can't tell me anything. I'm sorry I made you feel that way."

She shakes her head and comes over to my side of the table to give me a hug. "I'm sorry for not telling you."

"It's good. We're good," I remind her. "So tell me about him."

When she sits back down, her grin is electrifying. "His name is Zeb, and we met at work. He's a horticulturist who has been dealing with an infectious bug we found."

"Wait, we have a bug?"

She nods and takes a sip of her wine. "Nasty little shit, but anyway, Zeb has been dealing with it, trying to get rid of the creature and keep it away. I had to show him around the first day, and the next he came in and asked if I could kindly remind him where to go."

"And let me guess, you jumped his bones?"

Stella looks shocked, but only for a minute. "Actually, no. He asked me out, and at first I said no because of your mom and all, and it didn't feel right to be enjoying myself, in case you needed me. The next day we ate lunch together, and I told him what's going on and how I'm helping, and he said he'd wait until I was free."

"Wow."

"I know! Anyway, that did it. I took him up on his offer, and we've been seeing each other ever since. Want to know the best part?" She leans forward as if it's a secret, and I automatically mirror her position. "The sex is off the fucking charts. The man knows how to make my body sing like no other."

"Ugh, I miss sex."

"Call him," she says.

I look at her questioningly and shake my head. "Call who?"

"Cooper Bailey. Number twenty-five." She waggles her eyebrows at me.

"No. I'm not calling Cooper. Besides, he lives in Boston, and I live here. It'll never work."

Stella refills our glasses while saying, "You have nothing keeping you here, except for your job, which you can do anywhere, especially Boston. They have a zoo, and I know this because I already looked. I'd call him and see if you can ride that train again."

I throw my napkin at her. "I'm definitely not calling him and asking for sex." Although jumping between the sheets with him again would definitely be worth it, but I'm sure he's moved on. And if he has, I don't want to know about it. The rejection I felt, seeing him with that other woman, is enough to keep me here and away from anything that has to do with Cooper Bailey.

After dinner, we take our bottle of wine and sit on the back deck. I have to put this condo on the market because technically I'm not allowed to live here. I'm neither the right age nor am I retired.

"Are you going to help me pack?"

"Yeah," she says as she sips her wine. "Zeb will help, too. His muscles are big."

"I bet," I say, laughing. Stella takes it one step further and puts her hands up, showing me just how big. When the laughter dies down, her face softens.

"Let's go start packing your mom's room."

I have to look away. I don't want her to see me crying. "I can't."

Stella reaches for my hand, threading her fingers in between mine. "I'll be there with you. I know it's going to be hard, but it has to get done. We'll start tonight."

I hesitate for a bit before I nod. I don't know if it's the wine giving me the courage or what, but she's right. I need to do it, and I'll need her with me.

Stella has to drag me up the stairs. She stops briefly in the closet where she's been storing boxes and takes a handful down the hall with her.

"Wait, I'll do it." I stop her before she can open the door. As much as it's going to hurt, I want to be the one who opens the door first. With a deep breath, I close my eyes and twist the doorknob and step in.

Her room is basking in the late evening sunlight, creating a halo over her bed. I gasp and cover my mouth as Stella wraps her arms around my midsection.

"She's here," she whispers to me.

"I know."

"This is the right time." I want to disagree with her, but I can't. Deep down, I know she's right. Stella lets go and takes the boxes over to the bed while I stand there and look around. Everything seems frozen in time. My mom's room is still untidied, and her slippers sit by the foot of the bed. The afghan she used to keep warm is haphazardly draped over her rocking chair with a glass of water sitting on the small table.

The sound of ripping tape grabs my attention. Three boxes are on the floor, ready to be filled, and Stella is taping the next one. I want to ask her to stop so I can have some time, but I need to do this.

"We should put all her shirts in one box, pants in another," I tell Stella. "I want to keep her scarves, I think."

"Okay."

"Obviously I'm going to keep all her jewelry and pictures."

"I can call tomorrow and have the bed picked up."

I nod and am thankful she'll take care of that for me. I step into the closet and turn on the light. Rows of clothes hang there, untouched for months with a layer of dust on them. I reach for the box marked "personal" and pull it down and sit on the floor with it. I'm careful when I lift the dust-covered lid and place it right side up.

Inside is a stack of cards, each addressed to its recipient. As I look through them, I notice that these are all for her former co-workers and friends. These are friends that she pushed away when she was diagnosed with cancer. Part of me doesn't want to mail them for fear they may open old wounds that have since healed for people. But part of me knows I have to, to fulfill her wishes, even if I don't agree.

"Here, this one is for you," I say, holding up an envelope for Stella. She takes it and holds it in her hands for a moment before tearing it open and reading aloud. I try not to watch, but I can't take my eyes off of her.

> *My Dearest Stella,*
>     *I have known you almost as long as I've known my daughter, and not a day has gone by when I haven't loved you. Be strong for Ainsley, because she's going to need you when I'm not here.*

*Someday, you'll find happiness, and when you do,
please know that I'll be with you every step of the way. In
my jewelry box, you'll find a blue velvet pouch. This is my
gift to you on your wedding day. It's not much, but when
I saw it, I thought of you.*

*Love always, Janice*

Stella wipes the tears that have fallen and goes to my mom's dresser, pulling open the drawers of her jewelry box until she finds the blue velvet bag. The blue sapphire dangles from a chain, catching the fading sunlight just in time.

"It's beautiful."

"It is. I was with Mom when she found it. I didn't know she was buying it for you," I tell her as I lean against the doorjamb with my own letter in hand.

"Is that for you?" she asks, suddenly aware of what I'm holding. I nod and pull my lower lip in between my teeth to ward off the impending tears.

"Are you going to read it?"

I look down at my hand and back at her. She knows I'm fearful, yet curious as to what's inside the envelope. "I have to, right?"

She nods and reaches for my hand, pulling me over to the bed. When I was little, I used to sleep with my mom because she had the most comfortable bed. I reminded her of that not too long ago when I curled up with her in this one, only for her to tell me that her bed was so old and falling apart that she had put foam under her sheets for comfort. Now that I think about it, it must've been a comfort thing in the sense that I was always near her.

Carefully I slide my finger under the flap of the envelope and move it along until I can access the letter. It's five pages long, and the last thing I have in her handwriting.

> *To my beautiful, sweet, caring, and loving daughter, Ainsley,*
>
> *There are no words to describe the amount of joy you have brought to my life. You have been my light, my path, and the bridge that I traverse daily to a better life. When you came into my world, you changed me for the better and for that I will be forever grateful.*

She continues to go on about our lives together and how proud she is of me for going to college and getting my degree. My mom apologizes for getting sick—as if she could control that.

I continue to read about what she wants for me. She asks that I wear her earrings as my "something borrowed" when I get married and use the handkerchief that my grandfather always carried in his pocket but never used as my "something old." My mother encourages me to have children, travel, and find the love of my life, adding that it doesn't have to necessarily be in that order.

Stella and I both laugh at that.

> *And now for what you've been waiting for. For years, I've kept this secret out of love for a man I once knew and out of selfishness for fear you would choose him over me. I was young and foolish when I met your father, and I fell easily for his charm. By the time I found out he had another woman, it was too late, and you were already growing inside of me. He doesn't know about you,*

*Ainsley. I never got the chance to tell him. When I found out I was pregnant, he was long gone, and back then we didn't have the web to help us find people. I waited for him the next year, but he never returned.*

*He's the reason I have discouraged you from dating athletes. I was so angry and hurt, left as a teenager to raise a child on my own, that I wanted to prevent you from experiencing the same pain. I knew someday I would have to tell you this, but I never had the courage. I wouldn't be able to bear seeing him again, so I waited. I selfishly waited until I didn't have to face what I had done to the both of you. I hope that someday you will be able to forgive me.*

*His name is Wesley Wilson. He was a strapping young man, so full of charisma, and very handsome. You look a lot like him. He played for a baseball team, but for the life of me, I can't remember the name, but do remember they were from the northern part of the Midwest. If you decide to find him, please let him know that I'm sorry. I never meant to hurt anyone.*

I set the letter down on her bed and collapse in a heap of nothing. She kept him from me this whole time, and while I had an inclination, I had always hoped she didn't know who he was.

Stella leaves my side, only to return with a roll of toilet paper.

"Thanks."

"I'm sorry, Ainsley."

"I know. I am, too. I don't even know what to think."

"Are you going to look for him?"

I shake my head. "I don't think so. I don't know. What if he has a family and he doesn't want me? I don't think I can go through any more pain."

Stella holds me in her arms soothing me. It's some time before the tears stop and I'm able to function.

"I'll be right back. I have to use the restroom."

When she leaves, I pick up the letter again and reread the part about my dad. He was with someone when they met, which means they could still be together. He probably has a family and doesn't have room for me lurking around.

"Hey, do you have any tampons?" Stella yells from the bathroom.

"Under the sink."

"Nope, none."

"Are you sure?"

"Yep. There's nothing under here. Can you check your suitcase? Maybe you didn't unpack them."

I stand and start down the hall to my room, trying to remember when the last time I had my period. The date escapes me. In fact, I can't recall having one while in the hospital.

"I wadded up some toilet paper. Did you find one?"

I shake my head slowly.

"What's wrong?"

"I can't remember my last period," I tell her as anxiety starts to set in.

"It's okay. You were under a lot of stress. I'm sure your body just shut down."

Yes, that's it. My body went into preservation mode and stopped putting me through death once a month. Stella has to be right because there is no other alternative.

# TWENTY-SEVEN

## Cooper

It's hard to say if the change in managers has been a benefit to the Renegades or not, but it's definitely been one to me. I've known Wes Wilson for years, back to my early college days when I tried out for the U.S. Olympic Team. I didn't make the roster, but that was because there were other, more talented players than I was at the time. I never held a grudge or had any hard feelings. I also didn't expect Wilson to remember me, but he did.

While Bainbridge and I still switch off and on, I'm more on lately than he is. He calls it rookie luck. The odds makers call it talent. I'm not sure what I call it. All I know is that I'm happy with my playing time. I'm still working to make the position mine, and as much as I enjoy working with Bainbridge, I'm hoping he retires at the end of the season. I'm batting in the three hundreds, and my on-base percentage is almost double what Bainbridge is achieving. At the moment, we're a winning club, and in order to win, you keep what's working, and right now that's me. Regardless of who's playing, we're getting it done and are currently in first place with a four-game lead.

And I'm finding that I love Boston, even though I've never been a fan of wind, and Boston spring reminds me why. The fans here are amazing, the atmosphere is electric, and it feels like home. Once the off-season comes, I'll start house hunting, hopefully in the Back Bay area.

Most of the guys are already in the clubhouse when I arrive, prepping for the media explosion that is about to happen outside. Travis Kidd, whose locker is next to mine, is combing his hair trying to tame a pesky flyaway. My attire is simple: Put on some Renegades clothes and my ball cap, and call it good.

"Are you trying to find a chick?" I ask him as he continues to comb the same spot after he sprays it down.

"My picture will be taken."

"I take it you never look yourself up on the web."

Kidd drops his comb and glares at me. "When I'm playing, I don't care, but today is different."

Davenport slaps him on the shoulder. "Different because there will be women who forgot to put some clothes on and Kidd will be getting their digits."

"Thought so," I say, laughing right along with Davenport.

"Listen up." Our publicity rep, Talia, comes in, not caring if we're dressed or not. I suppose she figures we're at least decent since our day is starting with an autograph session, although she's been known to barge in.

"The lines are long so we want to move them along fast. We're trying to keep them off the overpass, but more people showed up than we had originally anticipated. Staff will be on hand to give you new markers when you need them. Fans will be handed an eight-by-ten color photo for you to sign, plus they can bring their own items. They are only allowed to have three pieces signed at a time before they have to get back in line. Don't worry about counting. The staff will be there to make sure fans comply.

"If you get thirsty, let one of us know. It's hot out, and we've moved you guys under the awning as much as we could. Once the line is complete, you're allowed to mingle if you want. That is the only time fans will be able to take pictures with you so we encourage it. Any questions?"

Most of us shake our heads, as she's pretty efficient with her details.

We follow Talia out and down to the street where fans start screaming our names. I wave, as do some of the other guys, and they get louder. I can tell pictures are being taken and can't imagine any of them will be decent. But who knows, everything will end up on social media anyway whether they're good or not.

There are twenty-five chairs lined up behind a row of tables. Talia and her staff direct us where to sit, as if we couldn't find our own chair when each one has a name tag on it. I'm not surprised to find all of the outfielders together, with me sitting next to Bainbridge and Meyers on my left and Kidd to the right of Bainbridge.

"The last time you did one of these, rookie, things were different." Bainbridge slaps me on the back as he says this. I can't tell if he's being an ass or if his comment is genuine.

"I didn't have many fans back then." I didn't, and I was at the end of the table. By the time people came through the line, they were tired and didn't really care about me.

"Yeah that's about to change." He points to the crowd, and there are fat heads with my face on them being moved up and down.

"Wow, that's freaking trippy."

"You made it, kid. Just don't let it go to your head," he says, reminding me that he's not only my teammate but also he's looked out for me from the get-go.

"I won't. I have a good role model."

He smiles, looks down at the table, and starts fiddling with one of the markers. Talia tells us to get ready.

---

Signing hours of autographs before a game is not recommended. I think the publicity department underestimated the number of people that were going to show up. And by the end of the event, Kidd walked away with twenty or more phone numbers. Three of which are dates for the upcoming week. I don't know how he does it, but the women flock to him. I don't know if I should be jealous or scared. I can't even find someone I want to spend time with. Our schedule is hectic, and it really takes an understanding woman to put up with it.

I change quickly and head out to the field. Even though I've been starting, I haven't stopped putting in the extra time with Bainbridge. We head out to center field with our buckets of balls and two bats. I end up going first, hitting one hundred balls into the mats that try to soften the impact that our bodies take when we collide with the wall during the games.

"You're doing good, Cooper. You've come a long way," he says.

"Thanks to you. You could've been a total dick and let me fail."

Bainbridge shakes his head. "That's not what's best for the club. We want to win, and if that means I'm on the bench, so be it."

I continue hitting the balls he's tossing, wondering if I'm ever going to be like him in that way. I was raised to look out only for myself, my teammates be damned, but Bainbridge has been trying to teach me otherwise.

"Have you thought about coaching?"

He pauses and looks at me. "Do you think I'd be good?"

I rest my bat on my shoulder and nod. "Hell yeah. I could never thank you enough for everything you've done for me when you didn't have to. I can't say I would've done the same thing if the roles were switched. I would now, though, because you've taught me what it means to be a team. So, yeah, I think you'd be a great coach."

Bainbridge seems to ponder this for a minute. "Maybe I'll think about it." Everyone knows he has a lot of shit going on at home, but he never seems to bring it to work.

We continue to work out until it's time for team activities to start. Inside the clubhouse, there's a buffet set up for us to munch on until it's time to get serious; this is something new with Wilson. Before, we'd go down and eat when we were hungry, but now we eat as a team and in the luxury of our clubhouse.

When I step out of the dugout, I turn at the sound of my name being called. My dad is right behind the dugout, grinning like a crazed fool. He's decked out in Renegades gear and has a crazy foam finger that he's waving around. I'm happy he's here just as long as he doesn't overstay his welcome. He needs to let me live my life and make my own choices, while suffering the consequences of my actions.

The game goes as planned, even though I rip my pants sliding into third and end up getting catcalled because people can see my ass in the outfield.

Most important, we win, putting us ahead of the Orioles once again. Unfortunately, both of us can't vie for the division title, and I'm hoping the Renegades are the sole leader of the American League East when it matters.

We decide to celebrate our victory at the bar across the street. It's become somewhat of a tradition for us, but tonight it's Kidd, Bennett, Davenport, my father, and I, sitting around a table shooting the shit. You'd be surprised how much we have to talk about after spending all day together.

Tonight, my father is leading the conversation, telling embarrassing stories from when I was kid. Like the time I climbed the tree in our backyard to watch the neighbor girl change her clothes because she always left her blinds open. My father sprayed me with a hose and made me go over and apologize to her, soaking wet. She later became my girlfriend for about a month until baseball started and I was never home.

My phone vibrates in my pocket. I contemplate ignoring it, but it won't stop. I pull it out, and my heart drops and then immediately speeds up, if that's even possible. Ainsley's name is displayed on the screen. Once the vibrating stops I start to breath again.

"You okay?" Daisy Davenport asks.

"Um ... yeah. I just need to use the restroom." My dad lets me out of the booth, and I navigate my way to bathroom, ignoring the people who are trying to get my attention. As much as I have tried to put Ainsley behind me, I've been unsuccessful. I've compared the few women I've dated to her, even though we've been over for months. But now that I've seen her name, I have to know what she wants.

I press her name on my phone once I'm down the hall and away from people.

"Hello," she says in a voice that I've missed.

"Hey ... uh ..."

"Hi, Cooper." Fuck, the way she says my name, it's like it was yesterday that I had her beneath me, tangled in my sheets with my hands all over her body.

"Hey, Ainsley."

"Look, I know you probably don't want to hear from me, but I'm in Boston and I need to see you."

"When?"

I don't care what the reason is. I don't care to know why she's here. The fact is that she wants to see me, and I'm going to go.

# TWENTY-EIGHT

## Ainsley

As luck would have it, my father is Wesley Wilson, the current manager of the Boston Renegades, making him Cooper's boss. I waited a month before I started to look for my father, and when I found him, it was like a weight had been lifted off my shoulders while a boulder was sitting on my chest. The moment I saw his picture pop up in my search I knew. We have the same eyes, cheekbones, and smile. The only difference is our hair color, but there is no mistaking that this man is related to me.

And now I'm currently in Boston so I can meet my father. I don't know how it's going to go, but my expectations are low. I had to call the Renegades' office to set up a meeting, using my position at the zoo to discuss the future of media day there. I need to see him, come face-to-face with him, so I can at least say that once in my life I met my father.

I chose a restaurant close to the stadium so I could meet with him and Cooper, albeit at different times, and not mess up their schedule. Last night when I spoke to Cooper, I thought my heart was going to burst. I had a long spiel planned, promising that I would take up only a few minutes of his time, but he agreed so quickly to meet me that I stammered through my words, giving him the time and location before hanging up. I thought I would be okay, hearing his voice, but I'm not. I miss him. But I know that things won't be the same for us. He's likely moved on. I've seen pictures of him with different women, and having a pregnant lady hanging around will cramp his style. I'll say what I have to and get on my way, letting him decide if he's going to be in the baby's life or not.

As for my father, it'll be his decision, too. I can't force a relationship, especially since I don't know if I want one or not. I may meet him and determine that he's an asshole and we'd never get along, except my heart is set on liking him, and I hate that it already seems to have made up its mind. Being here is such a risk, and any more rejection will likely send me into a tailspin.

I text Stella, letting her know that I'm at the restaurant and waiting for Wes. She begged me to let her come, but this is something I have to do by myself. My hand rests on my stomach, feeling the butterfly kicks that are currently going on inside. Finding out I was pregnant was a shock, but the real heartache came when I found out how far along I was. I had been neglecting my body and feared that I had hurt the baby, but all my tests have come back with glowing results, and the baby is thriving. I just wish my mother was here for all of this or that she at least knew before she passed that she was going to be a grandmother.

The hostess escorts Wes down the aisle toward my table. I know it's him because he looks just like me and I him. He's dressed similarly to the way Cooper dressed when I saw him away from the ballpark, with a red polo, khaki shorts, and a baseball hat.

"Mr. Wilson, I'm Ainsley from Naples Zoo. I was up in the area so I thought we'd meet and discuss next year's plan."

We shake hands, and he offers me the same smile that I've given him. "It's nice to meet you."

We sit down and give our drink order to the waitress: water for me, and a diet soda for him.

"I know that Cal Diamond used to do this event."

"Actually, this year was the first. The turnout was amazing, and the children really enjoyed getting to know the players."

"That's great." He lets out a chuckle mixed with a huff.

"Mr. Wilson, I'm going to cut to the chase." I pull out a picture of my mother and him from the time they knew each other and slide it over to him. It's a small snapshot that has faded over the years. "Do you remember her?"

He picks it up and rubs the scruff on his face. It reminds me of Cooper and the five o'clock shadow he always had.

"That's Janice Burke," I blurt out, not giving him a chance to answer me. "You are the Wesley Wilson that played for the Minnesota Twins?"

He nods. "I am," he says, without taking his eyes off the picture of him and my mom.

"And that's you in the picture?"

"It is." He pauses, and I shake my head, growing frustrated. Why can't he say something about the picture? About knowing my mom? I really wanted this to go smoothly and have a fairy-tale meeting, but it doesn't look like that is going to happen.

He sets the photo down and readjusts his hat. I'm trying not to cry but so desperately want him to remember my mom. "Please look again," I beg, my voice breaking. "You would've met her in Florida when you were playing."

He picks up the small photo again and studies it. I don't know if it's to appease me or if he's really trying.

"She had the prettiest hair I had ever seen. I remember it was red."

"Yes! Like mine, only darker."

Wes nods, rubbing his chin again. "I called her Janie. I always wondered what happened to her."

"What do you mean?"

He hands the photo back to me. "She disappeared on me. We were supposed to meet up one night, and she never showed. I was going to ask her to marry me."

"You were?" My voice cracks. I'm trying to remain composed, but my emotions are getting the best of me. "Then how come you didn't remember her when I showed you the picture?"

"I haven't seen her face in a long time. It just took a minute to jog my memory. How is Janie?"

I lean back in my chair and wipe away my tears. "Janice, or Janie, she's my mom."

"She is?"

I nod and continue. "And she died a couple of months ago, and that's why I'm here."

His face turns to stone; his charisma is now gone. "You came to Boston to tell me that some girl I was in love with twenty-some years ago is dead? Why would you do that?"

"Because you're my father."

I let those words sink in before I risk looking at him. His eyes are wide and his head tilts from side to side. He looks at the picture again, then back at me. I feel insecure and start to question whether or not he's truly my father. But deep down in my heart, I know he is because I can see him when I look in the mirror.

"Well, ain't that something," he says, leaning forward and taking my hand. "I have a daughter."

---

My meeting with Wes ended up going better than I had anticipated. He didn't question anything and didn't accuse me of having ulterior motives. We talked about life, what I was like growing up, and how his baseball career as a player never took off, but he's found his niche as a coach and manager. He apologized for not being there and added that I would've never been fatherless had he known.

I asked about his girlfriend, the one my mom spoke of, and he said he had fallen in love with my mom almost instantly and had broken things off with this girlfriend days after meeting my mom. He regrets not being able to say goodbye.

Deep down, I know my mother would've wanted this for me, and part of me is angry that she never tried to make it happen. If she had made the effort, her life could have been filled with happiness, and I would have had a dad. But there isn't anything that can be done to change the past. It is what it is, and now we can only move forward.

When Wes asked about my husband, I wanted to cry. I never thought I'd find myself in this position, yet here I am, in a similar situation to the one my mother went through. I'm not sure if I should call that irony or not, but it seems like the past is repeating itself. The one difference is that Cooper will know about the baby; what he does with that information will be up to him.

Wes stayed at the restaurant until I told him I had another meeting and prayed that he wouldn't run into Cooper. I have no doubt he'd ask Cooper what he's doing here. He'd be able to put two and two together easily, and I need to be able to tell Cooper without any outside interference.

Before Wes left, he told me that tickets will be available at the will call window if I want to catch a game while I am in town, and I was under strict orders, per my newly found father, not to leave without saying goodbye. That was something I could easily promise him.

My cheerful mood turned sour when I stood to meet Cooper as he came down the carpeted walkway toward my table. He was smiling until his eyes landed on my bulging stomach, and his steps faltered. Maybe I should've told him on the phone that I was pregnant, but the words weren't there.

"It's good to see you," I say as he comes forward to kiss me on the cheek, always a gentleman in my presence. I sit back down, thankful that the table can cover my belly, and he won't be inclined to stare at it.

"I only have an hour or so," he tells me. "It's game day, and I have to be on the field early." His words are matter-of-fact. Cooper doesn't want to be here. That much is evident by the way he looks at me.

I was a fool to think he'd be able to spare longer than an hour, leaving me no choice but to put us both out of our misery.

"As you can see, I'm pregnant."

"Yeah, that was pretty noticeable. I hope you're happy with him." He appears to seethe as he leans back in his chair. There's something different about him from the last time I saw him. He seems almost cocky, too self-assured. The man I knew questioned everything, and this one in front of me seems to have all the answers.

"The baby is yours," I blurt out, never taking my eyes off of his. For my own peace of mind, I need to see his reaction, even though I have no doubt that it'll break my heart. Of course I want the fairy tale. I want him to swoop me in his arms and profess his undying love, promising me a grand future, but that scenario is only a dream of mine. It's not my reality.

"Exactly how is that possible?" The tone in his voice scares me. The foolish girl in me thought this would be easy, and I'm unprepared for his anger.

"I'm sure you know how it happens, Cooper."

"I know how babies are made, Ainsley. I'm asking how exactly this is *my* baby, since the one time we had unprotected sex you assured me you were on the pill?"

I swallow the fear that's building in my chest and bite down on my quivering lip in hopes of warding off my impending tears. The last thing I want is for him to see me cry, especially over him.

"We had sex multiple times without a condom, and I *was* on the pill, but I was also under a lot of stress with my mother, and I don't know…accidents happen."

Cooper doesn't say anything; he just glares at me, so I continue. "Look, I'm not here asking for money or anything like that. I'm here to let you know that I'm pregnant and you're the father. I don't want my child growing up the way I did, not knowing who his or her father is, and I can at least say you knew."

He looks out the window at the passing cars. There are people on the sidewalks dressed in Renegades clothes and a few of them are wearing his number. He has a fan base now. It's easy to remember the day that I wore his shirt and the night that transpired after it, but that was another time in our lives.

"Please say something."

He shrugs. "I don't know what you want me to say, Ainsley. The last time I saw you, you were telling me to get the hell out of your life, so I did, and now you're telling me you're pregnant? It's a little hard to process right now."

"I understand."

"What do you want from me?"

I shake my head. "I just wanted you to know."

"Why now? Why today, and not months ago?"

Sighing heavily, I lean forward with my elbows on the table. "That last night we had sex, I was looking at myself in the mirror, questioning my actions. I had never had unprotected sex before, so I couldn't fathom why I would with you, especially after only knowing you for a week or two, and as I'm standing there running through my emotions, I heard a thud. My mom had fallen down the stairs, and I blamed myself because I was so preoccupied thinking about you, that I didn't know she was trying to get downstairs. We ended up in the emergency room. She had a broken ankle, but her CAT scan showed that the cancer was taking over. They gave her a month to live, and she lasted almost three. It took me a month to clean out her room, and by chance, Stella asked for a tampon because it was her time of the month, and that's how I found out I was pregnant," I ramble on.

"How could you not know you were pregnant? Aren't there signs women are supposed to know?"

"Yes, there are, but I was under a lot of stress. My mother, the only parent I've ever known, was dying, and I thought her being in the hospital was karma coming back to kick me in the ass because I started dating you against her wishes." I roughly wipe away my tears with the back of my hands.

Cooper runs his hands over his hat and face while groaning.

"I'm sorry."

"Sorry for what, exactly? Are you sorry that you ever agreed to go out with me, or the fact that you're pregnant?"

I don't like the way he phrases his questions because I'm not sorry for either situation. "I'm sorry that this is happening."

"Right," he says softly. "I gotta go. I'll call you later. When do you leave town?"

"Next week."

He nods and gets up without saying anything else. And for the second time in my life, I'm watching Cooper Bailey's backside as he leaves my life.

# TWENTY-NINE

## Cooper

I have been in some tough spots in my life, but none of them could ever compare to this. Give me an ace pitcher with my team down by three runs and the bases loaded with a full count, put the game on my shoulders, but don't make me face the stark reality that the woman I thought I could love is pregnant with my child, because I don't know how to handle it.

I guess the saying "it only takes once" is true. I was so stupid to trust the situation, but I wanted her, and when she offered herself to me like that I couldn't resist. And now I'm going to be a father. I don't even question that the child is mine. I know in my heart that this is one thing Ainsley wouldn't lie about.

"What has your schlong jockey in a bunch?" Kidd pushes my shoulder, and I fall into my locker. I shake my head, clearing away my thoughts. They should be focused on the game and not the news I was just given, but I can't get the image of Ainsley and her bulging belly out of my mind.

"Just thinking."

"Well, it better be thoughts of the White Sox."

"Yeah." I sigh. I'm not in the right frame of mind to play. I have no choice in the matter, either. I've started every game since Wilson took over, and I'm not about to take myself out of the lineup.

"Why are you so blue?" Davenport asks.

"I think someone kicked him in the trash hole," Kidd says, making me chuckle. I shake my head and start to get ready.

"You know, I'm going to start writing down all your one-liners and make a book out of them," I tell Kidd, who laughs.

"As long as I can be on the cover, I don't care what you do." He rubs his hands over his chest and winks at me. Davenport and Singleton start to laugh, which only pisses Kidd off, by the disgruntled look on his face.

I try to focus on getting ready, but it's hard. I want to call Ainsley, maybe go see her so we can talk, except I can't think of anything to say. The only question that comes to mind is, "Why?" and she doesn't even have an answer to that. Truth is, we fucked up, and now we have a child on the way.

"Fuck," I say, reaching for my phone. It dawns on me that I never told her how sorry I was that her mother passed away. I was too consumed with the fact that she told me I'm going to be a dad to consider her feelings.

I'm sorry about your mother. I meant to tell you earlier, but...well my mind is elsewhere.

I power it off and stash it in the corner of my locker. The last thing I want to do is reach for it continuously until I have to go out on the field.

I'm the last one out of the clubhouse, missing my ritual warm-up with Bainbridge. He gives me a funny look when I finally hit the field.

"Sorry, man," I say, offering him a weak excuse.

"You good?"

"Yep." I take off toward the field to start the stretches. Clearly I need to stop wearing my emotions on my sleeve and find a way to bottle them up. I know the guys know me better than anyone else, but this touchy-feely shit with them asking if I'm okay is really going to get on my nerves. I slip on my sunglasses in hopes that I can hide the agony I'm in. Maybe it'll be enough to ward off the questions so I can deal with the inner turmoil without an audience.

Everything is automatic for me, from warm-ups to taking the field and standing in the batter's box. My swing is slow and off the mark, and my throws to the infield are without precision. Each time I come in from the outfield, my father is yelling, telling me to pull my head out of my ass. I wish it were that easy.

No, what I wish is that she hadn't told me on a game day. Why couldn't she have waited one more week, or have told me two weeks ago when we had a day off? I get that maybe she doesn't know how our schedules work, but she could've asked.

But who am I kidding? It wouldn't have mattered. She called, and I went right to her because she still has a hold on my heart. We only dated for few weeks, and yet I let her in more than anyone else, and now I'm paying the price. It's showing in my game, and there isn't shit I can do to get out of the funk.

We end up losing, and that drops us to second place in the standings with back-to-back losses against the White Sox. And if that isn't bad enough, my father is waiting for me when I come out of the clubhouse. The look on his face is pure anger and completely unwarranted. I'm allowed to have a bad game. It's not a written rule but a known fact. Sometimes the other team gets the best of you. Or you get the best of yourself.

"Another performance like that and you're going to lose your starting spot."

I smirk and shake my head. "I won't. It was one bad night."

"You've had many," he says as he falls in step next to me.

"I'll be fine."

He grabs my arm and stops me from walking anywhere. He's lucky no one is around or people would start saying shit. Security doesn't take too kindly to the players being manhandled, even by their overbearing fathers.

"You need to be the best when you're out there every single time."

"I had a shitty night. It happens. I have a lot on my mind right now." As soon as the words are out of my mouth, I immediately regret them. I don't want him to know about Ainsley and the baby.

"Like what?"

"It's nothing."

Just then my phone rings and I make the mistake of looking at the screen to see who's calling. It's her, and unfortunately he sees it as well.

"Is that the woman from Florida?"

I nod, unwilling to give him a verbal answer.

"Why's she calling?"

I should tell him, right? He should know he's going to be a grandfather, even though I can guarantee I'll never let him be alone with my kid if he can't change his tune about Ainsley.

"She's in town."

"You need to stay away from her."

I shake my head adamantly. "Not gonna happen, Dad. She's pregnant and—"

"It's not yours," he interrupts.

"Excuse me?" I clench my teeth and grind out the words.

"Are you stupid? You're a rising star, with Rookie of the Year mentions and a multimillion-dollar contract. She's pregnant and in Boston? Even I can see the trap coming a mile away, Cooper."

Before I can say anything, he's on the phone and barking out orders to someone. I hear paternity suit, and that's when I walk away. I don't need to hear anymore.

I don't want to think my dad is right, but now that he's mentioned it, what if the baby isn't mine and she's playing me for a fool? What if I fall in love with the baby, raise him or her as my own, only to find out that I'm not the father? What happens then? Where does that leave me? What will that do to the baby?

———————◆———————

I contemplate calling Ainsley all night but don't have the guts to actually do it. Instead, I pace the floor thinking the same thought over and over again: Ainsley's pregnant. That thought turns into others; some are of us raising this baby while others have us fighting constantly and never getting along. Each one has the same outcome, though—the baby is mine.

But what if she's pinning this on me because I was there around the time she got pregnant? How do I know she wasn't with someone else? I can ask that, right?

Yesterday when I was talking to Ainsley, I knew the baby was mine. Standing here now, looking out through my window, I'm not so sure. We haven't seen each other in months, and I have no way of knowing if she didn't hook up with someone else. There are too many unknowns right now and I don't know what to do.

There's a nagging voice in the back of my head telling me that she wouldn't lie about this—not after everything she's been through. But I can't help but feel like she would do the same thing her mother did and just raise the child on her own, without any fatherly help, and I don't know if I want that, if I could be that type of man.

Late in the morning, I'm summoned to Wilson's office, no doubt to explain my fucked-up performance last night. With my tail between my legs and my pride on the line, I knock on his door before entering.

He's glaring; his face morphed into something I've only seen when he doesn't agree with a call, and now it's directed toward me. He stands and slams the door behind me. "Sit down," he barks as he sits back down behind his desk. "I've known you a long time, and I never expected you to lack character, but this is over the top. It's unacceptable behavior, and I won't stand for it."

I'm confused by his tone and the aggression behind his words. I had one bad game, which can easily be rectified.

I swallow hard and lift my chin so he can see that I'm serious. "It won't happen again," I tell him, even though it's not like I can prevent a loss; I can control only my performance.

"You're damn straight this won't happen again, especially on my watch. If you think I'm going to let you go around sticking your dick in whatever walks while you have a baby on the way, you've got another thing coming."

My mouth drops open, and he stands with his finger pointed at me. "You need to man up, Bailey."

"Um…"

"Don't act like you don't know what I'm talking about," he says, slamming his hand down on the table. "Ainsley's pregnant, and you need to take responsibly for your actions."

"Did my father call you?"

"No," he scoffs.

I put my hands up in the air, calling a truce. "With all due respect, Skipper, how do you know about Ainsley and the baby? I just found out myself yesterday before the game, which is why I thought you called me in here, to talk about my game performance, not some chick I banged in Florida."

My poor choice of words does not sit well with Wilson as his face turns red and his fingers clutch the ends of his desk. I'm starting to get pissed off wondering how he knows. If Aisnley somehow contacted my manager, she and I are going to have an exchange of words that isn't going to end up in her favor.

"Ainsley is my daughter," he says, sitting back down in his chair. I let his words sink in as my mouth opens to say something, but nothing comes out. "You have nothing to say?"

I shake my head. "She never told me that you're her father. In fact, she told me she didn't have one."

"Well, she does, and it seems my starting center fielder has gotten himself into a pickle."

I feel the walls start to close in around me. When I thought things were going well, namely my career, shit starts to crumble around me. I feel as desperate as when there's two outs in the bottom of the ninth and we're down by one run. I can swing for the fence and hope that I get enough velocity on the ball that it sails over the wall, or I can try for a double and pray that my teammate behind me can do the same.

Either way I'm in a hopeless situation.

# THIRTY

## Ainsley

We need to meet. Where are you staying?

Months ago a text like this from Cooper would've made my heart jump and my palms sweat, but now I feel nothing but dread. I know he met with Wes this morning. Wes made it very clear that he was going to talk with him, and it's not like Cooper can ignore a meeting with his manager. I asked Wes not to, to let Cooper and me figure it out, but he pulled the father card and I gave in.

After one day and over breakfast, Wes has made it clear that he'll be in my life, if I'll have him. Thing is, I want him to be. I want to have a father who I send a birthday card to or have stay at my house for Christmas. To have a father who will be a good grandfather to my baby. I've longed for a connection like this. I asked him if he wanted to take a paternity test to verify that he's in fact my dad and he said no, one wasn't needed, and that he felt it in his heart and could see it in my eyes when he looked at me.

When he asked about my husband again, I thought I could fake it and tell him that we're happy, but the sadness in my eyes must have been a dead giveaway. I caved, under his gaze, when he asked about the father of my baby, and I told him the story about how Cooper and I met. I had no idea Wes would summon Cooper to his office.

And now that meeting is over and Cooper wants to talk. Honestly, I don't know what to expect. I know what I want, but that may not be what's best for Cooper. I've seen the gossip columns and the pictures with other women. He's moved on, like he should have.

I type out my response, telling him where I'm staying and what room. He replies immediately, telling me that he's on his way, giving me very little time to prepare. In hindsight, I should've chosen a hotel farther from the stadium, but I was trying to make things convenient for myself when I met Wes and Cooper the other day.

The knock on the door startles me, even though it shouldn't. I hesitate briefly before opening the door. If I expected Cooper to be excited to see me, I'd been a fool. The man staring back at me with his arms resting on the doorjamb is not the man I remember. This one is hard with almost soulless eyes, while the one I was falling for months ago could make my knees weak with just one look.

I step aside and let him in, and mentally prepare myself for what's surely going to be a fight. The only other time I've fought with someone was my ex back in college. The day I found him cheating was enough to rip me to shreds and make me pound my fist into his chest. The combination of hurt and anger was too much to keep bottled in, and something in my gut tells me that Cooper is feeling that way now.

"Guess where I was this morning?" he says as he enters. I'm not sure if this is a rhetorical question or not, and I'm not sure how to answer.

"No? No guess?" he states when I don't answer him. "Help me out here, Ainsley, because I'm really getting confused. You tell me yesterday that we're having a child after months of not even seeing or speaking to each other, and then you go and tell my boss, who just happens to be your fucking father that you conveniently forgot to tell me about?" His hands flail, and his face is red. My heart beats rapidly, afraid of the words that are coming out of his mouth.

"It's not like that," I retort.

"What's it like, then? Because I'm having a hard time comprehending all of this. Wes Wilson is your father, and he just reamed my ass for getting you pregnant! I don't give a shit if he's on me about my performance on the field, but when he's fucking telling me to man up not even twenty-four hours after I find out about you and the baby, it's a bit damn, well, disconcerting."

My room is small and cheap and doesn't give us much space to move. I stand by the door while he paces back and forth. "I don't know." My words are weak, and my lip trembles. The last thing I wanted to do is upset him. "I found out that Wes was my father after my mother died. It was just dumb luck that he happened to be your manager."

"Dumb luck." He sighs. "How long have you known him?"

I take a deep breath. "I met him a couple of hours or so before you came to the restaurant. Once I found out who my father was, I knew I needed my baby to know its father, too." As soon as the words leave my mouth, I know they're taken wrong by the look on his face. I close my eyes, wishing I could take it all back.

"*Now* was the time to tell me? Yesterday you said you didn't fucking know!"

"I didn't mean it like that, Cooper." I plead with him to understand.

"How exactly did you mean it? You found your father and suddenly it dawns on you that I may want to know that you're pregnant? Were you even planning on telling me at all?"

"Yes."

"When, Ainsley? You're showing! Call me fucking stupid, but to me that means you're pretty far along. Is the baby even mine?" he asks as he sits down. He doesn't look at me, keeping his eyes focused on the ground.

"Yes, it's yours."

"How can I trust you?"

"I guess you can't," I say, defeated. "I understand if you want a paternity test. We can do one once the baby is born."

If that is what Cooper wants, I have no reason not to give it to him. I had hoped things would work out differently between us, something amicable, but I can see that isn't going to happen. If he doesn't trust me now, will he ever? I don't want to live my life with someone always second-guessing my actions.

I stand and go to the closet, pulling out my suitcase. Cooper is the only reason I'd stayed in Boston longer than I need to be here. Wes and I can build a relationship through e-mail and phone calls. I hope he'll understand why I had to leave Boston so suddenly.

"What are you doing?"

"I'm going home," I tell him as I take my clothes out of the drawers.

"So you're just going to leave? You come here to fuck everything up, and now that you've done that, you're going to bail?"

"What else was I supposed to do, call you?"

"You're not supposed to leave because I'm questioning whether or not the baby is mine. Jesus, Ainsley, we haven't spoken in months nor have we seen each other. Give me a break and let me process all of this. Fuck!" he yells, running his hands through his hair. "And the fact that you went to Wes...Do you even have any idea what that is going to do to me?"

"I don't understand what the hangup about Wes is," I tell him honestly. Shouldn't he be happy that I found my dad? That I have someone I can count on when I need a parent? When his baby needs a grandparent?

Cooper shakes his head and groans. "If I don't marry you, I'm on his shit list. Right now I can't even ask for a trade because I only have a few months of stats accumulated and they don't match my salary. If I marry you, I become his fucking pet, and the team hates me. Everything I earn won't be because of my hard work but because I married the skipper's daughter. You have no idea how completely fucked I am right now."

"It's not like you knew when we were together. Surely the team can't blame you?"

"It doesn't matter, Ainsley. They're not going to see it like that. My name is forever going to be linked to Wes and this baby."

"Then just bail, Cooper. I don't need you. This baby and I can cope fine on our own." I throw my hands up and start taking my clothes out of the dresser.

"You think that's the answer? To just fucking bail because that's what *your* father did?"

"He didn't bail. He didn't know about me, so he can't really be blamed for being an absent father, but if you..." I take a deep breath. "If you don't want this, fine. I can do it by myself. My mother did."

"Is that what you want?"

"Is it what *you* want?" I throw his question back at him. Even if Cooper doesn't want this baby, I do.

"I don't know."

"Well, that's just fucking great, now isn't it?" I scoop up my pile of clothes and toss them into my suitcase. I don't care about folding them. I just want to get the hell out of Boston and forget everything that has to do with Cooper Bailey.

"Stop," he says, grabbing a hold of my arm. When he touches me, it feels as if the chaos and anger around us calms down and everything feels right in my world, even though it isn't. I can't hold back the tears and find myself covering my face with my free hand to hide from him.

"Come here." He pulls me toward him, enveloping me in his arms as he sits on the edge of the bed.

He feels warm, safe, and like I'm meant to be here. I want to be closer, but my growing belly keeps us apart.

"I'm sorry," he says.

"For what?"

He laughs, but I'm not sure why. "For that night you came over and saw me talking to that woman, and for questioning whether this is my baby or not."

"I should've never said the things I did."

"Yeah? Then why did you?" he asks.

"Because I felt like my mom falling and dying was karma. She told me not to date you and I did anyway."

He holds me to his chest, rocking us back and forth. I try not to, but I can't refrain from nuzzling his neck. The way he smells draws in me and brings back the memories we shared, even though they were brief.

"I don't want you to leave," he whispers against my skin, igniting my desire for him.

"I don't want to leave, either." My fingers play with the ends of his hair as he sighs against me. "I've missed you." I know I'm opening myself up to more hurt when I say this, but I need him to know.

"I've missed you, too." That is when I feel his lips press against my collarbone. I bask in his feather-light kisses, needing more. "I have a road trip starting tonight, lasting six days, but then I have a day off. Stay, if you can?"

I pull away from him and sit on the opposite bed. "You want me to stay?"

"I do. I have a place not far from here. It has two bedrooms, is fully furnished, and in a safer neighborhood. You can stay there as long as you want, and when I get back, we can talk more, figure shit out. Unless..."

"Unless what?" I ask.

"Unless you need to go back. We're going to Texas and then on to Tampa Bay. I can stay in Tampa for a day longer."

My heart swells knowing that he wants to see me when he's off. "I can stay."

"Okay, good." He stands and moves over to the dresser and starts pulling out the rest of my clothes. "Go pack your bathroom. You're coming home with me."

I try not to act like a giddy schoolgirl but I can't help it. Once inside the bathroom, I fist-pump and shimmy my hips until I come face-to-face with myself in the mirror. My eyes are bloodshot and dark lines coat my skin under my lower lids. My image reminds me not to look into anything too deeply with Cooper. He could be doing this because I'm carrying his child and it's the responsible thing to do, not because he wants to be with me.

# THIRTY-ONE

## Cooper

I don't know what possessed me to bring Ainsley to my apartment, but I couldn't let her stay in that shithole. Maybe I could turn that around on Wes and ask him what kind of father lets his pregnant daughter stay in a roach motel. That would only bait him into calling me out on more bullshit, though.

Ainsley is currently looking around my apartment, like she did in Florida, although this place is much nicer. I'm happy she's here, in my place again. I just don't like the circumstances. I hadn't thought much about a reunion with her. I imagine, if I did, it wouldn't have been like this, with her pregnant.

I let her explore everywhere, even my bedroom, which honestly is where I'd like her to stay. I'm sure being with me is the last thing she wants. I know she said she missed me, but that can be simply because she's been going through a tough time or the fact that we ended on a bad note.

"Your bathroom is huge."

Her fingers run along the soaking tub. I thought I'd use it to quiet the ache in my overworked muscles after games, but I never have.

"Feel free to use the tub if you want. You can sleep in here too while I'm gone. I think this bed is a little more comfortable than the one in the other room."

"Thank you," she says as she continues her exploration. Ainsley moves into the kitchen and opens the refrigerator. "Okay, I expected nothing but cheese and beer."

"I'm not much of a drinker, plus I have a housekeeper who comes in every other day. She does my grocery shopping, laundry, and cleaning. Her name is Elaine."

"Does she cook for you?" Ainsley asks as she leans on the counter.

"No," I say, shaking my head. "I honestly don't cook a whole lot. Breakfast is usually the only meal I eat here. The rest are at the stadium."

"What about when you're off?"

I start to laugh. I wish we had days off. "Those are rare, except this month we have four. Usually we're lucky to get one."

Ainsley doesn't say anything else and continues to wander through my place. I could stand here and watch her or be useful. And as much as I'd love to just gaze at her all day, I decide to carry her luggage into the guest room.

When I step in, it feels wrong. I can't picture her sleeping here. I quickly turn around and take her stuff into my room, placing her suitcase on my bed.

"What are you doing?"

Turning at the sound of her voice, I feel a magnetic pull toward her. With three steps, I'm standing in front of her with her eyes searching my face for some sort of clue as to what's going on in my head. I take her in, trying to memorize what she looks like with her strawberry blond hair longer than it was when I last saw her. Her stomach is plump and carrying a child that I helped create.

Every time my gaze meets hers, my heart turns over in response. Urging me to kiss her, hold her, to do anything except stand there. It took me months to get over her, to not hear her laughter, feel her presence, and dream that she was next to me in bed. My game suffered because of her, and I'm not sure I can afford another relapse. I step away, guarding my heart instead of following it. It'll be safer that way.

"Don't." She reaches for me, taking hold of my shirt as it rests near the waistband of my shorts.

Ainsley watches me intently with longing in her eyes. Her cautious step forward is not lost on me. And neither is the sensation I feel as her fingers from her free hand play with the scruff on my cheeks.

"I won't be able to stop," I warn her. She's the last person I had sex with, even though I've been dating. None of the women I've met have done anything for me. None of them really compared to Ainsley or made me feel like she did by simply being in the room with me.

"I don't want you to stop."

My lips crash down on hers with savage intensity. My tongue plunges into her mouth, desperate to taste her, to reconnect with her. Fingers are in my hair, grabbing and pulling, while my hands cup her ass, bringing her as close as possible.

Her hand travels under my shirt, sending a jolt of electricity through my system. I jump, causing her to pull away from me and laugh. And that's when I see it—the lust in her eyes—and feel the uncertainty building within me. I cup her face and kiss her lightly on her forehead, nose, and finally her full lips, letting them linger there.

"I have to get to the stadium." The lie falls easily when it shouldn't. I still have hours, but I need to take a break. I need to process everything that is going on.

"Okay," she says softly. Her voice is laced with disappointment. "What time will you be back?"

Shaking my head, I sigh and step away from her. I need to have some space because if I don't, I'm liable to take her now. "I won't. Not until after the road trip is done. We leave right after the game."

"Oh..." Her voice trails off. "So I won't see you for six days?"

"I think it works out to be about seven...technically."

"Right." She sits down on my bed, only a few inches from me. The night we first shared comes rushing back to me. Her, in my shirt with my number pressed against her back, her milky white skin coming to life with my touch, and the way she held onto me with her fingers digging into my skin when we connected for the first time.

"Baseball season is tough, especially on families." I don't know if my words are meant to warn her off or what, but she needs to realize that I'm not going to be around a whole lot from March until October. I take a chance and look at her. Her eyes are downcast, and I can see the wheels spinning in her head. Maybe this is a good thing, me leaving for a few days so she'll know what it's like when I'm gone all the time.

"I'll call you," I tell her, kissing her quickly on the cheek and making a hasty exit. I need to get out of here before I do anything stupid.

---

I'm antsy as shit as I drive to the stadium. I hit every single light and car trying to make a left-hand turn against the afternoon traffic. Aside from the obvious reason for having my windows tinted, today was especially helpful because I was flipping people off right and left.

After I left my apartment I went over to Davenport's, only to find that he wasn't home. He's by far my closest friend on the team, and I need to talk to someone. As soon as I get my car parked, I'm hauling ass to the clubhouse, praying that he's there. I find him in the gym, working out with Kidd.

"Hey," they both say when I walk in.

"Can I talk to you for a second?" I try to act nonchalant about it, but Kidd eyes me warily. Ethan follows me out of the gym and back to my car. It's the only safe place to talk without someone eavesdropping. The last thing I want right now is for what I'm about to say to get out and rumors spread. Ainsley and I don't need that.

"You quitting or something?" he asks, once inside the confines of my SUV.

"Nah, man, but I need some advice, and I didn't want to talk inside the clubhouse."

"Okay, what's up?"

"Remember that chick I was digging in Florida at the beginning of the season? The one from the zoo?"

He nods. "Yeah, she was hot."

"Right, well we hooked up a few times, and now she's here… pregnant."

His mouth drops open before letting out a long, exasperated sigh. "Is it yours?"

"Yeah, it is, but that's not the worst part… she's Wilson's daughter."

"Are you fucking kidding me?"

I shake my head and keep my eyes focused on the outside world. I can't look at Davenport right now because I don't want to see judgment.

"Dude, does he know you knocked his daughter up?"

I nod.

"Wait, did we know he had a daughter?"

"No, man, and that's the fucked-up thing. Ainsley didn't even know he was her father until after her mom died."

"And now she's here? She just showed up on your doorstep?"

"Nah. She called me the other night. We were at the bar, she tells me she's in town, so I go meet her for lunch. And she stands up and the first thing I see is this chick that I really liked, pregnant. And I start to think about how I fucked up with her and now she's with some other dude and how I've lost my chance."

"Except it's yours?"

"Yeah, it's mine. I don't think she'd lie about it, especially after the shit her mother put her through with her own dad."

Ethan sighs, and we both stop talking. Telling him the story now makes it all more real, but still incredibly fucked up. If I marry her, play out the season and ask for a trade, I'm the bastard who took Wilson's grandchild away. If I marry her and stay, I'm the manager's favorite, essentially making me the most hated guy on the team. If I don't marry her, I can kiss my career with the Renegades goodbye.

"You're fucked."

"I know." I agree with him. "To make matters worse, I moved her out of her hotel and into my apartment, and then I almost slept with her."

"That will only complicate things," he says, shaking his head. "Fuck, I sound like a chick."

I can't help but laugh because right now we both do.

"Does your dad know?"

"Oh, yeah, my big-ass mouth blurted it right out to him. He doesn't know that Wilson is her father, though. Not sure how he'll take that."

"I suppose I'm out here because you want some advice?"

"Pretty much. I don't know what to do. My career means every-thing to me, but it's not going to matter what I do; any decision is going to be the wrong one. If I marry her, I'm Wilson's pet. If I don't, he fucks my career."

"What'd Wilson say?"

"Shit, he pulled me into his office this morning and ripped me a new asshole. Told me to man up."

"Fuck. I wish Daisy was here. She'd know what to do."

"I went to your place first. She wasn't home."

"Let me call her." Davenport pulls out his phone and calls his wife, putting it on speaker. He gives her the story, complete with the epic fuckery that is going on. Her audible gasps make me cringe.

"Cooper?"

"I'm here, Daisy."

"Marry the girl."

"Excuse me?"

"Listen to me," she says. "Marry her, but tell her and Wilson to keep their mouths shut about their connection. If he doesn't go around tell-ing everyone that he has a long-lost daughter and she doesn't tell every-one he's her father, no one, aside from Ethan and I, will know. Wilson's a good guy, and I honestly think he'll treat you fairly. You've earned your time on the team. Don't shortchange yourself or your talent."

"So you think I should marry her?"

"You're having a baby!" she yells into the phone, making Davenport and me laugh.

"Yeah, I guess I am. Well, she is. I did the fun part and she's doing the rest. Hey, can you do me a favor?"

"Anything. What's up?"

"Ainsley is at my place. Can you show her around the next few days, get her to fall in love with Boston?"

"You bet. I'll look after her. Don't worry about it, but I gotta run now."

"Bye, babe," Ethan says before hanging up.

A smile spreads across my face when I think about Ainsley and Daisy hanging out. "Your wife is something else."

"Tell me about it. You know she was a fan of mine. This woman would eyeball me something fierce during each game, sitting behind the visitor dugout. One game, I had finally had enough and had one of the ushers tell her I wanted to talk to her. We had a rocky start, but damn if I don't love her. She's amazing, and I thank my lucky stars for her every day."

"You guys gonna have kids?"

He shrugs. "When she's ready. She worked her ass off to get a degree, and even though she doesn't need to, she works. Daisy is independent as fuck, and I love her for it. Right now she's having a ball with my niece, Shea."

As soon as we see Wilson pull in, we get out of my SUV. Davenport heads back to the stadium while I linger in the parking lot for Wilson.

"Hey, Skipper," I say, as I meet him at his car. "Ainsley and I need some time to figure out the right course for us, but I need a favor from you."

"What's that, Bailey?"

"Can you keep Ainsley on the down-low? Not tell anyone that she's your daughter? I've got a good thing with this team and don't want to fuck it up."

"And you feel that her being my daughter will hurt your career here?"

He's a smart man and knows exactly how I'm feeling. I nod and kick a pebble away from me. "People already know we dated back in Florida, and I don't want shit fucked up."

He eyes me warily before agreeing. "Don't hurt her."

I shake my head. "I won't." I leave him at his car and hustle back to the clubhouse. It's not going to matter what I do, as long as I do the right thing for Ainsley and me.

# THIRTY-TWO

## Ainsley

I don't know how baseball players remain married. Cooper and I aren't even together, and I feel like a widow. True to his word, he calls every day, but it's more of a friendly call, and even though I've tried to get more out of him, he's very matter of fact about why's he calling—to make sure the baby and I are okay.

Today, I'm hanging with Daisy Davenport. After I was cooped up in this apartment for three days, she's taking me sightseeing and out to lunch with a little retail therapy added in for good measure.

Daisy is a cute little thing, a few inches shorter that me, but full of life and deeply in love with her husband.

"We're going to check out some sites before it gets too warm," Daisy tells me as she maneuvers the streets of downtown Boston. There's a crowd of people everywhere, and most of them are wearing some type of sports clothing. About a third of them are in Renegades gear, a few with Cooper's name on them.

"Bostonians love their sports teams, huh?"

"You have no idea," she tells me as she masterfully parallel parks her car. "After the marathon bombing, the community really came together. We were strong before, but now it's stronger. And the teams give back all the time. The guys are always down here, just hanging out. A couple of weeks ago, Travis Kidd had a kissing booth set up. Women lined up for miles to give him five dollars for a kiss on the cheek and a photo op."

"What'd he do with all the money?"

"It was a fund-raiser for the children's hospital."

My heart warms, thinking that Cooper could do something like that someday.

"Ryan Stone, he's the general manager, well, he's married to Hadley Carter, and she's down here a lot playing for the crowd."

"Oh, I like her music. Don't people bother her?"

Daisy shakes her head and points to where we're heading. "No, it's like we don't care that they're famous."

"Oh, God, I smell cookies." I rub my tummy, feeling as the baby flutters inside.

"Come on, they're delicious."

Daisy takes me into Quincy Market and has me weaving in and out of human traffic. The place is packed, and the smell of food has my stomach growling and my mouth watering.

"This place is like heaven."

She laughs and heads down a ramp and into another crowd. "It is, but Ethan and I don't come here a lot, at least not together." Daisy stops at the cookie stand and orders a dozen cookies. I want to ask her if those are just for her because, right now, I could get my own dozen and roll in another.

Daisy hands me a fresh cookie from the bag, and I swear I'm having an out-of-body experience when I taste the warm chocolate as it touches my tongue. "I've died."

"We'll come back through before we leave and get you another bag. They're amazing when you add vanilla ice cream."

I've never been much of a sweets eater until I discovered I was pregnant. I know it's all mind over matter and I figure, if I'd never have any cravings, I never accepted that I was pregnant. But I did, and now everything with sugar is my best friend, and chocolate, lots and lots of chocolate.

We continue to walk and munch on cookies, stopping at a few stores just outside the market. The cobblestone street isn't helping my back pain, though, and as soon as we find smooth pavement, I'm rejoicing.

"Are you feeling okay?"

"Yeah, I'm fine. I think it was just the road and walking unevenly." I stretch and rub the sore spot in my back to try to get rid of some of the pressure.

Daisy gets us two passes for the Boston tour, making me happy that we'll be seated for a bit on the trolley. As the tour starts, she points out different things that she finds interesting in addition to what the guide says. At various stops, we get off and walk through an old cemetery where revolutionaries are buried, buy nuts from the street vendor, and then tour the Old State House and the site of the Boston Massacre. By the time we're done, I'm exhausted and ready for a nap.

"Are you ready for lunch?"

"Yes," I all but beg. I want to sit longer than a few minutes and rest.

"I'm sorry. You're probably tired. Pregnant women get tired easily, right?"

"I don't know," I tell her truthfully. "Honestly, this is all new to me. I feel like I'm *just* now pregnant even though I'm showing. I didn't know until about a month ago, so I missed the first trimester because my mom was in the hospital and I was stressed out, but I'm sure you already know this." I know Cooper had to tell his friends something; otherwise Daisy wouldn't be here.

"Actually, I don't. Cooper only told me that you're pregnant, but I knew who you were already."

Daisy tells the hostess that we have two, and we follow her to our seats.

"What do you mean?"

"Well, I've known Cooper since April, when the guys came home. He stayed with us for a few days until he could get his apartment. He talked about you a lot."

"Was he drunk?"

Daisy looks at me oddly, and I shrug. Most guys don't open up about their feelings unless they've been drinking.

"No, he was just telling us how much he liked you and hated that you guys weren't talking."

"Oh..." I trail off, not knowing what to say. It was my fault we stopped talking. If I hadn't pushed him away, I'd probably feel like my life made sense right now.

The waitress brings our drinks, water for me, and iced tea for Daisy, and we place our orders. I choose a salad with a half sandwich while Daisy opts for the full salad.

"Can I ask you some questions about life as it pertains to baseball?"

"Sure, what's up?" she says.

"How do you do it? Cooper and I aren't even together, but I can't help but feel like I'm sort of lingering. I'm not saying we'll be together, but I'm concerned about what kind of life the baby is going to have."

"I stay busy by working, which takes up any of my free time, but I'm also a fan of the game and have season tickets that belonged to my grandfather, so I sit behind the visitor dugout. I don't miss any home games, rain or shine. And when Ethan's away, it's my chance to spend time with friends, go to the spa, and go shopping. On his days off, we're together. It works for us, but I knew what to expect going in."

"How long have you been married?"

"Oh, not long. We got married this past off-season."

"And you don't miss him?"

"I didn't say that. I miss him all the time, but we talk every day when he's gone and video chat at night. I'll watch the game on TV too so I can see him. This is his career, and he had it long before I came along, so I'm not going to tell him he needs to make a change. Besides, seeing him in his uniform, it does things to me." She winks, and I happen to agree with her. I remember seeing Cooper in the first game I went to and determined that baseball players are the hottest athletes in and out of their uniforms.

"What about the other women? The ones who constantly throw themselves at the guys?"

"I trust Ethan. If I didn't, I wouldn't be with him."

Do I trust Cooper? I don't know if I do. I can't let what happened between us in Florida sway my mind on whether or not Cooper is going to be a good father. Right now I have no reason to believe he won't be a good dad, even if he's absent for some of the baby's life.

But what kind of life is that for the baby? He or she will be able to watch their father on television while he entertains other kids but will only see him for three, maybe four months out of the year before he disappears again. I'm not sure I want that kind of life for my child. On the other hand, I want my child to have both its parents, which is something neither of us had growing up.

"When will you make the move to Boston?"

"I'm sorry, what?" Daisy's question breaks me out of my reverie.

"Your move to Boston? When will you be doing that?"

"Oh, I'm not moving. My home is in Fort Myers."

"Oh," she says, looking down at the table. The waitress appears at the right moment, bringing our food so we can occupy our time with eating and not the giant elephant in the room. I guess that's what's expected of me, that I should move here and be at Cooper's beck and call, but what kind of life does that leave me? I don't want to be his glorified babysitter so he can have a relationship with his child. I want a life, too. Call me selfish, but it's the truth. I know Daisy has a life, and it sounds glamorous, but she has Ethan. I don't have Cooper, yet. Maybe if I did, I'd feel differently.

We finish lunch with idle chitchat, making it hard for me to get a read on Daisy. I have no doubt she'll tell Cooper what I said, which will spur another heated debate between us. He has to know that I have no intention of staying here, even with my dad living here.

"Are you ready for some shopping?" Daisy asks once she pays the bill.

"Actually, I'm not feeling all that well. Can I have a rain check?"

"Yeah, definitely. My hours are flexible so anytime you want to get together, just let me know. We'll shop in New Hampshire, though, because it's cheaper."

I barely make it to her car before I start sweating. By the time I'm sitting down, I feel dizzy and nauseated.

"I don't think today's heat agrees with you," Daisy says as she pulls out into traffic.

"I think you're right." I keep my eyes closed as she navigates through the streets. "You'd think I'd be accustomed since I live in Florida."

"You're pregnant, Ainsley. Anything you're accustomed to is going to change because your body is changing daily. Foods you love may end up being foods you despise."

She's right, except I plan never to lose my love for cookies. I'm not sure how I'll cope if that happens. Stella called me lucky, bypassing the morning sickness stage, but I'm not so sure she's right. While my mom was in the hospital, I didn't eat a lot and felt sick often. I figured it was because my mom was dying and emotionally I couldn't cope with it.

Daisy parks along the street and walks me to Cooper's apartment. I invite her in because it seems like the right thing to do, but she declines, telling me she's going to head home and do some work, but if I need her to give her a call. I promise her that I will and thank her for a great morning as I close the door.

As soon as I crawl into bed, Cooper calls, just as he said he would.

"Are you having fun?"

"No," I tell him as I moan. "I'm not feeling well. Daisy just dropped me off."

"What's wrong?" He sounds worried, and I want to believe it's because of me, but I'm second-guessing myself on everything now.

"I don't know. I feel funny. I'm dizzy, and my stomach is nauseated."

"Is this morning sickness?"

"How do you even know what that is?" I ask.

"I've been doing some reading."

"Oh." My heart swells, and tears form in my eyes. I wish he were here right now.

"I miss you, Ainsley."

"Please don't say things like that if you don't mean them, Cooper. I may take your words the wrong way."

He sighs, and I can hear him adjusting the phone. "I've never said anything to you that I didn't mean. I do miss you. I've missed you for months when I tried to trick myself into dating other people. I've lied for months, telling myself I was over you when I wasn't. And even though you're in my bed, it's not the same and doesn't feel real."

I know what he means. Each night when I crawl into bed, I'm surrounded by everything that is Cooper, and I find that it's not enough.

"I miss you, too," I tell him, hoping he knows I'm telling the truth.

"I'll be home in a few days. Make sure you call Daisy if you need anything."

"I will, bye Cooper."

He pauses briefly before saying, "Bye."

He hangs up, ending our connection. I hold the phone to my ear longer than necessary before finally tossing it on the bed. I roll over and cradle my stomach, praying that Cooper wants to be in our lives, because I don't want to do this alone.

# THIRTY-THREE

## Cooper

The afternoon sun is blazing, and for the life of me, I can't understand why we had a noon start today. It's the bottom of the seventh, and we're down by two runs. For each run we bat in, they bat in two. It's a topsy-turvy type of game and exciting for the fans, if not so much for the players. We like a lead. We like things to be comfortable and not stress us out, unless of course you're the closing pitcher. They seem to like having the game on the line and will even lose the lead we've gained so they feel more like they are in control. If you ask me, that is just plain fucked up, and I sometimes want to wring the closer's neck. We work hard to give them that cushion; they just need to finish the game already.

I thought, with Ainsley being back in my life, my game would tank. However, that doesn't seem to be the case. This week on the road, I've racked up at least two RBIs per game and stolen three bases. I'm faring a lot better than I was during spring training when my father convinced me that she was too much of a distraction. Truth is, I probably wasn't ready for the bigs yet, but with the help of Bainbridge and the determination of Cal Diamond, I persevered and started performing the way I should be.

Singleton just singled to right, giving me a man on base to bring home. I look to our third base coach, for the sign, wondering if I'm hitting away or bunting. The infield shifts, expecting the bunt, but I'm supposed to stand in and take the pitch so Branch can steal, easy enough. I cringe when I see the meatball heading my way. I want to swing, but doing so could hit Branch right into a double play, or I could pop up and he'd have to go back to first. So I take it. My eyes close when the ump calls out "Strike," and I feel the ball whizzing by my face as the catcher for Tampa Bay throws down to second in hope of getting Singleton on the steal.

The base ump calls him safe, and our dugout cheers. We have a few fans in the stands as well who yell out their appreciation of Singleton. My eyes are on our third base coach again for the sign. It's a bunt. He wants to advance Branch to third. I get it. There are no outs, and we're down by two runs at the moment. The coaches will do anything to cut the Tampa lead in half.

I step in and show my bat. The infield adjusts slightly, but not too much, because they're smart enough to honor Singleton and his speed. As the pitcher warms up, I show my bat again, and everyone yells bunt. The pitch is high and outside so I pull back. The sign I get this time is the same, and I repeat my process of grinding my foot in and making sure I'm square to the plate. I take a deep breath, letting the bat rest on my shoulder until the pitcher shows that he's ready.

He starts his wind up. At the last minute I show I'm going to bunt. The ball hits the bat and I push it gently, absorbing most of the force in hope that the ball barely has any velocity to go anywhere. It stalls so much that I'm called safe at first. I watch the instant replay, showing the pitcher and catcher both going for the ball, with no play being made when the catcher finally comes up with it.

We are in perfect scoring position with a runner on third and now first. There's an air of cockiness when Kidd walks up to the plate. Once again signs are given from across the field. I'm stealing on the first pitch. Kidd pauses, adjusts his batting gloves, and steps into the box. He has a routine; it's ridiculous, but works for him.

I have a big lead. It's dangerous, but with Singleton on third, they don't want to get me in a rundown. They wouldn't be able to get us both out, and I know that is what the coaches want—they want Tampa to make a mistake and try to pick both of us off.

The second the ball is released, I'm hauling ass toward second. I slide, even though I have no idea where the ball is, and hear the ump call me safe. Asking for time, I stand and shake the dirt off my pants and readjust my cup. Aside from the jockstrap, the cup is the most uncomfortable thing I've ever had to wear. Kidd said he had a girl-friend complain to him once that a bra was more uncomfortable, so he tested it out and said he'd rather wear a bra than a cup any day.

Once the ball is back in to play, I'm clapping for Kidd. I take a few steps off second, getting comfortable in my lead. Kidd swings and misses, sending Singleton and me back to our bases for a moment. We step off and wait for the next pitch, and Kidd swings and drives the ball down the right field line. I'm in a dead sprint toward third with my eyes on our third base coach the entire time. His arm waves around and as I round third, my focus is on Singleton. He's going to guide me.

Tampa Bay's catcher crouches, and Singleton's arms lower, telling me to get down. I slide head-first around the catcher's leg and touch the corner of home plate with my fingertips. The ump yells "out," and I stand, about ready to argue with him, but I remember what hap-pened the last time I did that.

"Ump, there was no touch," I tell him calmly and repeat myself when Wilson comes out to ward off any issues between the umpire and me.

"Smith, there wasn't a touch," Wilson says. He motions for me to go back to the dugout, and I do, but I stay at the top of the stairs. When the opposing team scores or a play is in question that could affect the home team, the instant replay suddenly doesn't work. That is the case right now. The cameramen are showing the freaking mascot dancing around like a fool instead of showing the fans that I'm safe.

The ump confers with the umpire in the Replay Command Center, which is located in New York City, who overturns the initial call because the home plate ump is giving the sign that I'm safe. I watch the scoreboard change, tying up the game, before I step into the dugout where the guys commend me on excellent game play.

"Nice running." I give Singleton props with a fist bump.

"That bunt was deadly."

"Fucking lucky," I tell him as I down a cup of water and head to the railing to cheer on Bryce Mackenzie. I've never been a strong bunter so the fact that it laid down perfectly is a surprise to me. I'm usually a guaranteed out in that sort of situation.

Mackenzie goes down swinging, as does Bennett. Cashman grounds out to short, ending our half of the inning.

"Keep it tight, guys," Wilson says as we head to our respective positions. Meyers and I walk out together, bullshitting along the way. He's ready for our road trip to be over, and his big plan for tomorrow is to sleep. I don't know what my plan is going to be, but it will definitely be something to do with Ainsley. I think about telling the guys that she's pregnant, but I asked Wilson not to say anything, so I don't feel right letting the cat out of the bag, so to speak. Once Ainsley and I figure shit out, I'll let people know, but until then, my lips are sealed. Besides,

I don't feel like it's my news to share, but hers. Once it's out there, the damn BoRe Blogger will be all up in her business, and I don't think she wants that just yet.

In the end, we lose badly and are back on our plane by four in the afternoon. I text Ainsley to let her know that I'll be home around ten or so, but she doesn't respond before I'm forced to shut my phone off. We have wifi on the plane, but I choose to sleep on the way back so she and I can have a long talk tomorrow. My sleeping habits are all fucked up because of my schedule, and if I can get a nap in now, maybe waking up with her won't be such an issue for me.

I sleep through the flight, and once we're landed, we get on our charter bus and head back to the stadium. Well, some of us do. Daisy is waiting for Ethan, and their warm embrace makes me long for a relationship like that. Standing there like a Peeping Tom, watching them together, really makes me question what I'm doing with Ainsley. She's here and pregnant with my child, yet I'm keeping a safe distance between us. Why? Am I afraid she's going to run again? Maybe I need to give her a reason to stay.

The Davenports offer me a ride home, but I decline. I need my car, especially if I want to take Ainsley somewhere tomorrow. The ride back on the team bus is torture but only because I have someplace to be.

Back at the stadium, everyone mumbles their goodbyes as we go our separate ways. My drive home is short with minimal traffic on the road, and when I'm standing at the door to my apartment, everything shifts. I have a decision to make once I'm inside. It's going to be life-changing, and we may not want the same things. Ainsley and I need to talk and not let our attraction to each other get in the way. Lord knows, with the thought of her sleeping in my bed for the past few nights, my hand has been getting a workout. And don't even get me started on her breasts. I've noticed that they've gotten bigger and I really can't wait to watch them bounce up and down—that's if she still wants me.

When I step inside, all the lights are off except for the small glow coming from the bedroom. I move quietly through my apartment and knock gently on my bedroom door. She doesn't answer, but that doesn't stop me from entering.

Inside my room, candles are lit, and there are rose petals scattered over the floor and on the bed. Ainsley stands in the middle of the room with a long nightgown on. From where I stand, I can see her belly protruding, giving her shape. I set my bag down and step into the room.

"Welcome home," she says, staying in her spot. There's something different in her voice, a tone I can't place. Is she nervous that I won't like this or that I don't want her?

"I think this has to be one of the best homecomings I've ever had."

"Have you had many?"

I shake my head slowly as I stalk toward her. Her breathing catches when my hand cups her cheek. "None since I've met you."

A small smile plays on her lips, and I pray that was enough reassurance for her to know that I haven't been with anyone else.

"What do you want, Ainsley?"

"You," she replies softly.

"But for how long? Do you plan to go back to Florida? Or stay here?"

She closes her eyes and rests her head against my hand. "I want a family," she says as she meets my gaze.

"Do you see me in your family?"

When she nods, I lose all sense of reality and carry her to my bed. I lay her down gently with her hair fanning over the rose petals on the comforter. "You're so beautiful," I tell her as I kiss her exposed skin.

"Make love to me, Cooper."

"With pleasure."

Ainsley sleeps soundly next to me while my thoughts run rampant. All night I've thought about what I have to do, and I realize I don't want to wait. I slide out of bed carefully and get dressed in my closet. The few clothes she brought hang opposite of mine, bringing a smile to my face. I like that she hung her stuff up and made herself at home, even though this one will be temporary. We can't raise a family in an apartment and will need something bigger.

I check on her before I sneak out, making sure she's still sleeping. The temptation to crawl back into bed with her is great, but so is my quest. I shouldn't be gone long, but in the event that she wakes up, I leave her a note telling her I'll be right back.

It's after two in the morning, and the streets are empty except for those going home from the bar scene. That's never been me; even in college, I kept to the curfew and rarely went out during the off-season. Baseball was and still is too important to me.

I pound on my manager's door, knowing that I'll end up paying the price on Friday when I go back to work, but right now, I don't care. There's something I need to do, and it can't wait.

"What the fuck do you want, Bailey? It's two a.m."

"Yes, sir, but this can't wait."

He yawns and motions for me to come in. "Don't sit. You're not staying long."

I stand there under the scrutiny of my boss. "I'm here to ask your permission to marry Ainsley."

"What?" he scoffs.

"I'd like to marry Ainsley but would also like your permission."

He shakes his head and brushes me off. "Whatever, Bailey. Ask her. I'm going back to bed. Lock the door on your way out."

Wes Wilson, the man who busted my chops for getting Ainsley pregnant to begin with, walks out of the room and into his bedroom. When the door slams, I jump and quickly realize that this was easier than I thought.

The drive back to my apartment is quick, and before I know it, I'm shedding my clothes and climbing back into bed with Ainsley. She molds easily into my side with her ass pressing against my dick.

"Hmm, you're cold."

"Sorry, I had to run a quick errand." If that surprises her, she doesn't say anything. Instead, she reaches between us and grabs hold of me and begins to stroke.

"Ainsley," I warn, unsure if she's awake or not.

"Coop, I'm so horny," she mumbles in her sleep.

I rise up on my elbow and ask her to look at me. There's no way I'm taking advantage of a sleeping Ainsley. For all I know she could be dreaming.

"Look at me." Her eyes flutter open, and she smiles. "You're horny?" I ask, trying not to laugh.

"All the time."

"I can help solve that," I tell her, thrusting my hips into her hands.

"Please do." She stays on her side, moving her leg to give me access. I enter her, relishing in the feeling of being this close to her and knowing that when the sun comes up, I'm asking her to marry me.

# BOSTON RENEGADES

The Renegades have returned home from their road trip. Unfortunately this one didn't go as planned. After being gone for six days, the BoRes went two and four, losing the last game of the month to the Rays. The Renegades fell to the Rays 13–3, making that the biggest loss of the season to date.

The bats were strong from Bailey, Singleton, Mackenzie, and Davenport, but they weren't enough to overcome an early deficit.

Renegades have a much-needed day off before the Angels and Rangers come to town.

Don't forget to keep voting for your favorite player on the All-Star ballot. This is one election where your vote does matter.

The BoRes are 42–36 right now. They need to get smart, or what has started off as a good season will end before the wild card race.

# GOSSIP WIRE

Hadley Carter was photographed buying baby items. Her bump is just adorable. When asked, Ryan Stone stated, "I'm scared shitless but happy that we're starting a family."

The divorce between Steve and Lisa Bainbridge is final. No word yet on whether she'll stay in Boston or head home to Indiana. Sources tell me that Bainbridge was given full custody of their minor children. I'm sure the applications to be their nanny are coming in fast!

Branch Singleton has been seen out and about with someone new. No word on her identity, but they seem happy. Once we find out who the lucky lady is, we'll let you know!

And our favorite rookie may have a love connection on the horizon. It's rumored that his fling from Fort Myers is in town, but staff has been unable to verify.

The BoRe Blogger

# THIRTY-FOUR

## Ainsley

Waking up in Cooper's arms felt like a dream. I pinched myself a few times to make sure that I wasn't imagining everything. After watching his game, I called Stella, asking her what I could do to show him that I'm happy to be here, that I'm happy that I'm in his home. She laughed and told me to get sexy. It's hard to be or feel sexy when you're gaining weight and your stomach sticks out like beacon, but I tried, and thankfully he liked it.

He disappeared on me in the middle of the night. I woke, startled and scared, but when I went to look for him, I found the note he had left. I want to question where he went, but I figure I'm the one intruding on his life, and maybe he had to run to the store for something.

I lay on my side with one arm under my head and the other caressing my belly while I stare at a sleeping Cooper. The baby is moving around, kicking like a little soccer player. I still don't know where he stands about the baby, and it's killing me not to know. I don't want to pass up this moment, so I take his hand and place it on my belly. The baby kicks—it's soft but you can feel it—and Cooper's eyes flash open.

"What the hell is that?"

I swallow the fear that is building inside of me. "That's the baby."

"Holy shit. Does that hurt?"

Shaking my head, I fight back some tears. "No. It will when the baby is bigger, but not yet."

Cooper moves closer, keeping his hand on my stomach. Before I realize what he's doing, he's moved the comforter off of us and is eye level with my stomach.

"Can he hear me?"

"He?"

He looks at me with a devilish smirk. "Of course."

"What if he turns out to be a she?"

His smirk morphs into fear, and it sort of matches what I'm feeling. I don't want to get my hopes up that he's into this baby thing. That he wants us to be a family because that is what I want. When Daisy asked if I was staying in Boston and I told her no, I didn't like how I felt not having Cooper in our child's life. I grew up without a dad and he without a mom. Why would I do that to this baby?

"Honestly, Ainsley, I don't mind if it's a boy or girl. Obviously I'm partial to boys because of baseball, but if we had a little girl that looked just like you, I have no doubt she'd have me wrapped around her little finger like her mother does." As he's saying this, he's slowly moving up my body. He kisses me softly, locking our fingers together.

"I have to ask if this is real. Do you really want this?"

Placing his other hand on my hip, his thumb moves back and forth slowly along my skin. "I've thought about this a lot and what it means. This isn't something that either of us can walk away from. We both have to be responsible for the life we created, but it's more than that for me. I've told you how I felt about you, and that hasn't changed. Shit, up until two months ago, I was calling your office phone every day so

I could hear your voice. And that day you called me, I didn't even hesitate to come meet you.

"But when I saw you pregnant, I thought I had lost any chance at being with you. I was shocked and scared when you told me the baby was mine. I don't know how to be a dad or a husband. Hell, I'm probably not very good at being a boyfriend, but I'm going to fucking try until I get it right."

"Husband?" I squeak out.

"Yeah, husband." He gets off the bed and pulls me to the edge, helping me sit up, even though I can do it myself. When he gets down on his knee, tears well in my eyes.

"Ainsley, I'm going to make a lot of mistakes. I'm going to be gone a lot and you'll feel like you're doing it all, but when I'm here…when I'm lying next to you at night, you're going to know that you own me. You're going to know that I'm in love with you. I don't have a ring, but I don't want to wait. Will you marry me?"

I nod frantically and blurt out a blubbering "Yes." Cooper pulls me into his arms, kissing me with abandon. We scoot back onto the bed, and once again, I'm cradled in his arms. Cooper makes me feel safe. Feel loved.

"I asked Wes for permission to marry you last night."

"You did?" I don't think I could hide the shock on my face if I tried.

He nods. "I know he just found out, but I thought it would be important to both of us to have his blessing. We talked, and he's not going to tell anyone that he's your father."

"And that will make things easier for you?" I know he's worried about his career, and if we're going to be a family, I should worry as well.

"Yeah, I think this is how it has to be. I'm not saying you can't have a relationship with him: you can. And I want him in our child's life. I just don't want to broadcast it that he's your father."

"I can live with that."

⬦

After we shower and dress, I tell Cooper about my doctor's appointment and ask him if he wants to come. He agrees, even though I can see the fear in his eyes as we sit in the office waiting to be called back.

Today, he looks nothing like the Cooper Bailey I'm used to. Instead of his usual Renegades gear, he's opted for track pants and a hoodie, doing everything he can to hide who he is. I get it—he doesn't want our news spread all over the tabloids—but people are bound to find out sooner or later.

When my name is called, I grab his hand and drag him behind me. The nurse is laughing and says that she sees this all the time. The big macho men can't handle baby stuff and usually end up in the corner, away from everything.

In the room, the nurse goes over everything in my medical history from my doctor in Florida and asks Cooper some questions. When he brings up his mom, he pauses and shakes his head.

"I'll have to ask my father," he replies to the question about the type of cancer she had. When our eyes meet, we both see the same thing: worry. We've both lost parents to cancer. What does that mean for us, for our baby? Cooper kisses me on the tip of my nose, trying to ease my mind, but it doesn't work.

The nurse leaves, instructing me to change into the robe.

"I can see your ass," Cooper says, grabbing my cheek.

"Stop it."

I climb up onto the table and Cooper stands in front of me, playing with the stirrup. "Cooper, sit down before the doctor comes in."

He laughs and grabs my hips. "Look at this, it's perfect height. Maybe we need one for our house."

I slap him in the chest and grit my teeth. "Go sit down." He continues to laugh but does as he's told. I ignore his comment about "our house" because I don't want to go there yet. One step at a time, and besides, he just asked me to marry him today. We have time before we need to move.

"Good afternoon, Ms. Burke."

"Hi," I say as the doctor comes in. He's young and very handsome, and Cooper is by my side in a flash.

"So I understand you'll be transferring your prenatal care to Boston from Fort Myers?"

"Yeah, it's a sudden move."

"Let's go ahead and take a look. Lie back for me." I do and place my feet in the stirrups. When his hand disappears between my legs, I hear Cooper growl. I look at him, but he's focused on the doctor. I reach for Cooper's hand, squeezing tight, hoping to convey that I'm not enjoying any of this.

"Everything feels fine, but I want to get some images of the baby for our records and to make sure we agree about your due date."

"Wait, you mean an ultrasound?" I ask excitedly.

"Yes, haven't you had one yet?"

I shake my head rapidly. "No."

He smiles. "Well, then, I guess you're about to see your baby for the first time."

I look up at Cooper, who is somehow beaming and glaring at the same time. As soon as the doctor leaves the room, I pull Cooper to me.

"Are you jealous?"

"What, no," he scoffs, but he is unable to look me in the eyes. He sighs. "He was touching you."

"He's a doctor. He doesn't enjoy it like you do."

"You don't know that," he balks. I don't have time to counter his comment because the nurse and tech are back with the ultrasound machine. In a flash, my gown is opened, and blue gel is squirted onto my stomach.

And just like that the wand is pressed down and the whooshing sound of the baby's heartbeat fills the room.

"Your baby has a very strong heartbeat."

"That's because he's a boy," Cooper boasts.

The nurse presses a few buttons while moving the wand over my stomach. She turns the monitor to face us so we can see the baby. It looks like an alien life form growing inside of me.

"Do you want to know what you're having?"

Cooper and I both yell out yes, earning a chuckle from the nurse.

"Right here"—she points to the screen—"is your son and over here is your daughter."

"Wh...what?"

"You didn't know you were having twins?"

I shake my head and try to swallow the lump in my throat. "No... are you sure there are two?"

"Positive." The nurse moves away while the lab tech continues to take pictures. She's thumbing through my chart, making notes and shaking her head. "The doctor will monitor you throughout your pregnancy, and you should expect to deliver earlier than late November." She closes the file, coming to stand next to me. "Congratulations. I know you're in shock, but you're in good hands here. The babies look

healthy, and I've updated your chart. When you check out, the recep-
tionist will have your next appointment scheduled for you."

The lab tech hands us a few of the pictures before following the
nurse out of the room, leaving Cooper and me to the news that we're
not having one but two babies. When I look at him, he's white as a
ghost.

"Cooper?" I reach for his hand as I sit up, but he doesn't move.
"Hey."

"Uh?"

"We're done. I can get dressed now."

He helps me off the table and holds me in front of him. He lifts my
gown, inspecting my belly.

"How the fuck are there two babies in there?"

"Um . . . well, you see what happens—"

He shakes his head. "No, I know what happens. I remember sex ed
and all that shit. You're fucking tiny, Ainsley. We have to fatten you
up."

"No, I think I'm fine." I sigh and move past him, grabbing my
clothes so I can change.

"Babe, I don't mean it badly. I'm just saying that . . . fuck, I don't
know, but we're having twins—well, you are—I just put them there,
and we don't have any space. So get dressed because we need to go to
the jewelers, get you your ring, plus we need to house hunt."

"House hunt?"

Cooper steps to me, placing a chaste kiss on my lips. "We need a
house for our family or a really nice condo that has a yard like Ethan
and Daisy's. And I'm not buying it without you, so hurry your sweet
ass up because we have a lot of shit to do today." He swats my rear and
claps his hands together. I change as quickly as possible and follow him

out of the room, stopping to check out. The whole way back to the car he has me pulled as close to him as possible, kissing me every few steps.

"You know what?" he says, leaning me up against his car.

"What?"

"This morning, when I was asking you to marry me, I forgot one very important thing."

"What's that, Mr. Bailey?"

He pushes my hair behind my ear and kisses along my neck, my cheek, and finally my lips. "I love you, Ainsley," he tells me while looking into my eyes. "I love you, and these two babies that you're giving me."

# THIRTY-FIVE

## Cooper

As soon as I step off of the shuttle bus, the blazing heat causes sweat to pebble everywhere. It's fucking hotter than Hades in San Diego, and we have to play in this shit. I look at the other guys, Davenport, Singleton, and Sinclair, as they step out behind me, and their faces morph into this "what the fuck are we doing here" look, in obvious agreement with my assessment. Once I have my luggage in my hands, I haul ass into the lobby where the air conditioner feels like I've just stepped into the beer cooler at the local grocery store.

Pulling my phone out, I text Ainsley to make sure she's at the hotel. She and Daisy, along with Davenport's family, flew in early. Wes Wilson is here as well, even though he's not the coach of the American League All-Star team. He's actually here to be a dad to Ainsley, since their time in Boston is somewhat limited. Wes is a regular at our place for dinner when we're not playing, and he's been helping us look at houses, threatening us that he might live next door if there are two for sale in the same neighborhood.

When he saw Ainsley's ring, he was confused until I reminded him of my late-night—or early-morning, depending on how you look at things—visit when I asked him for his permission. He said he remembered, but he thought he had been dreaming or that I was drunk, so he didn't take me seriously.

I am dead serious about marrying her, and it's not because she's pregnant with my children, it's because I love her and can't imagine my life making any kind of sense without her. It doesn't matter that I've known her for only a few weeks. In the time we were apart, nothing else made sense except for baseball. Having her and baseball completes my world. The twins are just an added bonus.

I found out I made the All-Star team after we found out about the twins. I was still on this euphoric high of hearing their heartbeats and mesmerized by the ultrasound when Wilson called me into his office. He told me he had news, and I won't lie, I set the picture of the twins down on his desk to soften the blow. He smiled and said that he couldn't wait to be a grandfather and asked if I had manned up yet. I just shrugged and asked him what he needed me for, and that's when he said I was heading to San Diego. Of course, I was elated, but deep down, I had hoped that I'd have those four days off to spend with Ainsley. Thankfully, Daisy offered to fly with her and keep her company while I worked.

Ainsley tells me she's here, but out at the pool with the Davenports, and sends me a picture of Ethan's niece touching her belly. A slight pang of jealously hits me because Shea is spending time with her when I can't. I shake off the thoughts that I'm jealous of a toddler. If that's the case, I can't imagine what I'm going to be like when the twins get here.

After we're checked in, I change and head down to the pool. There seems to be a lively party going on with a few of the players from the other teams. We all shake hands and put aside any animosity that we have toward one another. Wives and girlfriends are introduced, and a rousing game of water volleyball gets underway. As the night wears on, things get rowdy. Some of the guys start drinking, but I refrain. I need a clear head for tomorrow's festivities, and I know that jetlag eventually is going to kick my ass.

"Are you ready to head up?" I ask Ainsley, who looks exhausted. I know she's only stayed down here because I was here, which meant we got to spend more time together. She nods and curls into my side as much as she can since the chaise lounges aren't that accommodating.

"Hey, Davenport, we're heading up." He nods, and Daisy signals that they're coming, too. With Ainsley's hand in mine, and the Davenports next to us, we make the trek back up to the rooms. Unfortunately, because the team is paying for my hotel, Ainsley can't stay with me, but she'll be with Daisy. Maybe Ethan and I can cuddle instead.

As soon as we step off the elevator, we come face-to-face with my dad. Everything inside of me turns to stone as my hand tightens around Ainsley's. I haven't really spoken to my dad since the day Ainsley told me she was pregnant, because I had nothing to say to him.

"What's this?"

My tongue is thick, and there's a lump in my throat that makes it hard to swallow. I follow his gaze down to Ainsley's hand, which is resting on my bicep, the hand that I placed a diamond solitaire on weeks ago.

"Didn't know you'd be here."

"Clearly, but do you honestly think that I'd miss your first time at the All-Star Game?"

The answer is no, and I should've thought about that beforehand, except I have nothing to hide. If he doesn't like Ainsley, so what? He'll figure out a way to coexist with her or he won't exist in my life at all.

"Dad, you remember Ethan and Daisy Davenport?" They shake hands, and he seems pleased to see them. "And this is Ainsley, my fiancée."

His face turns red as he glares at me. "We need to talk," he says, reaching for my arm, but I reel back and step in front of Ainsley.

"Whatever you have to say, you can say in front of Ainsley."

"This is a private family matter," he seethes. He looks at Ainsley, Daisy, and Ethan, and none of them flinch or move a muscle to leave.

"Ainsley's my family. So are Ethan and Daisy. Whatever you have to say, it can be said in front of them."

"*She's* not my family. *She's* a two-bit whore that trapped you into this relationship. *She* only wants your money. *She* doesn't give a shit about you. I'm not going to stand by and let you throw away everything you worked for because you were dumb enough to fuck this woman without a condom."

I feel Ainsley tense next to me, and I don't like it one bit. I hate that my father is like this. I take a look at her and see fear and sorrow in her eyes. She should never feel like that when she's with me.

"I'm only going to say this once, so you need to listen closely. Ainsley and I are getting married and we're starting family. I trust her, Dad, and wish you didn't have to be so pigheaded. But you are, and that leaves me no choice but to say this: If you can't accept my family, we can't accept you. The only time you will see me is on television or when you buy a ticket to a game. I will no longer support you. I will no longer be a part of your life. This is your call."

"You can't do that. You *won't* do that," he says, challenging me.

"I will. Oh, and if you ever call my Ainsley a whore again, I'll slap you with whatever lawsuit I can pin on your sorry ass. If you want a relationship with me, you will apologize to her. Until then, you are nothing to me."

I don't give him an opportunity to respond as I brush past him with Ainsley by my side. She's murmuring into my shoulder that she loves me, and all I want to do is pull her into my room and show her how much I love her.

When we get to the girls' room, I'm hesitant to let them go inside because my dad is still standing in the hallway, probably trying to figure out how he's going to live now. He's stubborn enough that I know he won't come around and see things from my side. I get that he wants what's best for me, but that's my choice, and I choose Ainsley.

Daisy assures us that they'll be fine, and promises they won't open the door for anyone, especially my father. Ethan and I both stand at the door until we hear the deadbolt slide before heading to our room.

"That was fucked up," Ethan says as we enter.

"That's my life. No one has ever been good enough for me in my father's eyes. When he found out Ainsley was pregnant and in Boston, he flipped and demanded I get a paternity test." I sit down, shaking my head. He put doubt in my mind about Ainsley and the babies, and I hated that. She never gave me a reason not to trust her. She was scared and alone when she came here, and I did nothing but question her.

"When my mom died, he changed and changed me right along with him. I was all he had. At first, I thought it was because he missed her, but I have come to realize it was because he wanted me to be something he never was."

My cell phone beeps with a text from Ainsley. For a moment I fear reading it, wondering if she's second-guessing our upcoming nuptials because of what just transpired with my father. We're supposed to get married while we are here in California, at Disney two days after the All-Star Game. If she backs out now, I don't know what I'll do.

Pulling up her message, I'm hit with the sudden urge to run down to her room and say fuck the rules, but I know I can't.

I love & miss you terribly. Thank you for sticking up for me.

She's thanking me for sticking up for her?

Why wouldn't I stick up for you? You're about to be my wife in a few days and you're the mother of my children. As far as I'm concerned you're the most important person in my life.

I send that back to her, hoping that she understands that it's not going to matter what my father says: *She's* my life.

I quickly type out another message. I don't want her to think that I didn't notice that part of her message and only focused on the negative.

By the way, I love you too.

Ethan tells me that he's going to go take a shower, leaving me alone to figure out what to do about my dad. There's a knock on the door that sends me flying over there hoping it's Ainsley. Only when I open it, it's my dad.

"What are you doing here?" Anger boils through my veins.

"I came to give you these." He hands me a stack of papers. I look down quickly, and my stomach rolls. *Prenuptial* is the only word that I need to read to know these aren't for me. I hand them back to him.

"Don't be stupid, Cooper," he says, pushing them back toward me.

"I love her. What part of that can't you comprehend? She's having my children."

"It's just one child. You can be active in his life and not have to marry her."

I groan loudly, growing irritated with him. "You know what? I shouldn't even tell you this, but maybe it will knock some sense into you. We're having twins, so it's not one child you're asking me to abandon, but two. And you know what? I'm not going to do it. I love her, she loves me, and we're going to get married. I'm sorry that doesn't work out in your life plan, but this is my life and it's what I want."

I start to shut the door, but he stops it and slams the papers down against my chest. "Read them. They make sense and will protect you."

Before I can crumple them up and send them soaring toward his head, he's down the hall. I let the door slam and look down at the papers. Instead of reading them, I rip them in half and throw them in the garbage. If Ainsley wants my money, she can have it.

# THIRTY-SIX

## Ainsley

I never thought my pregnancy would be public news or that anyone would care. Honestly, it never dawned on me that it would make a difference to anyone other than the few close friends we have. So when I arrived at Petco Park with Daisy and Ethan's family and we were ushered to our seats, I never thought in a million years that I'd find myself on the Jumbotron with the title of soon-to-be Mrs. Bailey flashing around my picture.

To say I was mortified would be an understatement, but I played it cool, pretending that it wasn't bothering me until they panned to Cooper, who was warming up. They put us side-by-side on the screen and change the caption to read "parents to be" before panning out enough to get my bulging belly. Half the crowd cheered, while a few booed. I get it; he was an eligible bachelor and women had hopes of landing him. But what stuck with me the most was Cooper's face and the sheer joy when he looked at the screen—essentially looking directly at me. It was enough for me to know that I don't need to be threatened by anyone else.

After last night, the encounter with his father left me questioning everything. Daisy and I spoke at length about her marriage and how she too comes from a broken family, about how Ethan was there when her grandfather passed away, even though she had pushed him out of her life. She said that some guys just get it, and we're the lucky ones.

I do feel lucky. Not because Cooper is a professional baseball player but because of the situation we're in. He could have easily told me to go back to Florida and to call him when the babies were born, but he didn't. I think the road trip he went on was good for him and exactly what he needed. I tried not to add any pressure and would have accepted whatever he decided. I was in no position to demand anything from him, though it would have torn me up inside had he not chosen us.

A few wives of the other players have come up to congratulate me on the pregnancy. For the most part, they're nice, but you get a few who toss a snide comment in every now and again. Daisy is quick on the rebuttal while I search for words that won't seem rude. She tells me that thick skin is important, and I shouldn't be afraid of hurting their feelings, because they're certainly not afraid to hurt mine.

The pomp and circumstance that goes into the All-Star Game is amazing. The vibe is infectious, and I find myself really getting into it. Since I've been in Boston, I haven't done much, except sightsee with Daisy and drag Cooper to my doctor's appointments, but I feel like I need to start going to more baseball games to support my man. Daisy says she loves it and has offered to sit with me on the visitor's side if I'm not ready to face all the wives. She says she gets a better angle of Ethan that way but also likes to see him when he comes in and out of the dugout. It's an offer that I'll likely take her up on until I'm comfortable enough to be there on my own.

Quitting my job and telling Stella that I won't be back to Florida was probably the hardest thing I've ever had to do, aside from losing my mom. Stella has been my best friend for most of my life and has been my rock for the past year, helping with my mother. I suggested she also move to Boston, but she quickly brushed that off, saying something about how unnatural copious amounts of snowfall is. I haven't told her that Cooper and I plan to live in Florida during the off-season. I want to surprise her when I show up at the zoo or knock on her door.

I have spoken to a few of the zoos in the area about a possible job, but Cooper said he would like me to stay home with the babies, or he's at least suggested that I don't need to work if I don't want to. But ultimately the decision is up to me. I don't know how I'll feel about not working in the long run, but I have to say it's nice to have the break right now. Daisy works, but she says it's to occupy her time, and her hours are flexible. She doesn't work if Ethan is home because their time together is too precious to her.

We stand when the teams are announced. Each player comes out of their respective dugout and stands along the baseline. Daisy explains that the American League is the home team this year, even though we're in a National League park, due to the fact that the National League hosted last year and will host next year. She goes on to say that it's supposed to alternate, but it hasn't been that way lately. I nod along, pretending to understand everything she is saying, although if I'm going to be a baseball wife, I better start brushing up on the history of the sport.

After watching a few of the players perform cartwheels in the outfield, I ask, "The guys don't take this game seriously?"

"No, they do. They're just having fun right now. The winner of this game determines which league will have home field advantage in the World Series. Naturally we want the American League to win because we'd have more home games and the chances of winning are better if the guys were to make it to the World Series."

"I see."

"No, you don't," she says, laughing. "It's okay. Cooper doesn't care if you know the game or not. He only cares that you're in the stands supporting him."

That thought makes me smile, and as I look over at the dugout, his head pops up. He waves at me, causing butterflies to take flight in my stomach. Either that or his kids are about to start kicking the crap out of me.

After what Daisy refers to as a one-two-three inning, our guys are up to bat. Cooper didn't start the game, but Daisy assures me he'll be playing in a couple of innings. Ethan is up to bat first for the American League, getting a standing ovation that is started by his father. I look at him and see nothing but pride for his son and everything he's accomplished, while Cooper's dad is trying to control his life. It's crazy how night and day some parents can be.

"Let's go, Unc," Shea yells as loudly as she can. If Ethan hears her, he doesn't acknowledge her.

When Ethan is called for a strike, her hands go up in the air, and she sighs. Daisy tells me that Shea is Ethan's biggest fan and will video-chat with him before each game to tell him what he needs to do.

"And he listens?"

"Of course. Shea is the apple of his eye. If she says jump, he will until she tells him to stop."

I look down the bleachers and see someone I don't recognize from yesterday. "Who's that next to Shana?" I met Ethan's sister yesterday when we arrived at the hotel.

"Oh, that's Mike, Shana's husband. He's not around much because of his job."

"What does he do?"

Daisy shrugs. "He's in the Army, but Ethan thinks he's Special Forces or something like that and just can't tell us. I honestly thought he really didn't exist, but he was at our wedding and stayed the entire month we were in the Keys."

I've always pictured Special Forces men to be huge, with bulged-out muscles, but Mike doesn't look anything like I've pictured. I suppose looks can be deceiving.

Daisy tells me that Ethan has a full count, and that has her with her hands clasped in front of her and rocking back and forth. Shea is egging her uncle on, telling him that he needs to figure it out. I can't help but laugh and wonder if the daughter Cooper and I are having will be anything like Shea. Yesterday when I met her, she was prim and proper, and today she's full-on tomboy. For her, it's probably the best of both worlds.

Ethan tosses his bat down and jogs down to first base. This makes the Davenports happy, and Shea is now sitting comfortably on her dad's lap. Ethan never makes it past first, though, as the other batters either strike out or the hits are caught.

"This is turning into a pitching duel," Mr. Davenport says. Daisy agrees with him while Mike offers his own comments. I haven't a clue what any of this means so I sit back and watch as Cooper runs out to center field in the top of the third inning. When his face is on the Jumbotron, I get giddy and clap for him.

When he told me that he had been chosen to play in the All-Star Game, I was happy. I didn't know what it meant until he explained the importance of it, especially since he hadn't been playing well for most of the season. And now he's out in center field, among his peers waiting for some action.

The first batter to step into the box is a big dude.

"He looks like he can crush it," I say to Daisy, who nods.

"He can, and center field is his favorite spot."

"Shit," I mutter. Even though I have faith in Cooper, I'd rather things be easy for him so he's not stressing out.

The batter swings and connects with the ball. It flies straight toward Cooper, but he's running toward it. I grip Daisy's arm thinking the ball is going to go over his head, but it's dropping fast. Cooper lies out, snagging the ball in midflight before landing and sliding on his stomach.

I stand, waiting to see if he has the ball. When he raises his hand, the stadium erupts in cheers and his heroic efforts are replayed on the big screen, causing everyone around us to shout even louder.

"Wow," I say as I sit back down.

"Is this really the first time you've watched him play?" Mrs. Davenport asks.

Embarrassment washes over me as I nod. "I saw him in Fort Myers once, but the rest of the games have been on television."

"Oh, sweetie, you really need to go to the games with Daisy. Cooper is a very good player, one of the best," she says, beaming with pride as if Cooper were her son.

"I'll make sure she's there," Daisy tells her mother-in-law, who smiles back in kind.

"I guess I've been missing a lot, huh?"

"It's okay. We still have a long season left."

In between innings, I volunteer to take Shea to the restroom. I have to go too but have been trying to hold out as long as possible. Walking hand in hand with her, I figure this could be a good test of my parenting skills. If I can keep track of a toddler, then I should be golden with newborns. It's a lie that I keep telling myself because there's no way I'm prepared for a baby, let alone two.

Once we've gone and washed up, Shea convinces me that she needs some cotton candy. I know I should probably ask her parents, but the thought of walking all the way back down and up the stairs again doesn't sit well with me, so we wait in line and she fills me in on her uncle's baseball stats. I'm amazed at how much she has memorized and find myself asking her if she's making them up.

"Nope. Mommy reads them to me at night before bed."

"Wouldn't you rather hear a bedtime story?"

She shakes her head. "I love my unc and want to know everything."

"I see."

We step up to the counter, ordering a pink cotton candy and seven waters. When everything is on the counter, I realize that I can't hold the waters and her hand at the same time.

"Shea, what does your mommy do when she can't hold your hand?"

"I have to hold her shirt."

Yes! "Okay, can you hold my shirt while we walk?"

She nods and grabs hold with her free hand, swinging her bag of pink sugar in the other.

"What are your babies' names?" she asks as we weave in and out of people.

"Yes, what are they?"

I stop in my tracks when Cooper's dad steps in front of me. I look around for security or anyone who can help, but they're all focused on their own tasks.

"Excuse me, please," I say, trying to step around him, but he just moves to block my path.

"Answer me."

"If you have something you need, you need to talk to Cooper."

"I would, but my son seems to be blinded by you and won't listen to reason."

"I'm sorry you feel that, Mr. Bailey, but I can't help you."

I attempt to move, but he blocks me again. I'm starting to feel scared. My heart is racing, and Shea is tightening her hold on my shirt, which is starting to pull on my neck.

"What's going on here?" Mike asks as he comes into view.

"It's none of your business," Mr. Bailey says.

"Except it is when you're scaring the shit out of my daughter."

I sigh in relief when Mike picks up Shea. She whispers something in his ear, which causes his face to turn red. He puts Shea back down, and she immediately grabs onto my shirt. Mike sizes up Mr. Bailey, and while Cooper's dad is bigger, Mike doesn't hold back. "I see that you have two options. You can either step away or I can carry you out of here."

If I'm not mistaken, Mike puffs his chest, and Mr. Bailey takes a step back.

"I'm not done with you."

"Oh yeah, you are. Because if I find out you come anywhere near her, I'll hunt you down and make you pay. I know who you are, and I know what went down last night. If you have a problem, I suggest you speak with your son."

Mike takes the waters out of my hand and steps behind me, motioning for Shea and me to walk toward the hallway that will lead us back to our seats. Once we sit back down, I start to cry, which alarms all the women around me. Mike calmly fills everyone in on what he witnessed and how he took care of it. I thank him, but it doesn't seem to be enough. I'd like to think that Mr. Bailey wouldn't hurt me, but I'm not so sure.

**BOSTON RENEGADES**

Well, folks, that was a close one. However, the American League prevailed with a 6–5 victory over the National League, securing home field advantage for the World Series.

Let's hope that our Renegades will be the ones hosting! They'll be in New York to face the Yankees, who are always a formidable foe, before having a nine-game home stand that brings Minnesota, San Francisco, and Detroit to Boston.

The American League MVP award went out to Mike Trout, who right now is considered the best in baseball, for his three-run homer in the top of the second.

It was a scorching day at Petco Park, but nonetheless the fans were treated to a well-played exhibition game. Let's give a huge shout-out to the National League contingent for hosting another great event!

## ALL-STAR WIRE

It seems that the All-Star Game was a family affair this year with the Davenports welcoming a new member into their fold—Ainsley Burke—who was seen not only sporting a pretty round belly but with a nice diamond on her ring finger as she sat with the Davenports during the game. No information on the impending birth or wedding, but when staff asked Cooper Bailey about this, he smiled and said he was very, very happy.

The cutest fan award goes to Ethan Davenport's niece, Shea, who was often captured by the Jumbotron yelling not only at her uncle, but at the other American League players as well, even going head-to-head with Mr. Trout as he walked to the batter's box. Mr. Trout commented after the game that no one in the business messes with Shea or they'd never hear the end of it.

Branch Singleton's son made an appearance and spent the day in the dugout with his father, playing batboy. Both Singletons had smiles on their faces all day.

After every pitch, Hawk Sinclair threw the ball into the stands, making him the most popular player of the day on both sides of the fence.

The BoRe Blogger

# THIRTY-SEVEN

## Cooper

One of the joys of having a few days off is being able to spend it with friends and family, and that is exactly what I'm doing now. Ainsley and I rented a convertible and are driving up the California coastline, enjoying the serene beauty.

I look over at my soon-to be-wife, with the wind blowing in her hair and the sun shining down on her, and wonder how I got so lucky. Never in a million years did I expect to fall in love with anyone at my age. Yet here I am about to marry this woman and become a father. To say my life changed as soon as I became a Renegade would be a massive understatement.

Reaching for her hand, I bring it to my lips and kiss it softly. When she smiles, every part of me lights up with happiness.

"Would you ever want to live here?" I ask her over the road noise and the radio. She reaches forward to turn it down but keeps our hands together.

"I don't know. I've always been an East Coast girl."

"There's no humidity here."

"True, but your job is in Boston."

"It doesn't have to be," I remind her. I'm still uneasy about Wes being her father and have talked to my agent about a potential trade. If one does happen, it'll be after next season when I can have solid numbers under my belt. However, being selected to the All-Star Game was a serious boost to my career and definitely something that could be used to my advantage in negotiations.

"We're a family, Cooper. We go wherever your career takes us."

"And what if I decided to stop playing baseball?"

Ainsley lifts her sunglasses and rest them on her head and does the same to mine. "Without crashing the car, look me in the eye, and tell me that you want to quit baseball."

I try to, but I can't. Quitting baseball is the last thing I want, but I want her to know that the option is there.

"Besides, Twenty-Five, I happen to enjoy watching you in your uniform."

I've had many nicknames throughout my years, but twenty-five is by far my favorite. She doesn't call me it often, but when she does, it's an instant hard-on for me. "Is that so?"

"Yeah, it is."

"Does that mean you're going to start coming to our games?"

"I am," she says as she puts both our sunglasses back down. "And I'm going to be as big as a whale when I do it, so you may want to get me two seats. Better yet, a recliner would be nice."

I laugh wondering what Ryan Stone would think if I put in a request for a recliner, then I remember his wife is pregnant, too.

"You know, I could always see if you can sit in the luxury suite with Hadley."

Ainsley shakes her head. "Nah, I'd be too busy being a fan girl and comparing bellies. I'll rough it with Daisy."

I continue to hold her hand even after she falls asleep. It seems that her stomach has grown in size ever since we found out we're having twins. The best part is that the babies are active, and when I talk to them, they like to kick. Ainsley says it doesn't hurt, but I can't imagine it feels all that great, either.

After the game, Ainsley told me about her run-in with my father and how Mike came to her rescue. I've thanked him, but it's not enough, and I plan to make sure he knows how appreciative I am once we get to Disneyland.

I wake Ainsley when we pull into the hotel, which is located in Disney. When she told me that she had never been to Disney World, even after living in Florida her whole life, I knew we had to fix this.

"Holy Batman," Shea yells as she gets out of Ethan's car. "Unc, do you see this place?" The Davenports' car pulls in behind us.

"I do, Shea, and I think everyone here now knows you've arrived."

"Come on, Flower," she says to Daisy, which is what Shea calls her aunt. "Mickey Mouse is waiting for me."

As Ainsley and I get out of the car, Shea continues to prod anyone who might be willing to take her to Disney *now* as opposed to later. Our plan is to get dinner and be there in time for their nighttime parade before tackling the entire park tomorrow. If I had any reservations about hanging with the Davenports, those were squashed when Mrs. D accepted the both of us with open arms and handed Ainsley two blankets for the babies.

"I think I'm going to skip the parade," Ainsley says after we check in. From the second I opened the hotel door to our suite, she's been curled up in bed.

I crawl in next to her, pulling her back to my chest. "Are you feeling okay?"

"Just tired."

"I'll let Ethan know we're staying in tonight. Besides, we have a big day tomorrow." I text Davenport, letting him know that we'll see him tomorrow, and set my phone on the nightstand before reassuming my position behind Ainsley. My hand rests on her belly, and the kicking starts. It feels harder now than it has the past few days.

"Are they hurting you?" I ask, as I press my lips to her shoulder.

"Today, yes. They're growing so much."

"I'm so sorry." I continue to kiss her until she turns and meets her lips with mine. It doesn't take long for things to get heated and for clothes to be shed. Sex, as of late, has been interesting, as we find positions that work and keep me off her midsection. Creativity has been an adventure. My new favorite position is spooning.

"You feel so good." The words tumble out of my mouth as I enter her, pushing her bent leg forward with my hips. I'll take this over the Starlight Parade any day. I make love to Ainsley, slowly and with as much emotion as I can pour into us. The only time I'm not looking in her eyes is when I'm kissing her, and I hope that she knows how much I love her.

"I love you, Cooper." Her words are my undoing.

———◆———

It's a little-known fact that you can get married in front of Cinderella's Castle if you're in Florida, but when you're in Anaheim, you get married in front of Sleeping Beauty's Castle.

When I suggested to Ainsley that we visit Disney with the Davenports, there was a twinkle in her eye that I hadn't seen before. We hadn't discussed a date, let alone set one, so I did some research and found the best place to hold a small ceremony. However, nothing I saw online is what I wanted to give to her. So after a few phone calls and a lot of name dropping, and with the promise of being able to use my image for promotional pieces, I was told we could get them to agree to close Sleeping Beauty's Castle for a little while so we can get married in front of our friends and family today.

Even though I thought this would be intimate, it's anything but. Once people figured out who we were after staring at Ethan and me for a bit, they quickly realized something was about to happen and started gathering. The fans are even asking us questions, which go unanswered. They want to know what we're doing here. In hindsight, I should've planned it better, but I didn't want a quickie wedding at the justice of the peace; I wanted to make this one memorable. We've talked about having another ceremony after the twins are born and she's comfortable fitting into a wedding dress.

As we wait for Ainsley and Wes to show up by horse-drawn carriage, Ethan and I stand here in casual wear. She didn't want anything fancy and balked at the carriage, but I asked her to appease her inner princess and take it for a ride. Besides, Shea was excited to get dressed up like Cinderella and ride in it, and I didn't want to disappoint her.

I stand tall when I hear the clip-clopping of the horse's hooves and see the carriage come into sight. This is just like the movies with the coachman on the back. Once the horses stop, he jumps to help Ainsley out of the carriage. Daisy, Shea, and Wes get off first before Ainsley comes into view. By all rights, Stella should be here, but a once-in-a-lifetime opportunity came up, and Ainsley didn't want her to miss it. I suggested we postpone and wait until after the babies arrive, but both women were adamant that we be married before their birth.

I didn't know what she'd wear, and now I feel underdressed. I expected a dress, but she looks radiant in the white summer gown that is flowing in the small breeze. Her bouquet is white and pink, while Daisy and Shea carry pink flowers.

Shea walks in front of her, followed by Daisy, who is filling in for her best friend Stella, with Wes walking Ainsley down the makeshift aisle to meet me. The cameras from the onlookers are snapping away, and they will undoubtedly provide us with enough photos on the web that we won't have to post any of our own.

"This is really over the top," she says when she reaches me.

"It's fun, and we're making memories. Besides, how many people can say they were married at Sleeping Beauty's Castle?"

She shakes her head. "I don't know. Not many, I suppose, since I thought this was Cinderella's."

"It'll be something to laugh about with the kids when we bring them here." I wink, hoping to ease the tension.

The minister starts in on his spiel, noting that we're giving ourselves to only each other, and that by joining in marriage, we're promising that we'll be true to our solemn vow.

"Do you, Ainsley Burke, promise to love, honor, and cherish Cooper until death do you part?"

"I do," she says with a smile on her face.

"Do you, Cooper Bailey, promise to love, honor, cherish, and obey Ainsley until death do you part?"

My brows furrow as I look him, but he shrugs and nods toward Ainsley. When I look at her, she's beaming.

"Obey, huh? You want to boss me around?"

"Just a little."

I shake my head, unable to contain my grin. "I do."

"By the power vested in me by the great state of California, I now pronounce you husband and wife. You may kiss your bride."

He doesn't have to tell me twice. I scoop her up and twirl her around, much to the delight of the crowd.

"I love you, Mrs. Bailey."

"Ah, I like the sound of that, Mr. Bailey."

I set her down, only for us to be mobbed by our friends. When I catch a glimpse of Wes, he's wiping at the tears falling down his face. I didn't know how much of a part Ainsley would ask him to play in the ceremony, but I'm glad he walked her down the aisle, especially since Stella couldn't be here.

We walk down the aisle, pausing when we get to the end. Fans clamor in front of us to get pictures. This is the least I can do for interrupting their vacation. When more questions are sent our way, Daisy takes it upon herself to answer on our behalf. I don't remember what Ethan says she does for work, something in publicity, though, so I'm confident in her ability to help us.

The Disney staff shows up, guiding us through the crowd and into City Hall on Main Street, where we officially sign our marriage certificate. Watching Ainsley sign her name with my last name does something to me, and it's hard to explain, but one thing I know for sure is that there won't be that many moments that will top it.

**BOSTON RENEGADES**

It's with heavy heart that we bring you this news.

One-time Manager Cal Diamond has passed away due to injuries he sustained in a car accident on the Tobin Bridge. Eyewitnesses reported seeing Diamond's car slam into the jersey barrier, head on, and did so without an attempt to swerve. It's being speculated that he suffered a massive heart attack behind the wheel. Fortunately, no one else was injured.

Diamond retired suddenly earlier this season due to health-related issues. At the time of his death, he was waiting for heart surgery. It is unknown why the surgery had been put off.

Our hearts go out to the Diamond family.

Tonight's game has been postponed.

The BoRe Blogger

# EPILOGUE

## Cooper

"Are you sure you're able to travel? Dr. Chen seemed to think that you'd go early." Ainsley rolls her eyes as she walks away from me. I've had a few injuries in my life, but none of them can even begin to compare to the amount of discomfort she's in. She's three weeks away from her due date, her back is arched—and not because I'm giving her pleasure—and she waddles. Bainbridge tried to demonstrate this pregnancy walk, but Ainsley's puts his attempts to shame.

"I'm fine," she yells out from the babies' nursery. I follow her into the room, which is done in soft yellows, blues, and pinks. The room is a hodgepodge of baseball, butterflies, and teddy bears, and topped off with an abundance of love. Two large pictures hang on one wall, each of our mothers. We want the twins to know that, if they were here, the babies would be loved and spoiled beyond belief. Not that Ainsley and I don't plan to spoil them ourselves.

Ainsley messes with the clothes we plan to bring the twins home in, folding and refolding them, pausing every few seconds to rub her back. We're supposed to leave for Florida later this afternoon to go tie up some loose ends with her mother's estate and to see Stella, but I'm second-guessing whether Ainsley should travel or not.

I go to her and start massaging her shoulders. Her neck falls to the side, and she moans, sending a jolt of electricity right to my crotch. We haven't been able to be intimate in about a month. She's pleased me in other ways, but I haven't been able to do the same for her, and I hate it.

"Hmm," I hum into her neck. Her skin blazes under my touch, something that hasn't gone away. I love how she's always so responsive to me, even when she's angry because of something I've said or done. I work the kink out in her neck, hoping that this will make her feel better.

"Do you want me to help you pack?"

She nods, leaning back into my embrace. Taking her by her hand, I lead her back to our bedroom and sit her down on the bed.

"Are you sure Dr. Chen said this was okay?" I ask again. It's not that I don't trust her. I'm finding it hard to believe that someone this pregnant can fly. "I really think we should cancel this trip, babe."

"I have to go. The new buyers want to close early."

"I get that, but Stella can do it. You can transfer power of attorney to her." It's taken longer than anyone expected for her mother's condo to sell, and when a suitable offer finally came in, Ainsley made plans to go back to Florida to complete the sale.

"I know. I just wanted to see Stella."

I get down on my knees and position myself between her legs. With my hands on her hips, I try to massage her muscles there as well. "Stella will be here when the babies arrive. She's promised you that. I haven't known her long, but she'll keep her word. Plus we'll be back in Fort Myers in two and a half months. I think you'll end up going only six weeks without seeing her." Leaning forward, I kiss her bulging belly, holding my lips there as long as possible.

I can't wait to meet the twins. For the past few months, they've been so active, causing Ainsley to be nauseated, that I really want this pregnancy to be over for her. She's been a trooper, never complaining and never missing a game after the All-Star break. She and Daisy have even become close.

The Renegades' front office threw a joint baby shower for Ainsley and Hadley. Ainsley was so starstruck that she fumbled through opening her presents and was more interested in seeing what Hadley was getting. Unlike us, Ryan and Hadley don't know what they're having. They decided to wait until the baby's birth and be surprised.

For me, I'm happy that we know, especially since we're having twins. Planning for one baby is hard enough, but when you're planning for two, you need all the help you can get. The twins are stocked up on winter wear, diapers, bottles, and those damn sucky things that that look like odd-shaped nipples.

Buying everything in double was easy. The hard part was buying their clothes. Every outfit I wanted was something to do with the Renegades, but Ainsley put her foot down, saying the kids needed to be able to branch out with other teams. I told her as long as it's New England football, basketball, hockey, and baseball, we're okay. The last thing I want is to be ribbed by fans because my kids are wearing some other baseball team, although the twins have received numerous outfits and blankets from my peers all with their teams' logos. I reminded them that their time would come when I thanked them.

Ainsley moans and places her hand on her side.

"That's it. I'm putting my foot down. You're not traveling. Stella can do it."

"But…" She can't even finish her sentence as one of the twins kicks again. They're still growing, and she's stretched as far as the eye can see. I'm afraid she's going to burst open like a water balloon.

"Babe, did you just pee your pants?" I lean back and find her pants drenched, as well as mine because of the way we were sitting.

"No, but I think my water just broke."

My eyes pop open as I let the words seep in. Lamaze class was pure torture. I hated going, but went anyway because it was important to Ainsley. The breathing technique is weird, and I question whether moms are actually able to use it. I didn't find it calming but on the verge of hyperventilation. I suppose it didn't help matters that I brought Travis Kidd with me one time. We had been out golfing on a day off when Ainsley reminded me that we had a class. I didn't have time to take him home, and I wasn't about to let him drive my car, so I made him go.

That was the biggest mistake of my life, although the women got a good laugh out of it. The instructor made him participate, and the sight of Kidd on the floor with his legs spread open, mimicking the breathing technique, was fucking hilarious. What I didn't count on was Kidd taking our adventure back to the clubhouse and using me as his partner while he demonstrated to the guys.

"I think I'm in labor," Ainsley says, stating the obvious.

I try not to laugh, but a chuckle escapes me. "Yeah, babe. I think you are." I kiss her quickly and shuck off my clothes, walking bare-ass naked into the closet to change.

"Asshole," she mutters.

"What's that?" I laugh.

"Six weeks," she says, reminding me it'll be six weeks after the birth before we can have sex. "You'll be begging me."

I bring her a set of new clothes and help her stand. "Ah, babe, you forget that we can still play, I just can't penetrate."

Ainsley slaps me but does so with a smile. Once she's changed, I call Daisy, Stella, and Wes while Ainsley cleans up, letting them know that we're on our way to the hospital. All three of them tell me their on they're way, with Stella already promising she'll be on the next flight out. My next call is to my agent, asking him to postpone the closing until later this week or see what he can do about getting down to Florida to sign the papers on Ainsley's behalf.

"Are you having contractions?" I help her into the car, making sure she's secure before I put the bags into the backseat.

"A little," she says, rubbing her side again.

"I'm supposed to remind you to breathe." I can't say it with a straight face. She knows how I feel about those classes.

"Shut up and drive, Twenty-Five."

It only takes a few minutes for us to get to the hospital. We pull into the valet parking area and I toss my keys to an attendant while another one helps Ainsley out of the car and into a wheelchair.

"You're my favorite player," the man says. I thank him and promise to come back later and give him an autograph. It's my automatic response. Shockingly, the man shakes my hand and tells me not to worry about it.

If Ainsley weren't pregnant, I'd love to push her down the hall in this chair and see how fast we could go, but the inner child in me has to refrain. I have no doubt she'd kill me once she popped these babies out. At check-in, we're taken to a room. The wallpaper is hideous with huge pink, brown, and white flowers.

"This is supposed to be calming," I tell her as I help her change and get into the bed. "I think we should change our walls to this."

"I think you've been spending too much time with Travis, and I may have to ban him from coming over to our house."

"You love Kidd, admit it."

Before she can answer, she's clutching her abdomen and scaring the shit out of me. "Babe," I say, trying to help her find a comfortable position.

"Oh God, Cooper, it hurts."

"Breathe, okay."

"Fuck breathing, get me drugs."

I'm torn between leaving her side and going to do what she asks. The nurse walks in just in the nick of time, saving me from having to leave her.

"Hi, Ainsley. How are you feeling?"

"She's in pain," I answer for her because she's currently gritting her teeth.

"That's to be expected. When did the contractions start?"

"She had a few minor ones on the way over, but she only mentioned pain as soon as she got into the bed."

"Let's take a look." The nurse helps Ainsley put her legs in the stirrups and disappears between her legs. When Ainsley cries out, I want to punch the nurse in the face for hurting her.

Without saying anything, the nurse stands, removes her gloves, and presses a button on the wall. Two more nurses come in and start hooking Ainsley up to various machines, pushing me out of the way.

"What's going on?"

"Your wife is about to deliver."

"Hold up," I say, putting my hands up. "The Lamaze chick told us that first time pregnancies could take hours."

"Everyone is different, Mr. Bailey."

Ainsley reaches for my hand, and I go to her, placing my head on her shoulder. "I hate you," she growls.

"I know, babe. I hate me too right now." I was prepared for her to say mean things to me. Bainbridge told me to brush them off and to just agree with her. Once the euphoria of childbirth kicks in, she'll be telling me how much she loves me because I helped create the two most precious people in her life.

"I need drugs," she yells out, but the nurse tells her it's too late. She disappears between her legs again and tells Ainsley to push. I remember from class that I need to help her sit up so she can bear down. When I asked Bainbridge what that meant, he said it's like taking a shit.

"Sorry, sweetie, but the baby is coming now."

"Babies," I remind her. "She's carrying twins."

"Yes, Mr. Bailey," she says, dismissing me. "You have another contraction coming, Ainsley. Let's push through it."

"What's this 'let's' shit, I'm the one pushing," she says as she starts grunting. I have to agree with her on that one. I have to give the nurse kudos for not engaging Ainsley in a tit for tat. I'm sure she sees a lot of it with her job.

"I hear we're about to have some babies today." Dr. Chen walks in wearing blue scrubs and a pink hat. I find it funny that he's color coordinating with the birth of our children. Right after him, a baby cradle on wheels is brought in.

"Has everyone forgotten that my wife is having twins?" I yell out, growing frustrated with the staff.

"No, Mr. Bailey. We try to keep the twins together. They've spent all their time next to each other, so it would be unfair to separate them now."

"Oh," I say, hanging my head in shame. The squeezing of my hand brings my attention back to Ainsley.

"We need a big push, Ainsley," Dr. Chen says as he takes over for the nurse.

"It's hurts," she screams out. "It's burning so bad."

"I know, but once the head is out, you'll feel some relief. You're almost there."

I chance a look between her legs and about lose my shit. Not only is it the grossest thing I've ever seen, but a man should never see what is happening to his wife's cooter.

"Okay, the head is out."

I look again against my better judgment and see a face with puffy cheeks and dark hair. The doctor works to clear the baby's airway before telling Ainsley to push again.

"Holy shit."

With another push my son is born, and he's letting the world know that he's arrived.

"Baby number one is a boy," the doctor says, placing him on Ainsley's belly. She starts crying, and I join in. The nurse hands me scissors and shows me where to cut his cord.

"Look at him," Ainsley wails as her hand touches every part of him. I know she's counting his fingers and toes, making sure they're all there. For the past few weeks, she's been having nightmares that limbs are missing, and every reassurance I've given her that the babies are perfect have fallen on deaf ears.

"He's perfect," I tell her. "Look what you did, babe."

"We did this," she coos, running her finger over his cheek.

"I did the fun part. You nurtured and brought him into this world." I make sure to give her all the credit because I really didn't do anything.

Sure, I catered to her every need, made sure she was always comfortable, and loved her with all my being, but she's the one who carried him and his sister.

"Ainsley, your little girl is on her way."

We were so sidetracked with our son that she didn't even notice her contractions. The nurse takes the baby so Ainsley can focus on delivering our daughter. This time I watch, stretching myself so that I'm still holding her hand but watching her give birth to the only other female that will make me weak in my knees.

With a big push, her head is out, and the process of clearing her mouth is done.

"Push, Ainsley."

And she does, freeing our daughter. The smallest of wails is echoed through the room, followed by her brother's booming cry.

The nurse sets her on Ainsley, and again the tears are flowing, and our daughter is getting a good once-over from her mother.

"She's gorgeous. Thank you, Ainsley." I kiss my wife deeply in front of the staff, not caring at all. Ainsley needs to know how much I love her and how perfect she's made my life.

The nurse takes our daughter while the doctor finishes up with Ainsley. In a flash, her gown is changed, her bed rearranged, and bags of ice are being added between her legs.

"We're going to give you something for the pain. It won't hurt the babies when you nurse. If you experience too much discomfort, let me know, and in about an hour, we're going to get up and walk and see if you can use the restroom."

I look at the nurse and then back to Ainsley. "They expect you to walk in an hour. I'd be down for the count after this."

"That's because you're a man."

I want to remind her that I'm strong, but the truth is I'm nowhere near as strong as she is.

The babies are brought to us, wrapped in blankets, one with a pink hat, the other with a blue. Both are put into Ainsley's arms, leaving me feeling a little left out. I get as close as I can to them, and watch in awe as she talks to the babies.

"I'm in love," she says, meeting my gaze.

"Me too," I tell her. "I didn't think I could love you any more than I did, but I do. The twins are icing on the cake, Ainsley. I can't thank you enough for making me a father." I lean forward and kiss her, smiling against her lips as the babies coo.

"They need names."

Names are the one thing we didn't discuss, opting to meet them first. I look at my son and daughter, eager to hold them, but knowing that Ainsley needs to bond with them, too, and I try to picture what will be perfect for them.

"Cal," I say, looking at my son.

"Cal?" she questions. I nod and wipe away a tear.

"He gave me a shot when I did everything I could to blow it."

"I like Cal," she says. "Cal Bailey is going to make a great baseball name."

"And now for our princess?" I run the tip of my finger over her cheek and laugh when she gives me her best Elvis impersonation.

"Janie."

"After your mom?"

She nods and tears start streaming down her face. "Yeah, she'd like that."

"Janie Bailey has a funny sound to it, but I like it. I like that her name will rhyme."

It's later in the day when people start to arrive, with Wes being the first. When he steps into the room, Ainsley is sleeping, and he finds me in the rocking chair with two babies on my chest.

"Hey, guys, your grandpa is here," I quietly whisper to them.

He beams when sees their faces.

"Wes, allow me to introduce you to Cal Wilson Bailey and Janie Corinne Bailey."

I've never seen a tough and rugged man like Wes Wilson cry until today. Once Ainsley and I decided on first names, the middle ones came easily. Cal got his grandfather's last name while Janie got my mother's first name. It was the easiest way for us to pay homage to our families.

Once Wes showed up, the visitors started flooding in, with Stella arriving just before visiting hours were over. The minute she saw Ainsley she was a mess, but it turned disastrous when she met the twins. I tried to warn Cal and Janie about their emotional aunt Stella, but I don't think they were listening. Needless to say, the minute Stella held the twins, I think they knew how important they are to her.

After everyone has gone, I crawl into bed with my wife and our babies, wrapping my arms around my family. Ainsley rests her head in the crook of my neck while Cal and Janie sleep on her chest.

"Life can't get any more perfect."

Even though I agree with her, I can't help but say, "Well, the Renegades could win the pennant!"

# BOSTON RENEGADES

The family at the BoRe Blogger would like to congratulate general manager Ryan Stone and his wife, Hadley Carter, on the birth of their son. No name has been released as of yet.

We also want to congratulate center fielder Cooper Bailey and his wife, Ainsley, on the birth of their twins, Cal and Janie.

The three newest members of the BoRe family were born on the same day, same hospital, and one room away.

Ethan and Daisy Davenport report that all three babies are perfectly healthy, and the moms are doing fantastic!

Welcome to the family!

The BoRe Blogger

Please turn the page for a preview of
the next book in Heidi McLaughlin's
Boys of Summer series.

## *Grand Slam*

Coming in Spring 2017

The one I'm eyeing for the night bends at her waist and lines her pool stick up with the cue ball. She slowly pulls the wooden rod through her fingers until the tip finally connects. The hard white plastic ball rolls toward her target, hitting it perfectly and stalling as the blue-striped ball rolls into the pocket. I let out a massive sigh and lean on my stick, waiting my turn. I should've known better when she approached me, asking if I wanted to play a game or two of billiards with her. I know better than to let a good-looking woman hustle me out of money, but I wasn't thinking with my right head. I never am, and once again I'm letting my balls get busted, no pun intended, by a pool shark.

"Sweetheart, are you going to let me play? My balls are getting lonely." If she thinks I'm crude, she doesn't say anything. In fact, she looks at me from over her shoulder and winks before shimmying her ass toward my crotch. My internal groan is epic. I've been watching her bend, lick her lips, show me her ample cleavage, and shake her ass for almost an hour. Not to mention that she brushes against me each time she passes me. And the touching isn't subtle. I can read her loud and clear, all the way from her tight-as-sin jeans to her plunging neckline.

"I can't help it if you suck."

"Do you?" I ask, stepping in behind her. My crotch is lined up perfectly with her ass, earning me another hair-tossing look over her shoulder.

She stands and turns to face me, resting her ass on the edge of the table. "What do you have in mind?" Her finger trails down the front of my shirt until she reaches the buckle of my belt. The tug is slight, but definitely felt. Message received loud and clear.

"What's your name?"

"Are names important?"

"Of course. When I demand that you come for me, I need to know what to call you."

"Demand?" she questions.

"I'm greedy like that," I tell her, placing my cue stick against the table as I step closer to her. I lean in and try to get a whiff of her perfume, but a mix of the stale air from the bar and the beer on her breath makes it hard to tell what she's wearing. I do love a woman who takes the time to dab the perfect scent on her skin, though.

"Blue."

"My balls aren't blue, darling, and haven't been in years."

"No, my name is Blue."

"That's a very unique name," I say as my hand rests on her hip.

"What can I say? I'm a unique woman, Travis."

Ah, she knows my name. That's usually how things go for me. Rarely am I given the opportunity to introduce myself. Everyone knows who I am, and while I enjoy the fruits of my labor, sometimes anonymity would be nice. One day, I'd like to talk to a woman who doesn't know that I'm Travis Kidd, right fielder for the Boston

Renegades and one of the town's most eligible bachelors. "You know who I am?"

"Doesn't everyone? I'm a Boston girl; I know my Renegades."

I nod and reach for my beer. It's the off-season, and technically I shouldn't be here. I usually head south for the winter but opted to stay home this time. After a long season, one that saw my former manager die and one of my closest friends on the team become a dad to twins, I thought I'd stay around and see what the winter had to offer. Aside from the cold, I haven't found much, except Bruins hockey and Celtics basketball. Those games have been the highlight of my time off.

The pickings among women have been slim. Without trying to bag on the female population, it's evident that they're seasonal as well. Right now, the puck bunnies, gridiron groupies, and court whores are in full effect, and the cleat-chasers are resting like the rest of the baseball world. Maybe I should've been a dual-sport athlete. This way I would've had the best of both worlds.

"Travis?"

"What?" I ask, mentally shaking the cobwebs out.

"Where'd you go? It's your turn." Blue nods toward the table, and I look over her shoulder to see the cue ball sitting there.

"Why don't you help me?" I know how to play the game of pool, but since she seems to be a pro, why shouldn't she show me? I would have happily slid up behind her and taught her how to handle her stick, but she took the fun out of it.

Instead, she's off to my side and leaning into me, giving me a perfect sideways glance down her shirt. I smirk, ignoring everything she tells me, and watch as her mounds of flesh move each time her hand does. They're real, that's for sure. None of that fake silicone shit on this chick.

"And that's how it's done," she says, righting herself. She continues to slightly lean over the table, though, jutting her chest out for me to ogle. I cock my head to the side and wink before taking aim at the cue on the table.

My first shot goes in, and the second quickly follows. I line up the third, and that is when I see a raven-haired beauty nursing a drink at the bar.

Saylor Blackwell is off limits to anyone her agency represents. That includes me. Although I wish it didn't. Saylor is the one I would've switched agents for if she told me to, but I fucked that up much I like I screw everything up. When she needed me, I wasn't there. And I haven't spoken to her since.

It's my dumb luck that she's sitting at the bar with her long, slender legs crossed, and she's dressed like she recently got off work. Her eyes are set on the television, ignoring the gaggle of men staring at her. I remember that she was a hard nut to crack back when I wanted to know her better. I can't imagine what she's like now that she's more successful.

My last shot is sunk into the corner pocket. "Eight ball, right side," I say, nodding in the same direction I plan to send the black ball in order to finish this game. I'm in a rush now, eager to speak with Saylor. I know I shouldn't but I can't help myself.

"Where ya going?" Blue calls out.

"To the bar. Rack 'em," I tell her. It's not a lie. I am going to the bar but with the intention of speaking to another woman. I'm smooth, though, and I can easily play it off while I order another round of drinks.

"Two, please." I put up two fingers as I motion toward the bartender. Leaning in, I know I'm blocking Saylor's view of the television, which is all in my game plan.

"Hey, Saylor."

"Travis," she says coldly. We have a history. A small one, but it's there. I often remember the night we spent together and the regret that was on her face when we were done. I had never been kicked out of an apartment before that night. Usually, once I'm satisfied, I leave. With Saylor, everything was backward. It's like she used me to scratch an itch, and once I took care of that she didn't need me anymore. "What brings you in?"

She looks everywhere but at me. "I'm meeting a client."

"And nursing your what?" I take her drink from her hand and sniff. "Scotch? When did you start drinking the hard shit?"

*That* gets her to look at me. Her glare is deadly as her blue eyes penetrate mine. "As if you know anything about me."

"I know enough."

"You don't know shit, Travis Kidd. Go back to your booty call. She's looking at me like she's ready for a cat fight, and I assure you, you're not worth fighting for."

Saylor turns, giving me the cold shoulder. If I weren't so stunned by her outburst, which I did not deserve, I'd tease her. But I have a feeling that there's something bothering her, and I'm the last person she needs making shit worse.

With the bottles of beer between my fingers, I go back to the pool table where Blue is indeed throwing daggers at Saylor's back.

"Down, kitty. She works for my agent." I run my hand down her arm, trying to defuse the situation. Jealous women usually turn me off, and this should be my sign to hit the road, except I'm an idiot and want to stay, mostly so I can watch Saylor.

Taking Blue by her hand, I lead us over to the stools, and I sit down, pulling her between my legs. My hand is planted firmly on her leg right under her butt check. It's a risky move, especially with all the cameras around, but I don't care right now. It's the off-season. I'm allowed to have a little bit of fun.

"You have nothing to be jealous over," I tell her. If anything, I'm trying to appease her.

"Okay."

"We good? Wanna go back to kicking my ass at pool?"

She looks over at the table and nods. "You rack, and I'll break." Blue saunters away, giving me space to watch Saylor, who turns and makes eye contact with me. I wish I could tell what she's thinking. Is she second-guessing her harsh words? I am. I want to go back over and offer to pick up her tab. Or ask how she's getting home. It's late, and the roads are shit. If she's driving, she shouldn't be drinking. She has a kid who depends on her.

"I'm ready," Blue says, thrusting the stick in my face. Her words catch me off guard. Is she ready to play another game or two of pool? I hope so because I have no intention of leaving as long as Saylor is at the bar. Or is she ready for me to fuck her and never ask for her number? Because that is bound to happen as well.

I break, sending the balls off in every direction. Four drop. Two of each, giving me the choice of what I want to be. Blue is yammering in my ear about the setup and which would be the best. Her angles work only for her, though, and I see that I can run the table on her if I line up correctly.

"We should've bet," I tell her as I walk around the table.

"I'd hate to hustle you out of your money, Travis."

I laugh off her comment and proceed to clear the table. She huffs when the eight ball falls into the designated pocket.

"Well, would you look at that," I say, taking a bow. Blue pushes me lightly and falls into my arms. Her lips are on mine before I can push her away, and doing so now would be embarrassing for her, so I kiss her back and find myself opening my eyes to watch Saylor watch me.

As soon as I pull away, Saylor is sliding off the barstool and heading toward the door.

"Be right back. I need some fresh air." A true gentleman would have invited his lady friend outside, but that is not who I am.

"Do you need a ride home?" I ask as soon as I see Saylor standing near the curb. "And what happened to your client?"

"He canceled."

It didn't strike me as odd earlier when she said she was meeting a client, but it does now. I've never met anyone from the agency at a bar, let alone this late at night.

"How about that ride home?"

"Travis," she draws out my name and then drops her head into her hands. Without thinking, I pull her into my side. "Come on, Saylor. It's a ride. Nothing else."

"What the hell is going on? I thought you were taking me home!" Blue speaks loudly enough for everyone on the block to hear.

My arm drops, and Saylor steps away from me. I turn at the sound of Blue's voice behind me.

"I'll be in. Give me a minute." I smile, hoping to placate Blue, but it doesn't work.

"I see some things never change," Saylor says as she steps off the curb and waves at a cab, only to be passed by.

Shaking my head, I push my hands into my pockets for a bit of warmth. If I'd known Saylor would be out here when I returned, I'd have run in and grabbed my jacket. "It's not like that."

"What, do you like her or something?" The sound of Blue's voice grates on my nerves. Saylor looks over my shoulder and rolls her eyes.

"Or something," I say, without taking my eyes off Saylor.

As soon as a taxi pulls up to the curb, Saylor is sliding in.

I make a split-second decision to get in with her, but not before Blue yells at me. "Where the fuck are you going?"

I answer her by slamming the door shut. I have Blue on the outside screaming and Saylor looking at me like she's going to kill me. She opens the door, and I hear, "Fuck you, Travis Kidd. You'll pay for this." And before I realize what's happening, Saylor is out of the car and the cab is speeding down the road.

# Acknowledgments

To my editor, Alex, I say thank you. I think I've experienced every emotion while editing but can honestly say that I'll be a stronger writer because of you. Thank you for taking a chance on me and my love for baseball. I can't wait to work with you again.

To my agent, Marisa, I can never thank you enough for this opportunity. Working with you has been life changing, and I am forever grateful.

To my usual crew, as always, thank you for everything that you do to help bring each idea to life. Yvette, Amy, Georgette, Tammy—you guys put up with a lot of harebrained ideas, and I appreciate it. Audrey, Tammy, Sonja, Amber, Rebecca, Jamie, Jackie, Jill, Kristen, Amanda, and Veronica—you guys work so hard to make sure everyone knows about my stories. Thank you.

To the countless fans, readers, and bloggers, thank you for spending countless hours with our creations.

To my family—as always, I appreciate everything you do.

# ABOUT THE AUTHOR

Heidi McLaughlin is a *New York Times* and *USA Today* bestselling author. Originally from Portland, Oregon, and raised in the Pacific Northwest, she now lives in picturesque Vermont with her husband and two daughters. Also renting space in their home is an over-hyper beagle/Jack Russell, Buttercup, and a highland Westie/mini schnauzer, JiLL.

When she isn't writing one of the many stories planned for release, you'll find her sitting courtside during either daughter's basketball games.